Praise for *We Can Be Heroes*,
also by Catherine Bruton:

'Remarkable. Witty, wise and compelling' *Sunday Times*

'Astonishing, inventive . . . A remarkable piece of work'
Books for Keeps

'Deserves high praise for its clarity and feeling.
Thoughtful and well-written' *Evening Standard*

'This is a book with high ambitions – it tries to do many
things and pulls them all off – tender, sad, but also tense
and exciting. An excellent read' Alistair McGowan

'An important book: brave, honest, funny and very
tense' Bookbag

'Wonderful' Thirst for Fiction, blogger

'An astonishing debut' Julia Eccleshare, Lovereading

'Outstanding . . . A big, brave debut' *The Bookseller*

'Sensitive and explosive' *Inis*

'Funny and very realistic' Sally Nicholls, author of *Ways
to Live Forever*

'Hugely entertaining. Perfect for fans of Michael
Morpurgo and Frank Cottrell Boyce' Red House Books

After graduating from the University of Oxford, Catherine Bruton began her career as an English teacher and later went on to write feature articles for *The Times* and other publications. *Pop!* is her second novel for Egmont, following *We Can Be Heroes*, which received high acclaim. Catherine lives near Bath with her husband and two children.

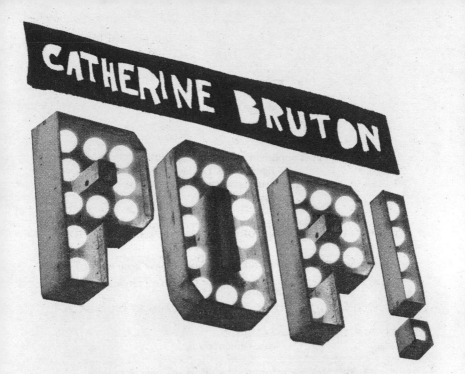

CATHERINE BRUTON

POP!

EGMONT

EGMONT

We bring stories to life

Pop!
First published in Great Britain 2012
by Egmont UK Limited
239 Kensington High Street
London W8 6SA

ISBN 978 1 4052 6133 3

1 3 5 7 9 10 8 6 4 2

www.egmont.co.uk

A CIP catalogue record for this title is available from the
British Library

Typeset by Avon DataSet Ltd, Bidford on Avon, Warwickshire
Printed and bound in Great Britain by the CPI Group

51029/1

EGMONT

Our story began over a century ago, when seventeen-year-old
Egmont Harald Petersen found a coin in the street. He was on
his way to buy a flyswatter, a small hand-operated printing
machine that he then set up in his tiny apartment.

The coin brought him such good luck that today Egmont has
offices in over 30 countries around the world. And that lucky
coin is still kept at the company's head offices in Denmark.

*For Pookin, Moppet, Jubber, Woodley and Clarey-
poppleskin (not forgetting the baby monkeys!).
With love.*

Contents

First Round

Rules of Talent TV No. 1:
Come up with a great story

Elfie

I've always been good at making up stories. I get it from me mam. She reckons the more outrageous you make a story, the more likely people are to believe it – and she's had plenty of practice at telling whoppers, so she should know.

Me mam's always been obsessed with TV talent shows – you know, the ones where a load of wannabes compete to become a star? I think she reckoned she was going to be discovered one day and be an overnight singing sensation. I said you'd never catch me dead doing one of them competitions. But if I ever did, I knew I'd win no problem. Cos I'd worked out the formula, see. Forget about talent, there are a few simple rules every contestant must follow if they want to go all the way: The Rules of Talent TV.

The first rule is that you have to come up with such

a cracking back story that the whole nation will jam the phone lines to vote for you. Cos everyone who enters a TV talent show has a story, haven't they? At least, the ones who get through to the final round always do. It might be a battle with cancer or drugs, or a dead dad/dog/goldfish who told you to 'follow that dream!', or a crippling stutter or stage fright or one-legged-ness or just chronic ugliness . . . it doesn't matter: if you want to win, you need a healthy dose of misery in your back catalogue.

Not that I'd have needed to make much of it up, mind you. My real life was tragic and miserable enough, mostly because of me useless, walkabout, good-for-nothing mam. In fact, I reckon storytelling was about the only good thing I ever got from her. That and our Alfie.

Only if you ask Jimmy Wigmore he probably wouldn't agree. He'd probably tell you that my stories and my crazy plans were what landed us in so much bother in the first place. And . . . I suppose he might have a point.

Jimmy

I first saw Elfie Baguley when I was eight years old. Her family had just moved into the house opposite and she was doing handstands up against the wheelie bins, flashing her knickers in full view of the whole estate. I reckon I sort of fell in love with her right there and then.

When we were kids we hung out together all the time, out on the marshes by the power plant. Our dads worked together at the plant so Elfie reckoned that made us family – sort of. We would rescue baby frogs and play at being fire-eaters or pop stars (Elfie), or pretend to be escapologists and crop-circle makers (me). We smoked home-made dandelion cigarettes, graffitied our names in crayon under the railway bridge and dug for oil next to the river. Elfie even camped out there one time when her mam did a runner. Her dad didn't find her till the next day.

I taught Elfie how to swim off the muddy banks of the Mersey, and she taught me how to play hooky and steal strawberry laces from the corner shop.

One time she persuaded me to numb her ear with a frozen fish finger and then pierce it with a safety pin. Another time, she tattooed her name on my arm with a permanent marker and it didn't come off for weeks. And I was the only one she ever talked to about her runaway mam.

But in the last year or so everything had changed. The developers came and built more affordable housing by the marshes. Then the immos came from abroad and took loads of the contract jobs in the factory and the local men – my dad and Elfie's dad included – started striking about it and spending all their time down at the picket line outside the factory, shouting at the scabs who refused to strike. And Elfie got all cool and trendy and even more mouthy, while I just got big-footed and tongue-tied and really, really good at swimming. And although we were still best mates, things were different somehow.

Oh, and Elfie's mam started going walkabout again. She'd stopped her invisible mam act for a bit when she was pregnant with Elfie's baby brother, Alfie, but after he was born she started it up again. 'The human yo-yo', Elfie calls her. Each time she did one of her disappearing acts, Elfie came up with yet another new scheme to distract her from the 'mindless tragedy of her life'. That's the way Elfie talks these days: like she's in an American teen drama, or one of those daytime chat shows.

Elfie's plans got more and more mental each time. Which wasn't good news for me cos her schemes are usually a bit dangerous, sometimes illegal and they always – always – get us into a heap of trouble.

But at least they're not boring. Life with Elfie never is.

Agnes

When no one talks to you or even looks at you, when everyone just pretends you aren't really there, after a while you begin to wonder if you have actually become invisible. Or if you might forget how to speak: like if someone *did* speak to you, you would open your mouth and nothing would come out, because all the

7

words you had stored inside your head had dried up.

That's how it felt when we moved to England and my dad started working at the power plant. Nobody looked at me; nobody spoke to me. I heard them whispering behind my back, saw the looks they shot at me when they thought I didn't notice, read the words they graffitied on my locker. I hated being invisible; being mute. I felt like I was dissolving into silence.

Rules of Talent TV No. 2:
Get yourself a dream and follow it

Jimmy

My dad wants me to be an Olympic-medal-winning swimmer. Long distance. He reckons everyone should have a dream, and this is mine apparently. I train for two hours every morning and the same in the evenings. Elfie reckons if I spent any more time in the water, I'd have gills.

So that's how I ended up staggering bleary-eyed out of our house at 4.45 a.m. (you have to get up really early to fit in two hours' training – plus two buses each way – all before breakfast) on the day of Elfie's mam's fourteenth bail out.

It was still dark and my dad was blabbering away about training sequences and lap times as usual, but I wasn't really listening. I was half asleep, still dreaming of underwater turns and flickering blue tiles 10 feet below water.

My dad was just closing the door, real quietly
so as not to wake my mam, when Janice Baguley
– Elfie's mam – came bursting out of the house
across the road, shattering the early morning silence
by screaming at the top of her voice and dragging
a pink suitcase the size of a small car. My dad and
I both stopped dead and watched as she stumbled
out on to the pavement, wearing a rainbow-coloured
jacket covered in sequins, electric-blue platform heels
and a pink skirt that made Elfie's school skirts look
modest (and that's saying something!). Her suitcase
must have been heavy cos it got caught in one of
the paving stones and she started tugging at it and
yelling, 'Effing case!'

Elfie's dad appeared behind her in the porchway,
wearing just his boxers and a T-shirt. His hair was
all messed up and he looked pale and washed out
compared to Elfie's mam. 'Don't do this to the kids
again, Jan,' he was saying.

Elfie was right behind him in a short nightie with
teddy bears on it and a massive pair of fluffy purple
monster slippers. She was carrying Alfie in her arms.

'Just let her go, Dad,' she said. 'We're better off without her.'

Elfie's mam stopped battling with the suitcase then and swung round angrily. 'I'm a giver,' she said, with an angry flick of her hair. 'That's my problem. I give too much of meself until there's nowt left. And nobody appreciates it.'

'Yeah, it's all give, give, give with you, in't it, Mam?' Elfie yelled back.

'I gave you the best years of me life, young lady!' Elfie's mam snapped.

'Pity whoever gets the worst, then,' said Elfie.

If you didn't know Elfie as well as I did, looking at her right then, bouncing her baby brother on her hip, eyes narrowed, nose scrunched up, you might have thought she really didn't care about her mam at all.

'I've been a good mam to you!' said Mrs Baguley.

'Yeah? What sort of good mam stages a walkout on her own kid's birthday?' asked Elfie. 'Or had you forgotten I turn fourteen today?'

Elfie's mam opened her mouth to answer, her

bright pink, glossy lips forming a perfect 'O', but nothing came out.

'Thought so,' said Elfie. Then she put her hand gently on her dad's sleeve. 'Come on, Dad.'

Clive Baguley is a big man. He's head of the strike committee so no one round here messes with him. But at that moment he seemed smaller somehow. Deflated, like one of those wrinkly balloons you find in a corner a few days after a kids' party.

'It's the middle of the school holidays, Janice,' he said limply. 'What am I meant to do with the kids?'

'Take 'em down to your precious picket line and give 'em a placard to wave,' Elfie's mam replied.

Across the road, in Mrs Newsround's house, a light had come on and a curtain twitched in an upstairs window. She's not really called Mrs Newsround, that's just what Elfie calls her cos she's the estate's official news-gatherer, which Elfie reckons is a fancy way of saying a nosey old cow who likes spreading gossip.

'I need you, Janice,' Elfie's dad was saying.

'And I need my freedom!' shrieked Elfie's mam, tugging again at her giant pink suitcase. The wheel was still caught in the crazy paving.

Elfie's dad stepped out on to the pavement and tried to grab it off her. Under the custard yellow light of the streetlamp, his face looked lined and old. 'The kids need a mother,' he was saying.

'Just not the one we've got,' Elfie said loudly.

'I gotta think about what *I* need for once, Clive!' Elfie's mam wasn't letting go of the suitcase and she tried to yank the wheel free again, glaring at Elfie's dad through aquamarine eyelashes.

'But I love you,' said Elfie's dad, making another grab for the case.

'Then set me free,' said Janice, in an over-the-top voice like she was auditioning for a soap opera.

And they started having this tug of war, which would have been kind of funny if it hadn't been for the look on Elfie's face – she'd let her don't-care expression slip for a moment – and then little Alfie started crying and calling out, 'Mam! Mam!' but his mam wasn't taking any notice of him.

'Come on, son,' said my dad. 'None of our business this.'

He started moving off and that's when Elfie caught sight of me on the opposite side of the road. She flushed pink beneath her freckles and just for a second you could see how gutted she really was. I gave her a sort of smile and she shrugged. Then she put her don't-care face back on again, flicked her hair, scrunched up her nose and looked away.

Suddenly, the wheels of the giant pink suitcase came loose and Elfie's mam went flying backwards, almost tripping up over one of her electric-blue heels.

Alfie screamed.

Somewhere in the distance a car alarm went off.

A voice shouted out from a nearby window, 'Will you keep that bleedin' racket down. Some of us are trying to sleep!' It sounded like Mrs Tyzack, the single mam with a bunch of ginger kids who are always making a racket out on the streets. Elfie would say that her telling other folks to keep the noise down was 'hippo – flipping – critical!'.

Elfie's mam swayed for a second, then got her balance back. She gave her new 'do' a little shake, pursed her lips and stuck out her boobs and, for a moment, she looked just like Elfie.

Alfie was whimpering so Elfie started bouncing him on her hip even harder, making his little blonde head bob up and down like a rag doll's.

'Fine,' said Elfie's dad. 'Just go.'

'And we'll get the locks changed this time!' Elfie added.

Elfie and her mam stared at each other, and they almost looked like sisters having a fight (only I would never dare say that to Elfie, cos she hates it when people say she looks like her mam). Then Elfie turned back to her dad and said, 'Come on, Dad. She's not worth it.'

Three hours later, after I got back from swim training, I found Elfie sitting on our front doorstep with a buggy and baby Alfie.

'Do you want to play mams and dads?' she said.

'Happy Birthday, Elfie,' I said.

And that's how it all started.

Agnes

I learned to speak English by collecting words, picking up the phrases people threw in my direction and storing them in my brain for the future. People threw insults mainly: 'Immo', 'Ey-tie', 'Scatty foreign cow', 'Immigrant scum'. The words were new to me at first. They weren't in the pocket dictionary my dad gave to me when we moved here, or they had a dictionary meaning that didn't seem to fit ('scatty' meaning absent minded, 'scum' meaning froth or dirt on top of a liquid). It didn't take me long to find out what the words really meant: 'Scatty' – filthy and disgusting, 'Scum' – worthless, 'Immo' is an abbreviation of immigrant, 'Ey-tie' is an insulting term for an Italian person (even though we're actually Portuguese).

Yes, I gathered a whole collection of weird Merseyside words. Which was good, because it made my parents think I was settling in and making friends. My dad laughed when I used them, told me I was turning into a 'little Scouser'.

He wanted me to learn English. So that's what I did.

Rules of Talent TV No. 3:
Always have a plan

Elfie

I needed a plan. Bigger and better than any of the ones I'd come up with before. Because even for me mam, walking out on my actual *birthday* was a new low. She'd done it on Christmas day once (I was six and she shouted, 'And there's no such thing as Father Christmas!' as she stormed out the door) so I suppose I shouldn't have been surprised really. Or gutted. But I just wanted not to have to even think about it and that's where the plan came in.

'So I guess you already know me mam left again,' I said.

Me and Jimmy were sitting under the old bridge down on the marshes. We had our backs against the arch, bums perched on the rock-studded concrete, staring up at the metal girders. You could still see bits of our names written over and over in waxy zigzags from the time we'd pretended to be graffiti artists when we were in Year Four.

'How many times does that make it now?' said Jimmy.

'Thirteen,' I said. 'Fourteen if you count the time she went to Blackpool for the day and left me in the ballpark at Ikea.'

'What about the time she put you on the Mersey Ferry and left you doing the round trip to Birkenhead for five hours?' said Jimmy, who was sitting with his long legs curled up into his body, like one of those plastic bendy men. 'Does that count?'

I remembered crouching under the lifeboat as the sun went down over the Mersey. 'That one definitely counts.'

It was cold and damp and cloudy – just the sort of day crap things are meant to happen on. Not the way it's meant to be in the middle of August when it's the school holidays.

I reached into the pocket of me dad's coat. He'd forgotten to take it out with him, so I'd nicked it. It was one of those donkey jackets, thick as a blanket with plastic bits on the shoulders and elbows that can't ever have been cool. But it was warm, and it smelt of sweat and cheap deodorant, just like me dad. I rummaged around in the pocket and fished out a packet of cigarette papers and a tea bag.

'When did you start smoking?' said Jimmy.

'Only since me dad stopped being able to afford tobacco,' I said, shaking the tea bag in his face. 'I don't much like real ciggies but you should taste one of Elfie's tannin specials.'

'Why? What're they like?' He stared at the tea bag like it was something he'd never seen before in his life.

'Better than them dandelions we used to smoke. They were gross!'

Jimmy laughed a bit then (he doesn't laugh much. I reckon it's all the chlorine) and I laid out the cigarette paper on my bare knees, bit open the tea bag and sprinkled the contents along the small white strip of paper.

Jimmy just watched. Jimmy Wigmore was always watching me in those days. He thought I didn't notice, but I did. I didn't mind though. Apart from me dad and our Alfie, Jimmy was the only person in the world that I could actually rely on.

'Things must be bad if your old man can't afford baccie any more,' said Jimmy.

'Yeah, well no one round here's exactly rolling in money, are they?' I said. Me dad had been on strike for nearly three months by then. So had Jimmy's dad, and half the men in town. The other half were out of work – cos the foreign workers had come in and got all the contract jobs. Let's just say, our estate isn't exactly full of lottery millionaires and big-bonus bankers.

Jimmy wrapped his arms round his giant legs, which are about a metre longer than mine, and said, 'Does it . . . um . . . actually work?'

'Me dad says it doesn't help with the nicotine withdrawal much but it's cheap. So do you want some?' I said, waving the white tube in his face.

'Nah,' he said, pulling a funny expression. He's got a long face – everything about Jimmy is long and lanky – but he still looks a bit babyish with his blue eyes and little kid's smile. 'Are you sure it isn't, like, bad for you?'

'Smoking tea? No idea,' I said. 'Can't be much worse than drinking it though, can it?' I stuck the tea-bag ciggie in my mouth and reached for the lighter me dad always keeps in his jacket. Only, instead of the lighter, my hand closed over a piece of paper. I pulled it out. Another red bill: telephone this time. 'Looks like a final reminder,' I said, watching the crumpled document flap around, caught in the wind coming off the river. 'Wonder when we'll get cut off?'

Jimmy looked away, staring out at the mud-brown water. From here, on a clear day, you can see way over to the oil refinery on the other side of the Mersey and out to the North Sea beyond. If you look east, you can see the soap-flake smoke coming out of the washing powder factory a mile upriver. If the wind is blowing west you can smell it too – burnt soapsuds, like a washing machine on fire.

'It doesn't exactly help that me mam had every reality TV show on speed dial,' I said, digging my hand back in me dad's pocket again and this time finding the cigarette lighter. 'Last year she voted for those triplets on *Pop to the Top* over three hundred times. Y'know, the ones with the sticky out ears and weird pouty mouths? She kept voting even after they got kicked off. She reckons it might be some kind of record.'

I flicked the lighter and watched it spark. Then I held it up to the red bill and tried to set fire to it (which isn't as easy as you'd think on a windy, rainy day, even if you *are* camped out under a bridge). Finally, the paper caught and I watched it blacken and curl. For some reason it made me feel a bit better.

'How long d'you think she'll be gone this time?' asked Jimmy as I stared into the flames.

'Well, she took the pink suitcase but she left half her middle-aged-tart clothes,' I said, watching the orange flames lick closer and closer to my fingers. 'So, who knows.'

'She always comes back in the end though, doesn't she?' said Jimmy. He unfurled his daddy-long-legs limbs and stretched them out over the concrete so you could see his massive flipper feet at the end. Seriously, Jimmy Wigmore has the biggest feet you have ever seen in your life. I reckon that's why he's like a swim champ, or whatever, because he's actually got the legs of a giant frog, or a merman.

'Only cos me dad always takes her back,' I said, dropping the burning letter and watching it fall on to the concrete. I picked up the tea-bag cigarette, stuffed it between my lips then bent down to try and light it with the burning bill. 'You know,' I said, as the taste of tannin hit the back of my throat (it was gross, but there was no way I was telling Jimmy that), 'if it were me, I'd have the locks changed.'

Jimmy glanced at me and then looked away again quickly, going pink. 'People will put up with a lot from someone they love,' he said.

'Yeah, well,' I said, exhaling quickly and ignoring the fact he'd turned bright red. 'He might like getting his heart trampled on by me mam's gladiator stilettos, and I'm so used to it I don't even notice any more, but it's Alfie I worry about.'

We both glanced over to where Alfie was tottering through the damp marshes, picking up stones and who knows what else, talking to himself in baby language.

Alfie is the cutest kid you'll ever meet. Not like

me when I was a baby – I've seen the pictures and I was well ugly. But Alfie, he looks like an angel, with blonde curls and green eyes and a nose like a midget gem. He could win any beautiful-baby contest hands down. He's the best thing that me mam ever did – in fact, he's the only good thing she ever did – and I love him more than anything in the whole world.

I turned back to Jimmy. 'What kind of sadistic mam calls her kids Elfie and Alfie, anyway?' I said. 'That says it all, that does!'

'Maybe she didn't realise?' said Jimmy.

'Or maybe she'd just forgotten my name,' I said. 'Or forgotten she even had another kid. That'd be typical that would. It's not like she had much trouble forgetting my birthday.' My tummy did a weird little flip when I said that. 'Anyway, I'm not going to stand around waiting till he's old enough for her to break his heart.' The river was choppy today, with the wind whipping up little waves on the mud and the rain battering the surface. 'Which is why we need a plan,' I said.

Jimmy looked up quickly. 'What this time?' he asked, a pained expression on his face.

'Not sure yet,' I said. 'But there's no need to look so worried. I reckon we've got to go for something really big this time. Epic.'

Jimmy groaned.

I ignored him. 'Not just summat to fill in time for the rest of the summer holidays – cos, let's face it, neither of us is being whisked off to Disneyland, or even Legoland, any time soon. And not just summat to take my mind off me mam either. Nah, this time I reckon we need a plan that's so massive it'll change our lives forever.'

'Such as?' said Jimmy, the anxious expression still on his face.

I glanced over to where Alfie was playing with some mangled bit of old metal and smiling to himself. The sun had come out from behind a cloud and he was all bathed in light, looking more like a grubby angel than ever. Then I thought of how he'd called out, 'Mammy! Mammy!' that morning and how she'd just ignored him and turned away.

'I dunno yet,' I said. 'But you know me: I'll think of something!'

Agnes

When we first moved here I thought the power station looked like a fairy-tale castle, with its eight cooling towers stretching into the sky. When it was all lit up at night it would make the clouds glow orange for miles around. My dad says you can see the lights of the towers over a hundred miles away.

My dad also once said that crossing the picket line every day was like being the prince in *Sleeping Beauty*, cutting through a forest of thorns to get to the princess. He laughed when he said it, like it was all just a joke.

But it stopped being funny after a while. Some days, he came back with cuts and bruises where the strikers had thrown things at him. And at night we heard them outside, shouting things, throwing stuff at the house. Once they put human faeces through the letter box. Another time they threw bricks through the lounge window. Often they emptied dustbins full of rubbish in our front garden.

And it was the same at school: ink flicked in my face, nail varnish in my hair, once even a used tampon in my school bag. Everywhere, feet tripped me, elbows bumped me, people glared at me.

At least it was different in the summer holidays, away from all that for a bit. But it still didn't seem much like a fairy tale. Not any more.

Jimmy

'Are you coming then, or what?' Elfie demanded.

'Where to?'

'I think better when I'm on the move,' said Elfie, who was already on her feet and patting cement dust off her bum while stamping out her tea-bag cigarette with the heel of one of her mam's peep-toe stilettos. Her dad's old donkey jacket hung so low over her bare legs she looked like she wasn't wearing anything underneath. I knew her dad would go mad if he saw her dressed like that, but I didn't think now was the time to say so.

Without bothering to argue (like I said, no point), I just scooped up Alfie, who was busy crushing snails and licking them, and shoved him, squirming and squealing, into the buggy.

I followed Elfie back across the marshes, avoiding the power station and the picket lines. She marched along at a hundred miles an hour, waving her arms around and muttering to herself (she said she was waiting for her light-bulb moment) while I traipsed behind, bumping Alfie's buggy over the rocky ground, trying to keep up. Alfie was giggling like he was on some kind of fairground ride (which is actually a pretty accurate way of describing a day with Elfie) and chanting, 'Effie! Effie! Effie!' the whole way.

Alfie is Elfie's number-one fan. Sometimes I reckon he must think she's his mam, cos she looks after him way more often than his real mam does. Even in term time, Elfie's mam was always getting her to bunk off school and look after Alfie so she could go shopping or to the bingo.

'So, I'm trying to think of our best plan yet,' Elfie shouted, twirling round and walking backwards, which looked pretty lethal in her mam's shoes. 'Do you remember the time we swapped the door numbers of everyone on our street?'

'How could I forget?'

'Or the time we broke into the power station and hung them Everton flags on the eight towers,' she laughed. She was still twirling, pulling funny faces at Alfie every time she spun round, which made him scream with laughter.

'What about the time we tried to make crop circles in the marshes?' I said. 'Yeah! That was a good one. We even made the local news that time!'

Suddenly, she stopped spinning and stood still for a moment. We'd reached the edge of the new housing where most of the immos live beside a narrow strip of floodplain littered with debris left behind by the developers – lumps of concrete, bits of metal, bottles and cans.

'That's it,' said Elfie.

'What is?'

'TV!' she announced with a massive grin.

'What?' I said.

'We need to get ourselves on TV! That's the plan.'

'Uh – right . . .' I said, feeling uneasy. I glanced over at the immo houses. As well as the broken windows and upturned bins, there was graffiti all over the walls saying stuff like: 'F-off Johnny Foreigners!' and 'British Jobs for British workers'. There were even a few swastikas around. 'So what exactly have you got in mind?'

Elfie flopped down on to the rubble–strewn grass and looked thoughtful. 'I'm thinking reality TV,' she mused. 'What about the one where they lock you all in a house for a month? That'd be cool. People would vote to keep me in there just to *save* me from having to endure a tearful reunion with me mam.'

'You said no one watches that since it moved channel,' I said, leaning over the buggy. Elfie says I shouldn't stoop – so does my mam – they say I shouldn't be embarrassed about being tall, but it's hard not to be self–conscious about your height when half the kids at school call you Giraffe Boy (and the other half call you Finding Nemo).

'Good point. What about the jungle one then?' she said, picking up a lump of rubble and throwing it in the air. 'I could eat bugs and wrestle snakes. That'd be a bit like living with me mam an' all!'

'That's only for celebs,' I said. Alfie had started complaining the minute we stopped moving, so I rocked the buggy to and fro to try and cheer him up.

'Yeah, but half the people who go in are total nobodies,' said Elfie, still tossing the rubble from hand to hand, spraying herself with white dust as she did so. 'They go in a wannabe and they come out a star – least that's what they all hope.'

'Maybe you could do that one about people who've got talent,' I said, jiggling the buggy even more furiously as Alfie started to wail loudly.

'Duh! The clue's in the title,' said Elfie. 'You've got to have a talent. And I don't.' She clutched the piece of rubble and stared at it. 'I mean, at least you can swim. Me, I can't do anything much.'

And I wanted to say, 'Of course you can. You can mend broken frogs' legs and make crop circles using a toddler buggy, and break into the power station and, and . . . and you're the coolest, craziest, brilliantest person I know.' But, of course, I didn't.

Instead I said, 'You can sing. I mean, everyone can sing – right?'

'I can sing better than you but that's not saying much.'

'Well then, you could do *Pop to the Top*.'

Elfie was staring down at her mam's dust-covered mules. 'Nah, that's just some local thing they screen after the regional news. What I'm after is national exposure.' She kicked her feet, sending bits of earth flying.

'Loads of people watch it, though,' I said. 'Cos Liverpool is supposed to be, like, the home of pop music. That's what my dad says anyway.'

Elfie just shrugged. 'I s'pose.'

'Think of The Beatles and Kerry Katona and the sporty one from the Spice Girls and all them lot. They all come from Merseyside.'

'Yeah, and so does Rick Astley and some random band called Half Man Half Biscuit,' said Elfie, scrunching up her nose so her freckles all squiggled around. 'Not to mention The Reynolds Girls!'

'Who are they?' I said.

'Exactly!' said Elfie.

I paused, then said, 'Isn't *Pop to the Top* judged by that Scouse pop legend your mum totally fancies?'

'Even though he's old enough to be her dad!'

'And that lad who won last year is number one in the American charts and hanging out with all the stars and everything.'

'Could be cool, I s'pose,' said Elfie, tugging at the broken strap on her mam's shoe.

I paused. I was running out of ideas and I wasn't even sure why I was trying to persuade her anyway. Elfie always does this: argues back for no particular reason, or if she does agree with anything I suggest, she usually claims it was her idea in the first place. But then I thought of something else.

'And I read that this year there's a £25,000 cash prize,' I said.

Elfie looked up from fiddling with her shoe. 'Now you're talking!' Her eyes were twinkling suddenly. 'That's what I call a plan!'

She grinned at Alfie, who stopped wimpering for a second and giggled.

'I mean, with that kind of dosh, I could clear me dad's debts and have some left over to sign him up for a dating agency,' Elfie went on. 'And I could get some decent stuff for Alfie, and . . .'

Only she stopped then and wrinkled up her nose. She's got this dead cute nose. Like Alfie's only with loads more freckles on it. 'Only one problem,' she said. 'I can't actually sing.'

'You just said you could.'

'I said I could sing better than you,' she said. 'But that don't exactly make me Mariah Carey!'

And then the weirdest thing happened. Elfie said it was fate, or our destiny calling or something. Whatever it was, it was totally freaky because, right then, Alfie stopped crying again. And that was when we heard the girl. Singing.

Rules of Talent TV No. 4:
If you don't have any talent, find someone who does

Elfie

Everyone's heard of 'show-stopping performances', right? Voices that are supposed to make grown men cry, or shatter glass and that? Well, the first time I heard Agnes sing, it was definitely a baby-stopping performance. I swear, the minute she started warbling, our kid quit crying and me and Jimmy both stopped talking at once.

I'm no vocal coach but I *had* spent fourteen years living with me mam's Talent TV obsession so I reckon I was an expert on uncovering hidden talent. And this kid was proper good. And when I realised the singing was coming from one of the immo houses, I *knew* we were on to a winner. Cos, like I said, you need a good story if you want to make it in Talent TV, and here was a mind-blowing back story staring us right in the face.

So that was when I came up with my best plan EVER!

I turned to Jimmy and said, 'D'you hear that? That's destiny calling, that is.'

'What?' said Jimmy, looking confused. I sometimes wonder if his whole alphabet consists of question marks. I imagine them swimming round his brain like little black fishes.

'Never mind, come on,' I said, making my way over to the house where the singing was coming from. 'Let's go check her out.'

For a moment he looked as if he was going to say no, but Jimmy Wigmore knows better than to argue with me – especially on one of me mam's walkabout days – so he just sighed and followed me over to the high wooden fence surrounding the houses.

'Gizza leg up then,' I said.

He pulled another face then bent down and made a cradle out of his hands.

'Just like the time we graffitied the bridge,' I said, stepping into it and pulling myself up.

Jimmy groaned. 'Only you weigh more these days!'

'You trying to say I'm lardy?'

'No, I . . .' he spluttered, his face going bright red.

'Good, cos we both know who'd win if this turned into a scrap.'

The girl had started singing a different song – a slower one this time with long warbling notes at the end of each line. She sounded even more amazing than before and I kept thinking about what Jimmy had said about the £25,000 prize. I had little £ signs dancing round my head as I tried to push myself further up the fence but I still couldn't actually see anything.

'Can't you push me up a bit more?' I said.

'I can't go any higher,' Jimmy puffed.

'What's the point of all that swim training if you don't even get any muscles?' I said, standing on my tiptoes on his hands, then bending my knees and launching myself as high as I could and hooking my elbows over the top. Jimmy grunted with pain below.

The girl was in the kitchen, with her back to me. But I could see she wasn't some middle-aged dinner-lady diva. She was just a skinny kid, with long black hair that went right down to her bottom. She looked sort of familiar.

Suddenly, she stopped singing and turned round and stared right at me. That's when I recognised her. She was the immo kid from school. The one who started in our year last term. The one nobody ever spoke to.

Then my foot slipped, I lost my grip, screamed and went tumbling backwards off the fence, kicking Jimmy in the face as I went. When I looked up from the ground, Jimmy was clutching his eye and groaning.

'This is great!' I said, grinning.

'Great for what, exactly?' he said, still wincing.

'My plan!'

'Right,' said Jimmy, looking unconvinced.

'Don't stand there looking like you've just swallowed an armband. Come on!'

'Where are we going?' asked Jimmy.

'Getting ourselves a new immo bezzer.'

'But what about your dad?' said Jimmy, still looking dazed and confused. 'What about Alfie?'

'Who do you think I'm doing all this for, you divvy?'

Agnes

I've moved house more times than I can remember. My dad's worked on contracts all over Europe: Germany, France, Belgium, the Ukraine. Sometimes for as little as three months, sometimes for over two years at a time. I've been to school in six different countries, had lessons in four languages. But this is my first time in England.

It's hard always being the new kid; always having to make new friends. And even though I'm good at picking up languages – like a magpie, my dad says – when I'm around new people my throat goes dry and my mind goes blank.

When I came to England it didn't matter. No one cared that I had nothing to say and that I wasn't any good at making friends. Because nobody wanted to talk to me anyway.

But everything changed when Elfie Baguley turned up on the doorstep and said: 'Wanna play pop stars?'

She was wearing this massive black coat over a teeny-weeny jeans skirt and a pair of tattered sandals that looked about two sizes too big for her. I knew if my mum saw Elfie she'd say she looked cheap – the word 'sloobag' rolled out of a little box in the back of my mind, like a ball in a lottery machine.

She had Jimmy Wigmore with her. I knew him from school, too. Tall, gangly, a bit shy and sort of sleepy looking. He was bright red and blinking furiously with embarrassment. His long floppy hair dangled over big puppy-dog eyes and his ears, which were bright red too, stuck out at right angles from his face.

I glanced from Elfie to Jimmy, and then at the crying child in the buggy and tried to figure out what they were all doing together. And why they had been spying on me. And what they were doing standing on my doorstep.

'I'm Elfie,' the girl announced loudly. She had freckles all over her face and too much lipgloss on.

'I know,' I said.

'Oh! You can speak English.' She looked surprised.

'Yes,' I said.

'What's your name, then?' She scrunched up her nose and, although she was dressed as if she was about twenty-five, she suddenly looked like a little kid who had raided her mum's make-up.

'Agnes,' I replied.

'You what?'

'You would say, "Agg–ness,"' I said, quietly, glancing at Jimmy who was jiggling the buggy to and fro. 'We say, "An–yez."'

Elfie pulled another face, which made all her freckles squish together. 'Whatever.'

'Why you –' I hesitated, searching for the word, '– looking on me? Spying me?'

'We weren't spying on you,' said Jimmy quickly. He was rocking the buggy to try and stop the baby crying. It wasn't working.

'I see you,' I said quietly.

Elfie huffed loudly and said, 'We weren't spying. We were listening. To your singing, if you must know.'

'Why?'

'Cos your voice is OK, that's why.'

'Oh,' I said. 'Thank you.' But I wasn't sure it was a compliment the way she said it.

'The baby liked it too,' said Jimmy, blushing and

staring down at his long feet again. Even though it had started to rain he was just wearing a T-shirt and a pair of cut-off shorts and his long limbs stuck out of the arm and leg holes like a scarecrow.

'That is what you want?' I said, eyeing them both nervously. 'For me to sing to baby?'

'Don't be daft,' said Elfie. 'I want you to teach me.'

I glanced at Jimmy again but he looked as confused as I did. 'Teach you what?' I said.

'Effing long division and Spanish conjunctivitis verbs!' she replied, raising her eyebrows sky high. 'What do you think? Singing, of course.'

I looked at her sparkly lipgloss, her not-quite-clean hair. 'Why?' I asked.

'You'll see.'

'If you no tell me, why I say yes?'

'Because you're an immo and everyone hates your family, and it's the summer holidays and you've got no friends and nothing better to do,' she said with a told-you-so face.

I glanced at Jimmy who was hiding behind his fringe. 'What he name?' I asked, nodding at the crying baby.

Jimmy blinked madly then opened his mouth to speak but Elfie piped up. 'Alfie,' she said.

'Oh,' I said. 'He is yours?'

'Do I look old enough to be his mam?'

I shrugged. Jimmy caught my eye and blinked some more. 'Where his mother, then?' I asked.

'She's on tour with an R 'n' B diva megastar, if you must know!' said Elfie. I glanced at Jimmy again but he was looking down at his feet. 'Yeah,' Elfie went on, with a little toss of her head that made the plastic beads on her neck shake. 'She's in charge of that American diva's backstage demands – she wants rose petals in the loo, someone to stir her coffee anticlockwise, champagne for her dog's bathtub, gold loo seat, puppies and kittens on tap – that sort of thing.'

She stared right at me as she said it, like she was daring me to call her a liar. Jimmy didn't seem to know where to look. The baby had stopped crying and was sucking furiously on one of his fists.

'Right,' I said.

'So, you going to teach me or not?'

'Um – OK,' I said.

'Just OK?' said Elfie, twirling the plastic beads round her finger and staring at me.

'If I say yes,' I said, catching Jimmy's eye again as he looked up. 'You will talk me at school?'

'Don't be daft!' said Elfie, pursing her lips. 'This is strictly business – and top secret. So, are you going to let us in, or what?'

'Baby needs new nappy,' I said as I led them into the sitting room. It seemed strange, them being in my house. I hadn't had anyone over since we'd moved here and I could feel my throat going dry and the words in my brain getting fuzzy as Elfie Baguley stood in the middle of our sitting room, checking it out with a look on her face like everything smelt funny.

'I'm rationing his nappies,' she declared.

'Rationing?' The word was new. It sounded odd on my tongue.

'It's what British people did in the war when you lot were bombing us,' said Elfie. 'Don't you know anything?'

'I don't think they *were* bombing us, were they?' Jimmy mumbled quietly, his big ears going red again. 'Wasn't that the Germans?'

Elfie raised a single curved eyebrow and the pink in his ears spread all over his long face.

'Bombing?' I said. Another word I had not heard before.

'Yes! War – bomb – bang – boom!' said Elfie, waving her arms around.

'I no understand.'

'I thought you said you spoke English,' said Elfie, with an exaggerated sigh. 'Where – are – you – from – anyway?' she went on, talking really slow.

I felt my face flushing just like Jimmy. 'Por – tu – gal,' I replied, also really slow, staring right back at Elfie for a moment then looking away.

Jimmy giggled. Elfie glared at him and then back at me.

'Yeah? Well, your lot had that Mussolini and were big pals with Hitler during the war, weren't they? I listen in History, see? I'm not a complete divvy!'

I love the word 'divvy'. It means stupid, idiot,

foolish. I like the way it sounds when Elfie says it, a faint purr on the 'v' sound.

'I think that was Italy,' Jimmy said.

'Italy – Spain – Portugal. Whatever!' Elfie snapped. 'Anyway, no – money – for – nappies,' she said extra loudly. 'Don't – mention – the – war!'

She walked over to the mantelpiece, all grumpy and glaring. Jimmy caught my eye and sort of smiled. I sort of smiled back.

Elfie picked up a picture of me and my mum and dad from the shelf. My mother is small and dark, like me. People say my dad looks a bit like a Hollywood heart-throb – only shorter. Elfie peered at them both, suspiciously.

'Don't look much like you, do they?'

People are always saying how much I look like my mum. And how I have my dad's eyes. But I kept my mouth shut and said nothing.

'Guess all the beautiful genes skipped a generation,' she said, putting the picture face down on the shelf. She raised an eyebrow then glanced at Jimmy who was blinking madly again. Then she turned to me, like she was waiting for me to say something back. And I wanted to think of something clever to say – to call her a divvy, a scatty cow, a ho-bag (all words I have collected) – but nothing came out.

Just then Alfie started to wail again.

'Baby is hungry?' I asked quickly.

Elfie rummaged around in her pocket and brought out a half-eaten packet of cheesy Wotsits. 'Those should do for a bit,' she said, handing them to Alfie, who stopped crying immediately and grabbed them in his little chubby fingers, a smile breaking out on his grubby, teary face.

Elfie's expression changed when she looked at her little brother. She didn't look so hard somehow when she smiled at him and pulled a silly face. Alfie giggled and shoved the powdery tubes into his mouth, showering himself with luminous orange dust.

Elfie pushed her tongue out at him and he laughed. 'He loves Wotsits!' she said. 'Me mam reckons they count as dairy products cos they got cheese in 'em!'

'Right,' I said.

Then her expression changed again and she put on

her tough face like before. 'So, any road, let's get on with the plan.'

'Plan?' I glanced at Jimmy who shrugged and gave me a look as if to say, *Don't ask.*

'So, I've decided that for once in your life, Jimmy Wigmore, you're actually right about summat,' Elfie went on.

'Really?' said Jimmy. 'What?'

'We're entering *Pop to the Top*!'

'Oh,' said Jimmy.

'What is *Pop to the Top*?' I asked.

'Bleedin' heck!' cried Elfie, giving me a pitying stare. 'Where have you been living for the past five years?'

And I could have told her that I'd been living in seven different countries and never stayed in the same town for more than two years, only she didn't give me the chance.

'It's only the biggest regional TV talent show in the UK!' she said. 'Last year's winner is now a global superstar. And it's judged by one of the biggest names in pop. And we're gonna win it!'

'We are?' asked Jimmy.

'Don't be a divvy! Not you, Jimmy Wigmore,' said Elfie, shaking her head. 'My girl band. Only it's more of a duo than a band. Teen-girl pop-duo sensation – that sort of thing. Two girls and a microphone.' She nodded her head in my direction and gave Jimmy a significant look. 'Singing across the cultural divide. Getting it yet?'

Then Jimmy and Elfie both turned to stare at me and I felt my brain fuzzing all over.

'You and Agnes?' said Jimmy.

'Bingo!' said Elfie, who was grinning now.

'But you say you want me *teach* you sing,' I said.

'She's right. You never mentioned anything about her actually singing,' said Jimmy, catching my eye.

'It's obvious innit,' said Elfie. 'She's got the voice. I've got the looks – and the business brains. It's a winning combination. And with a £25,000 prize up for grabs, I reckon this could be the plan to end all plans.'

'You'd have to share the prize if you sang together,' said Jimmy, who was blinking madly.

'Yeah. We'd share it three ways,' said Elfie. 'Me and her are the talent and you can be our manager and roadie and groupie and stuff. So, I wonder what we should call ourselves? I was thinking "Scab girls", or "Scabbers". You know, because of the strike – and cos our dads hate each other. What do you think?'

'I think your father love it,' I said quietly.

Elfie turned to look at me again. She narrowed her eyes and raised her eyebrows. 'Oh, so the immo understands sarcasm!' she said.

Jimmy shot me a warning look.

'What do you know about my dad, anyway?' said Elfie, defensively.

Everyone in our town knew about Elfie's dad. 'He start the strike.' I paused and then said, 'My father say he keep it going, too.'

Elfie paused and then said, like it was no big deal, 'That's right. The Militant of the Mersey, my old man!'

'My father also say –' I hesitated again – 'that he do all the graffiti and the bricks through windows.'

Jimmy closed his eyes, like he was waiting for an

explosion. But Elfie just responded with a shrug and another flick of her hair. 'Don't believe everything the estate gossips say,' she said. Then she grinned widely and added really quickly, 'But you're right about one thing, kid. If me dad knew I was even here, he'd go ape! Not cos of where you're from, mind – me dad's no racist. But it's cos of your lot that we're in this mess, isn't it?'

'My dad says we're not even supposed to talk to immos,' said Jimmy apologetically.

'Exactly,' said Elfie. 'But sometimes you've got to ignore your parents for their own good. Plus, it adds a whole new level of excitement to the plan. So, are you up for it or not?'

I hesitated. 'If I say no?'

'You won't,' said Elfie. 'Hanging out with me and being a secret pop star will be too much to resist. So, what d'you reckon, Agg-ness?' She plastered a big smile on her face and I was sure she had deliberately mispronounced my name.

I hesitated, biting my lip. 'I think we called "The Juliets",' I said eventually.

Elfie gave me a funny stare. Jimmy looked up, his eyes wide with surprise. Alfie giggled.

'Because of Shakespeare,' I said, biting my lip some more. 'I listen in English, too.'

Elfie raised a single eyebrow. 'Fine,' she said with a theatrical sigh. 'Whatever. We've got two weeks to get ready so you'll have to be up for a pretty intensive rehearsal schedule. And once you're in, you're in. No backing out.'

'OK,' I said.

'Pinkie promise?' Elfie said, holding out her hand with just her baby finger extended.

'I no understand,' I said, glancing at Jimmy.

'And you'll have to give up saying that all the time, too,' said Elfie impatiently. 'It's well irritating!'

'It means if you break your promise –' Jimmy hesitated – 'Well – um – you're supposed to cut your little finger off and feed it to the fishes in the Mersey. It's sort of Elfie's idea.'

'Really?' I asked nervously.

'Yeah, really,' said Elfie huffily. 'Come on. You gonna swear or not?'

Nobody apart from my parents had really talked to me for weeks and weeks, and I had all these words swilling around unused in my head, nobody to share them with. So I held out my pinkie finger and linked it with hers. And made my promise.

Rules of Talent TV No. 5:
Get your friends and family
behind you

Elfie

I might be good at making stuff up, but I wasn't lying when I said me dad would go mad if he knew I was hanging out with an immo. A lot of what Agnes said was right: me dad's head of the strike committee and he's well mad at the immos cos he reckons they've robbed local men of jobs. Only that makes him sound like a total nightmare, and he's not really. The thing is, he's like two different people. Most people know him as this total hard-nut ball-breaking bully boy, but that's because they only see the man on the picket line.

But the man I know, the dad who comes home every night, is totally different. He's just a softie who looks like a wrestler but acts like a pussycat. Or a doormat: me mam's own personal doormat.

Me dad's been in love with me mam since he was

fifteen. They met down the roller rink in Warrington one Saturday night. He says he saw her skating backwards wearing a pair of black Bauer Turbo roller skates with neon laces, shaking her shaggy perm under the revolving lights from the disco ball, and he fell for her there and then. They closed the roller rink down six months later and built a load of flats. She's been messing him round ever since.

And no matter what she did, he always seemed to forgive her. That's what got to me. He was hard as nails when it came to laying down the law on the picket line, but when it came to me mam, he was a total pushover. It was like he'd used up all his fight and there was none left to stand up to her – even when she was breaking his heart and hurting Alfie and doing my head in. He just let her walk all over him every time.

She'd been over to the house and taken more of her stuff while I was out. I knew because when I got back Mrs Newsround shouted out to me across next door's garden, 'Saw yer mam with her pink case earlier,

Elfie. She going off on holiday, is she?'

'Nah! She's got a job as personal stylist to the Queen Mother,' I shouted back.

'I thought the Queen Mam were dead?' said Mrs Newsround. She was out pretending to water her roses.

'That's what they want you to think,' I said. 'But for your information she's hanging out with Elvis and Princess Di in Benidorm.'

Mrs Newsround had her mouth open to reply but before she had a chance, I said, 'Anyway, gotta go. Tattie-bye!' and shoved Alfie's buggy into the front porch, slamming the door. Fight gossip with gossip – that's my rule.

Me mam had taken loads of stuff this time. There were empty spaces all over the house. On the mantelpiece there was a gap where the photo of her meeting Ireland's second biggest boy band had been – she'd left the one of me and Alfie. Upstairs, the bathroom scales were missing, so were her Slendertone waist trimmers, and the pile of celeb magazines from by the loo. She'd taken more of her clothes, too, and left the drawers hanging out, things scattered all over the bedroom floor.

The house still smelt of her though, as if she'd left tiny droplets of her perfume lingering in the dust. Alfie must have noticed it because as soon as we walked in the door he started to cry and say, 'Mammy?' which nearly broke my heart and made me even more mad at her.

I picked him up and cuddled him, nibbled his nose – cos he likes that and it makes him giggle – and then I let him nibble mine with his little wet mouth. I closed my eyes and listened to the sound of his little sucking breaths so close to mine and it made me feel a bit better somehow.

When Alfie was first born I used to pretend he was my baby and I was his mam. I almost wish I was, cos I know I'd never let him down the way she does.

I wanted to tidy up before me dad got home so I gave Alfie another pack of cheesy Wotsits and that seemed to make him forget about her for a bit. Then I moved stuff around so you couldn't see the gaps where she'd taken things and when me dad got back we both pretended like nothing had really happened.

'Good day at school?' he said.

'It's the summer holidays, Dad!'

'Oh, yeah.' He picked Alfie up and threw him in the air in the way that always makes him giggle. 'Did you do anything nice?'

I shrugged. 'Hung out with Jimmy Wigmore.'

'You still mates with the swim kid?' He raised an eyebrow. He doesn't approve of Jimmy much cos he says his dad is weak-chinned and halfway to being a scab cos he voted against the strikes at first. 'What d'you get up to then?' he asked.

I thought about what we'd actually done: how we'd printed off the application forms at Agnes's house and I'd faked all our dads' signatures on the parental permission bit. And how we'd argued about songs (Agnes thought smaltzy ballad, I thought lesbian Euro disco, Jimmy thought classic Beatles or Elton John – I won!). And how we'd moved on to what to wear because Agnes was going to need some serious styling. Only of course I didn't tell him any of that. Cos if hanging out with Jimmy Wigmore made him frown, being bessie mates with an immo would send him off the scale.

So I just said, 'Not much.'

'Which means you've got another of your crazy plans on the go,' me dad said with a smile. 'Never boring with you around, is it, Elfie love? What is it this time?'

I just shrugged and tried to do a kooky grin.

'Well, I hope that Jimmy Wigmore knows what he's let himself in for,' he said.

'I told you – we're not doing anything.'

Me dad was looking over at the shelf where there's a photo of him and me mam on their wedding day. Dad used to be dead good looking when he was younger – not film-star good looking like Agnes's dad, more in a dodgy 90s Scouse band member kind of way – and he still sort of is, only he looks loads older and tireder these days.

'Jimmy's dad wasn't at the picket line today,' he said.

'Oh.' I looked at him. He had a funny expression on his face.

'Maybe he was just sick or summat?' I suggested.

'Maybe,' he said, putting Alfie down and flopping on to the sofa.

He flicked on the TV and sat playing with Alfie while I made him some food (fish fingers, smiley faces and spaghetti hoops) and brought it in on a tray. Alfie had fallen asleep on the sofa. He was filthy and still in his grubby jeans and T-shirt but he looked dead cute.

The football was on. Liverpool, me mam's favourites, versus some Euro team with a funny name. Me dad's usually really into the football but that night it was like he wasn't really watching. I suppose he was thinking about her.

I got my own food and brought it in on a tray, and we both ate without talking for a bit, pretending the food was OK (I'm the world's second worst cook – me mam is officially number one). Dad swore at the telly occasionally cos Liverpool were losing to the foreign team – even though he's been an Everton man all his life. Unlucky in love and in football, I guess.

'I need some money for nappies, Dad,' I said after a bit.

'For God's sake!' he yelled, as the Liverpool striker hit the cross bar.

'I thought you hated Liverpool?' I said.

'Yeah, well there's British pride at stake here,' he said, putting down his unfinished plate of food on the floor.

'Who are they playing?'

'Some Portuguese team I can't pronounce.'

'Like the immos?' I asked.

'Exactly,' he said. 'Only half the reds are frigging immos themselves. Look at that squad list – they sound like British names to you? They haven't an ounce of Mersey pride between them.'

'That's probably why me mam supports them, then,' I said.

That was the first time either of us had mentioned her all day.

Me dad paused. 'She'll be back, you know,' he said.

'I thought she said she was going for good this time,' I muttered, looking down at my chipped nails and trying to sound like I didn't care.

'She always says that, doesn't she?' he replied. 'But

your mam and me, we're like Superman and Lois Lane, or Princess Leia and Luke Skywalker. We're meant to be together.'

I didn't point out to him that neither of those couples had happy-ever-afters (or that Luke and Leia are actually brother and sister!). Or that I didn't even want me mam to come back. He looked too gutted.

'Oh!' He leapt to his feet, hands on his head as Liverpool conceded a stupid goal.

He sat down again and put his arm round me. 'How much money did you say you need?'

'Just for nappies and stuff,' I said.

He rummaged in the back pocket of his jeans and pulled out his wallet. 'Here,' he said, passing me a tenner.

'Thanks.'

I took the note from him and shoved it into my skirt pocket, then curled myself up next to him, my head resting on his shoulder, just like I used to when I was little. I didn't mention that we also needed more baby milk. Or that there was no food in the fridge. Or that we were out of loo roll. And I didn't mention about the red telephone bill, either. Instead, I tried to think about bringing home my share of the £25,000 prize so me dad could stop worrying about money for a bit.

Later on, after the football had finished (Liverpool lost 3–0), I crept into bed with Alfie. That's what I do when me mam walks out cos I want him to know that I'm not going anywhere. That I'll always be there for him. And cos lying close to his warm, soft body and listening to his baby breaths purring in the darkness somehow makes me feel less alone too.

Jimmy

At first, my dad wanted me to be a runner cos I was tall and someone said to him that I might be like one of those Kenyan runners who always win gold in the Olympics. He started making me try out in county competitions from when I was about eight. I even placed number twelve in the county for the 800 metres one year. Only that wasn't good enough for my dad.

So he enrolled me in the local swimming club. It turned out I was good. Better than good.

Right from the start, I loved swimming. I loved being in the water. I seemed to function better there than I did on dry land. My big flipper feet that had tripped me up on the running track seemed to help me slice through the water. 'Like fins,' Elfie Baguley said. And, as usual, she was right.

By the time I was eleven, I was swimming thirty-two miles a week. Which sounds like a lot – and it is – but it never seemed like too much to me, somehow. I just didn't seem to get tired. Then the local coach recommended that I join a bigger club, so I started training at the Olympic-sized pool on the other side of Liverpool. It means getting up before five and travelling miles but I don't mind that either. Now I do more like forty miles a week, which Elfie tells me is the aerobic equivalent of running more than 160 miles on dry land. I don't know how on earth she figured that out, or even whether she's just making it up, but basically it's a really long way.

I spend over twenty-seven hours a week in the

pool; most nights I dream that I'm in the water, and at school I watch everything through a sea of chlorine. Sometimes, I fall asleep in class because I just can't keep my eyes open. That's the only bad thing about it really. As soon as I get out of the water, I'm back to being weird gangly me, the kid who trips up on his own big feet and smells of chlorine and snores in the back of geography.

But I can put up with being called 'Nemo' and 'The Little Mermaid' and 'Flipper' cos when I get back in the pool, I feel at home again. And anyway, my dad wants to give me the chances he never had and I don't want to let him down.

'Where have you been, son?'

My dad was standing in the middle of the sitting room when I got back from hanging out with Elfie and Agnes. He had my training bag slung over his shoulder.

I glanced at my watch. I was late. I'd never been late for training before. Ever.

'Um . . . just out,' I said, feeling my face start to burn. 'With friends.'

'You're late for training,' he said, quietly.

'I'm really, really sorry. I lost track of time and . . .' I reached out for my kit bag.

He hung on to it and kept staring at me. 'Nearly half an hour late.'

I glanced at my feet nervously. My dad never gets mad at me. Not really. 'I'm sorry, Dad. Like I said, I lost track of time.'

'You don't have that kind of time to waste at the moment,' he said with a sigh. 'There are national trials coming up in Wolverhampton: Olympic target squad selections.'

'I'm sorry,' I repeated. 'It won't happen again.'

'Let's go then,' he said quietly.

We headed out on to the street where a gang of about five little kids were racing round on hand-me-down bikes, doing Evil-Kenevil-style jumps over a load of recycling boxes.

'Bye, Mam,' I called, as I pulled the door to.

'She's already gone,' he said.

'To work?'

'She got a few extra shifts at the bar.'

'Right,' I said.

Since the strike started, my dad hadn't been bringing any money home and I knew it really, really bothered him. I heard him and my mam arguing about money at night when I was lying in bed, thinking about butterfly arms and white tiles far, far beneath the blue.

I glanced over at the Baguley house. The curtains to their sitting room were open and I could see Elfie and her dad on the sofa, watching TV. 'So, you and Elfie Baguley are – what? Friends again now?' he asked.

'I guess.'

'Or more than that?' He glanced sideways at me and I felt myself go red. My dad and I never talk about stuff like this. 'Is she your girlfriend now?'

'No, Dad!' I said quickly, my cheeks getting even hotter now.

'Because you do remember that all she ever does is get you into a heap of trouble,' he said.

'Yeah, Dad. I remember.'

'And she'll do the same again if you let her.'

'She just wants me to help her with something,' I said.

'Course she does,' said Dad. He shook his head and stared down at his feet.

One of the kids – the ginger one – was racing towards one of the jumps, yelling like he was going into battle. I watched as his brother's old bike – way too big for him – went flying up in the air and then came down with a crash in the middle of the recycling boxes.

'I just hope for your sake she's not like that mam of hers,' my dad was saying.

I watched the ginger kid disentangling himself from the pile of plastic and metal and laughing wildly. For some reason it made me think of Elfie setting fire to the red bill and choking on her tea-bag cigarette.

'Anyway, my point is that you don't need distractions at this point in your career,' said my dad, firmly.

'I know, Dad,' I said. 'But . . .'

'But nothing. You don't want to go throwing away all your hard work for some girl. Especially not *that* girl!'

He didn't say anything else after that. He didn't need to. And I didn't know what to say either so we walked the rest of the way in silence.

Agnes

Our home in Portugal is by the sea. Lots of tourists go there to see its high cliffs staggering down to sandy beaches and blue seas. It's a place where the sun always shines and you can hear people talking in many different languages. That is where we lived when I was small and where we still live when my father is between contracts.

When we are away, my father rents the house out to tourists. Sometimes we find the things they have left behind: an earring under the bed, a broken bucket, or a pair of goggles by the pool: reminders that the house is not ours alone.

I learned to love words at the seaside, too. Playing on the beach listening to the tourists speaking in different languages, tossing words to each other casually, like a beach ball. I picked up the words they threw around and collected them like shells.

My dad came back from work early that day and he was in a good mood. 'Let's drive out to the coast,' he suggested. 'We have maybe a couple of hours of light left and there is something I want to show you.'

Me and my dad have always done things together, ever since I was little. My mum calls us the *duo terrivel* (the dreadful duo!) and says it's a good job there's at least one adult in the family. But she smiled when my dad said he was taking me out. Said it would do me good, and glanced at my dad in that way she's been doing recently. Like they're both worried about me.

'Come on, *sapeca*!' said my dad. *Sapeca* means 'nice but naughty'. It is one of my dad's pet names for me. One of my favourites.

So, we got in the car and headed towards Liverpool and then out along the north coast road. All the way, my dad talked about the history of the region, local industry, the climate, because he always wants me to find out as much as I can about the places we live. My dad likes us to talk in English. He reckons this will help me learn the language and he says it helps him too. He is a collector of words, just like me.

We stopped in a place called Crosby, and parked where the grass-strewn sand dunes finally give way to a vast, damp, sandy shore. It had started raining, and there was a sharp wind blowing inland from the Irish Sea. 'See the beautiful English summer!' my dad said as we sat in the car for a bit, building up courage to step out into the wind. 'Come on, then.' He laughed. 'You said you missed the sea!'

We climbed out of the car and braved our way across the dunes. We were quiet for a while; we had our hoods pulled tightly over our heads and, in any case, the wind made it hard to talk, whipping the words straight out of our mouths.

At first I thought I must be imagining the man: a black, solitary figure, standing twenty metres or so out into the surf, staring towards the horizon. He looked like someone walking to a cold watery death, or wading out to rejoin his fishy ancestors in the deep. I was about to cry out when I noticed another, twenty metres or so to his left, standing even further out. He had grey surf lapping round his waist. And then another, and another – solid figures, evenly spaced along the tideline, each as still and staring as the last, each in the same position of contemplation.

I turned to my dad. 'What are they?' I yelled above the wind.

'Sculptures,' he shouted back. 'I thought maybe you would like them.' He gestured out along the shoreline where I could see more of them now, some almost completely submerged in the sea, others standing upright on the sandbanks. 'Come on,' he said.

We had to take our shoes off to wade across the wet sand. The rain wasn't that heavy, but the wind whipped it against us so that it stung our skin. Beneath my feet, I could feel the indentations that the waves had made in the hard cold sand.

'There are one hundred figures spread over three kilometres of the coastline,' my dad yelled. 'The artist calls them "Another World" – Mundo Outro.'

The closest figure was buried up to its knees in the sand. From a distance it had looked black, but as

I got closer I could see it had been cast in a kind of bronze which, even in the grey early evening, gave off an eerie amber glow. It was taller than I expected, too: even with half its legs submerged, it was taller than me.

My dad was a few metres behind me. 'What do you think, *anjo*?' he shouted. *Anjo* is another of his names for me. In English it means 'angel'.

'I don't know,' I said. And I didn't. My feet were in the surf and I felt the freezing brine cut into my toes and soak the bottom of my trousers. I walked round to face the Iron Man. He had an odd, blank expression on his face.

'What do you think they are looking at?' he shouted.

'Maybe they remember homes far away across the sea,' I said, thinking of my own home, on a different coast, facing out to a different sea.

I think he wanted to say something then. Ever since the holidays started, I know he has been worrying about me. When I was at school I could pretend I had some friends, but since term ended it is has become more and more obvious that I don't. And I love my dad and I hate it when he worries about me, so I said quickly, 'I had some friends over today.'

'Really?' he said, still looking at the bronze figure, trying to act like this wasn't a big deal.

'Yes,' I said. 'Elfie and Jimmy. They are in my same form at school.'

'That's great, *anjo*,' he said. 'Your mother worries that you may be –' he hesitated – 'finding it hard.'

'No, Dad,' I said, looking down at my bare feet which were turning slowly blue with cold. 'Everything is fine.'

'I told her so,' he said, wrapping an arm around me and pulling me close. 'She worried the strike may be making things harder for you. At school, and . . . with the other young people.'

'Is not a problem,' I lied.

'That's what I said. I told her kids your age do not worry about politics.' He laughed. 'Just the old men my age who have playground scraps. I'm glad to hear everything is OK.' Then he pulled me in tight and kissed me on the head and we stood for ages like that, watching as the receding tide drew back to reveal acres more sand, releasing more and more of the figures on to dry land.

The sun was starting to go down, and a low red light was catching in the puddles left behind by the sea, marking out in orange and mahogany and ochre the wave patterns on the sand.

'Do you know what they make me think of?' my dad asked. The wind had dropped so he no longer had to shout. 'The statues, I mean.'

'What?'

'They look like they are on strike!' He grinned.

I smiled, thinking of the crowds of men down by the entrance to the power plant. The ones who threw rocks at the buses carrying the scabs across the line every day. I thought about Elfie's dad and Jimmy's. Were they the ones throwing rocks, I wondered? Elfie had said her dad would go mad if he knew she'd even spoken to me. I was the enemy she said.

'So,' said my dad. 'What is your friend with the funny name called again?'

I hesitated for a second. I had never really lied

to my dad before, but Elfie had said I was sworn to secrecy. That it was essential to the success of the plan. 'Elfie,' I said. 'Elfie Smith.'

Rules of Talent TV No. 6:
If your real family won't get behind you, make up a new one

Elfie

When I was little I used to pretend I was adopted. Or swapped at birth. You know, like my real mam was actually some massively famous pop star who'd been forced to give me up and had been searching for me ever since (or maybe she was a film legend, or an It-girl or even all three – you've gotta aim high, right?).

I used to imagine she'd come for me one day, turn up on the doorstep and have a big showdown with me mam. She'd tell her she didn't deserve a daughter like me and then we'd drive off into the sunset in her big white limo and she'd say, 'I'm your mam now and that woman is never gonna hurt you again.'

In my fantasy, me dad then came to live with us (in our massive mansion with a pool and jacuzzi) and, by some amazing twist of fate, it'd turn out he was actually my real dad after all. And then we all lived happily ever after.

It got a bit more complicated when our Alfie was born and with everyone always saying how much I look like me mam. And we definitely have the same weird toenails which I figure rules out the adoption/swapped at birth possibilities.

So I came up with this new fantasy which involved me dad divorcing me mam and finding me and Alfie a new stepmam who baked fairy cakes, combed nits out of hair and turned up to watch school concerts. I figured that since practically half the kids in my class came from broken homes it didn't exactly seem fair that my parents wouldn't just do the sensible thing and split up.

I wasn't exactly sure how me going on Talent TV was going to make me dad dump me mam, but I had this crazy idea it might. And even though I'd always said I wouldn't appear on a TV talent show if you paid me, I figured at least if we won the prize money I could hire someone to kidnap me mam and sell her to the circus, or summat. And then it'd all be worth it.

Jimmy

Five minutes after I got back from training the next morning there was a ring on the doorbell and there, standing on the doorstep, was Elfie with baby Alfie in tow.

'You're early,' I said. I looked down at my bare feet, the skin still slightly puckered from the pool.

'I'm sorry,' she said grumpily. 'Is this not a convenient time for you?'

'No, I didn't mean that,' I said, stumbling over my words. 'I only meant . . .'

'All right! All right! No need to get your knickers in a twist,' she said. 'Are you coming, or what?'

I quickly pulled on my coat and trainers and called to my dad that I was going out.

'Don't be late for training this afternoon,' he shouted back.

'I won't.'

Elfie raised an eyebrow. She reckons my dad is a pushy control freak. I've tried convincing her otherwise but she just tells me I'm brainwashed.

I stumbled out of the door, and followed her down the path. I figured she must have got dressed after her dad left for the picket line because I doubt he'd have let her go out like that otherwise. It looked like she was wearing her mam's clothes again cos they didn't really fit her properly. She had on a miniskirt that was all baggy round her hips and a boob tube which her boobs didn't really fill (although there was NO way I was telling her that). Then she had her dad's massive donkey jacket on top of it all, and she still had on the same make-up from yesterday, only now it was smudged and dirty looking.

'Doesn't your old man ever let up on you?' she was saying.

'He just wants me to be the best,' I said, drawing level and shortening my stride so as not to outstrip her. My legs are about a foot longer than hers. I don't think she realises I have to walk deliberately slowly when I'm with her and I wasn't about to tell her that right then, either.

She paused and looked at me, her nose scrunched up. 'And if it turns out you're not?'

I shrugged. 'I dunno.'

'That sucks!' she said. 'I'm glad he's not my old man. I'd just be a colossal disappointment.' Then she started off again, pushing the buggy in a funny side-to-side motion, deliberately stepping on the cracks in the paving stones. 'Step on the cracks, break your mam's back!' she said with a grin. 'Crackety-crack!'

Alfie giggled as the buggy swerved.

'Um, how's *your* dad?' I asked warily. She seemed in far too good a mood which was never the best sign with Elfie.

'Grand,' she said, still hopscotching over the cracks. 'Why wouldn't he be?'

'Only, you know –' I hesitated.

'What?' She turned round and gave me a funny look.

I could feel the blood rushing to my face. 'You know – with your mam going.'

She paused, just for a moment. 'Oh, yeah, that!' she said, shrugging and starting up her dance again. 'He's over it already and so am I!'

I didn't know what to say, because I knew she was

gutted about it really. But I also knew she'd go mental if I said so.

I always feel funny walking through town with Elfie Baguley. Cos she's so – not cool, exactly – but, well, she's Elfie and I'm just Jimmy Wigmore. I'm sure people must look at me and Elfie and wonder what we're doing together. Sometimes I wonder myself.

Anyway, we kept on walking for a bit, across the main road and in the direction of the marshes. Then Alfie started crying. 'What's wrong now?' said Elfie. She always talks to Alfie like he's a grown-up. She reckons he understands everything she says to him but he didn't seem to be listening because he just kept crying.

'Maybe he needs his nappy changing?' I said.

'Yeah, well, have you got any idea how expensive nappies are?' she replied. She'd stopped skipping and was dragging her feet as she walked.

'No,' I shrugged.

'And have you ever tried shoving a jumbo pack of Pampers up your top without some security guard seeing?'

'Um, no,' I said again.

She kicked up a shower of dust with her bejewelled feet. 'Figures,' she said. 'Lanky string of spaghetti like you, you'd look like a flippin' kebab. Sooner we win that prize money and get airlifted out of poverty the better, I reckon.'

'Um – about that, Elfie,' I said, nervously. 'I've been thinking and I'm not sure it's the best plan.'

'Why not? We can be rich, my friend!' she said, doing a little skip which I think was supposed to be her being rich.

'Yeah, but your dad . . .'

'He'll forgive us when we win.'

'But what if we don't?' I asked.

'Did you hear the immo sing?' she said.

'Um – yeah?'

'Well then, enough said. We've struck gold with those immo vocal chords, Jimmy Wigmore. The girl has serious star potential. She just needs a bit of styling by yours truly and she'll be oozing x-factor, I'm telling you.'

I couldn't really disagree with her about Agnes's

singing. She was pretty amazing. It was the rest of the plan I wasn't sure of. 'It's just –' I started to say.

'Look,' said Elfie firmly. 'I'm not saying this won't be an emotional rollercoaster, as they say in the business!' She grinned. 'But it'll be the ride of your life, Jimmy Wigmore!'

I was about to try and object when she exclaimed, 'Oh no! That's all we need!'

I followed the direction of her gaze and saw two girls from our year at school walking towards us on the other side of the road. They both live on the estate but I mostly try to avoid them. I went to duck behind a tree, but Elfie yanked me back out again. 'Too late trying to hide, kiddo,' she said. 'We'll just have to front them out.'

She was right: they'd already clocked us and they were giggling like mad.

'Oi, Elfie!' called the blonde girl who was called Kirby and who lived just down the road from us. 'What you doing with Jimmy the Fish?'

Kirby and Elfie have been sworn enemies ever since the time in Year Three when Elfie stole Kirby's pants and put them in the teacher's desk. And then Kirby got back at her by telling everyone Elfie's mam had French kissed our headmaster behind the trolley park at Lidl (which she still says is true to this day, and with Elfie's mam you never know).

'Are you and the dolphin boy, like, going steady now?' giggled Kirby's friend who calls herself 'Pinkie', although everyone who went to primary school with her – including me and Elfie – knows her real name is Penelope Penney (yes, seriously!).

They were both giggling, and I could feel myself go the colour of ketchup. But Elfie just stuck out her chest, tossed her head like a supermodel and put on her best 'Merseyside Wag' voice. 'Don't be daft!' said Elfie. 'He's just my manny.'

'What's one of them?' asked Pinkie.

'Duh! A male nanny,' Elfie said, giving her a look. 'I should have thought it was obvious!'

'Never heard of one!' said Kirby, narrowing her eyes. Elfie reckons her mam copied that pop star who named her kids after the places where they were conceived – only Kirby's mam can't spell.

'Can I help it if everyone round here is so out of touch?' Elfie said in her poshest voice. 'Mr and Mrs Golden-balls have a manny – and so does that pop star with the pink afro, who goes out in just her knickers.'

'Does she even have kids?' said Pinkie.

'Keep up, sister!' Elfie said, raising her eyebrows as far as they could possibly go. 'Anyway, Jimmy's my manny, and he's looking after my kid brother, a] because he's had a crush on me since Year Three and b] because I don't like changing nappies, and all that crap.'

I started to blink madly, which is what I always do when I'm nervous (Elfie says it freaks her out), and if it had been physically possible to go redder without exploding at that point, I reckon I probably would have.

'Where's your mam then?' asked Pinkie.

'She's away a lot with work at the moment,' said Elfie, with her best freckly smile.

'Yeah? Remind me what it is she does again,' said Kirby, smirking.

I held my breath and waited for it.

'If you must know she's working as a make-up artist for the world's oldest country and western singer,' said Elfie, two small spots of colour appearing amid the freckles on her cheeks.

'Really?' said Kirby, grinning at Pinkie.

'Yeah. Those country and western babes trowel it on so thick most of the make-up girls end up with repetitive strain injury after a couple of weeks,' Elfie went on in a sing-song voice, her head tipped to one side like it always is when she's making up her craziest lies. 'But me mam used to do make up for "King Facelift" himself, so she built up her Polyfilla muscles and now Miss Tennessee 1905 always asks for her.' She finished with one of her big fake grins.

'Funny that,' said Kirby. 'Cos my sister reckons she saw your mam dancing at Club Halo in town on Friday.'

'She must have a twin sister or a lookalike or whatever!' said Elfie quickly, the pink spots darkening in her cheeks.

'Must be, cos the woman she saw was dancing with some immo who looked half her age.' Kirby flashed a nasty grin. 'Dancing real close, apparently.'

Elfie's smile slipped, just a fraction. 'Well, she must have seen wrong, Kirby,' she said. 'Because me mam's applying cement to Miss Glam Gran Alabama's facial cracks as we speak.'

And then, before either of them had a chance to answer (because even Elfie knows when she's pushed her luck), she said, 'Anyway, gotta go. Alfie's got pilates, followed by his baby Mandarin class. Can't be late! See you around!'

Then she grabbed me by the arm and gave them a cutesy little wave as she tugged me off in the direction of the marshes. 'Come on, our Jimmy,' she said.

'Yeah, ta-ta, our Jimmy,' I could hear Kirby shouting, as Elfie dragged me at top speed round the corner.

'Yeah! Bysie-bye, our Jimmy!' shouted Pinkie. 'Did the chlorine make your ears go like that or was it hanging out with Elfie what did it?'

And then they both burst into fits of laughter like she'd said the funniest thing in the world and Elfie stormed ahead so fast I had to hurry a bit to keep up with her.

'Are you OK, Elfie?' I asked, glancing back at Pinkie and Kirby who were still staring in our direction and laughing.

She stopped suddenly and turned round to look at me. 'You don't really think me mam's hooked up with an immo, do you?' Her face was still pink under the freckles and she was staring right at me.

I blinked a bit because I didn't know what to say. Like I say, with Elfie's mam you never know. 'They probably just said that to wind you up,' I lied.

She looked down at her feet. Her sandals looked old and shabby, missing most of their sparkles.

'I hope so,' she said quietly. 'Cos me dad's got enough to worry about already. If he finds out she's dating the enemy, I reckon it'll destroy him.'

Agnes

The other thing about nobody talking to you is that you have loads of time to sit and watch and listen. And you notice things – things people don't want you to notice. So that's what I did. I watched and listened and I collected bits and bobs about all the kids in my class at school. The same way I collected words.

So, I knew that Kirby Winstanley's parents were getting divorced. I knew that the eldest Tyzack boy didn't really have an ASBO like he claimed and I knew that Pinkie Penney couldn't read properly, which is why she always went to the nurse when we had to read parts in English.

I knew things about Jimmy Wigmore too. I knew that he did stuff for Elfie: like finishing her homework and painting over the graffiti about her mum that someone wrote in the toilets. I also knew that Jimmy sometimes fell asleep in geography and that he gets eczema on his arms and face because of all the chlorine and I thought that was why he kept his hair long, so no one could see it.

I also knew that he was the one who climbed up on the roof of the science block and got my coat the time someone threw it out of the window, though when I tried to say thank you he denied it.

I thought I knew stuff about Elfie Baguley too.

Because there were always rumours going round school about Elfie's family: about her dad, who they said has a tattoo of the eight cooling towers on his bum; and her mum, who was supposed to have been dropped from the original line-up of the nation's biggest girl band and had an affair with the deputy head (or a boy in Year Ten, depending who you ask). There were rumours about Elfie herself too. Lots of them: that she got her name because her mam and Pixie Geldoff's mam had a dare; that she once did time in juvenile detention; that her dad wasn't her baby brother's dad; that she was the one who did the scab graffiti on the immo houses.

Yes, there were loads of rumours about Elfie Baguley. Only Jimmy said she made half of them up herself. And once I started hanging out with her, I didn't know what to believe any more.

'You cannot wear that!' said Elfie when I showed her what I was planning to wear to the audition.

We were down by the river, under the railway bridge, where we'd been meeting to rehearse every day for the last week. Jimmy said it was their den. Elfie said it was our *Pop to the Top* campaign headquarters. Mainly, it was somewhere we could go where no one was likely to see the three of us together (or the four of us since Elfie usually had Alfie with her too). She'd introduced loads of security measures – like a password we had to say when we turned up at rehearsals, because she reckoned that secrecy was essential to the success of the plan. 'She says it's a copyright issue,' Jimmy explained. 'She reckons if her ideas get leaked people will try to copy them or something.' He shrugged when he said this, then went bright red, like he always does when he talks to me. And then he shut up and didn't even look at me for about half an hour.

We now had just over a week left until the first round of auditions and Elfie reckoned some of the acts would have been practising for months, so she said we needed an intensive programme of rehearsal. But the more I thought about the competition, the less I thought I'd be able to do it. I lay in bed at night trying to imagine singing with Elfie – on a stage, in front of people. The idea made me feel sick. Made hundreds of moths dance in my stomach. I told Elfie that morning but she said it was too late, she'd already sent in our application forms. 'And anyway, you pinkie promised.'

'But I –' I tried to explain but I didn't have the words.

'Clearly you do not understand pinkie promises,' said Elfie. 'If you back out now you get your finger hacked off – obviously – but you also get cursed for life.'

I opened my mouth to argue.

'And I will be personally in charge of the cursing,' said Elfie. 'Now stop whinging, cos we need to start thinking about your makeover.'

'Makeover?' I said, feeling the moths dance some more. I tried to catch Jimmy's eye but he was staring really hard at the graffiti on the arch of the bridge.

'Flippin' heck! We really need to work on your vocabulary!' said Elfie huffily. 'A makeover is when I make you look a bit less like a skinny geek and a bit more like a supermodel, all with the aid of me mam's magical make-up cast-offs.'

She pulled a giant floral washbag from the changing bag hanging off Alfie's buggy. It was overflowing with broken make-up compacts, leaking lipglosses and crumbling multi-coloured eyeshadows.

'Being a pop star is all about image,' she went on, yanking out even more stuff: a spangly dress, a pair of tassel-fronted sandals with enormous heels and the biggest bottle of hairspray I'd ever seen.

I didn't say anything. I didn't know *what* to say.

'So, I figured you'd need a bit of styling,' she went on, holding the dress up against me. 'No offence, but this Spanish Goth look you've got going on is not exactly going to cut it on national TV.'

'She's Portuguese,' said Jimmy quietly. 'And it's local TV, Elfie.'

'Whatever. It has viewing figures in the hundreds of thousands and first impressions are everything, so we need to bling this one up a bit! You could be sort of pretty if we put a bit of slap on you.'

It was raining and even under the bridge it was damp and cold. I stared at the clothes she was shaking in front of my face, trying to imagine how I would look in them. 'Sort of pretty' she had said, but with a curl of her lip that made me think she didn't really mean it. Jimmy had gone red again and was looking anywhere but at me.

'What's the problem?' said Elfie.

I didn't answer. I'd never worn anything remotely like Elfie's mum's dress before and I couldn't imagine myself in it. I shivered a little, just looking at it.

'Look what I'm planning to wear,' said Elfie, taking off the massive black men's jacket she's always got on to reveal yet another micro miniskirt and handkerchief top. Jimmy stared so hard I thought his eyes were going to pop out.

'What if I don't want to look like you,' I murmured.

'You should be so lucky to look like me,' said Elfie, throwing the dress at me. 'But you can hardly look worse than you do at the mo, so stop your fretting and put it on.'

I glanced at Jimmy again but he took one look at me holding the gold dress, blinked about ten times and then studied his giant feet like they were suddenly the most interesting things in the world.

'What's up now?' Elfie was staring at me. She had her hair in a side ponytail and she'd plastered on some deep red lipstick, sparkling green eyeshadow and bright spots of rouge on her cheeks. She did look kind of amazing in an over-the-top sort of way. I wished I could put her mum's dress on and look like her but I knew I wouldn't. Jimmy obviously knew it too and that was probably why he wouldn't meet my eye.

'Nothing,' I said. 'Where you want me change?'

'Well not here, obviously,' said Elfie. She pointed to the other side of the bridge where there was a clump of bushes.

I didn't bother to argue any more. I might only have been hanging out with Elfie just over a week but, just like Jimmy, I already knew there was no point in disagreeing. So I took the dress from her and trudged out into the rain.

'We'll put a bit of slap on you after,' Elfie yelled from under the bridge. She was perched with her bum on the cobbled concrete, legs twirling in the air like she was on an imaginary bicycle. 'Lipgloss and a load of eyeliner and you won't recognise yourself.'

I slid behind the bushes and stared down at the dress, already feeling cold and damp. It was drawing towards the end of August but it felt like autumn. 'Is it OK for your mother?' I asked quietly.

'You what?' Elfie yelled.

I glanced out and saw Elfie's legs stop pedalling for a moment. I looked at the dress again. 'Your mum. Is it OK for her that I wear dress?'

'Course it is,' she answered with no hesitation. Then her voice changed a bit. 'I mean, the twin lesbian starlets she's working for give her so many hand-me-downs she hasn't even got time to wear them all.'

'You say she work for R and B star?' I said. I could feel the fine mist of the rain bring up goosebumps on my skin. I pulled the dress hurriedly over my head.

'Yeah, yeah! She works with all the big names,' said Elfie, quickly. 'In fact, last year at the Brit Awards it all kicked off cos that psycho supermodel with the big nose and the pop diva who's into adopting monkeys got into a massive cat fight because they both wanted me mam to do some of her pre-show reiki on them.'

'Reiki?' I asked. I closed my eyes, pulled the tiny

dress down as far as it would go then stepped out from behind the bush.

Elfie was now leaning on one of the bridge supports, reclining like she was on a sun lounger. Jimmy was crouched down, fiddling with his dad's battered old MP3 player: Elfie had put him in charge of backing music.

'You know, hands on healing stuff,' Elfie went on, barely looking at me. 'She's got this gift. Like a spiritual thing. I think I've got it, too. She hears voices, channels the spirits and that. Aren't I right, Jimmy?'

Jimmy looked up then and saw me. His pale blue eyes went wide as buttons. 'Um – yeah,' he said. His face was a glowing red jellyfish and his mouth was open, like a freshly caught mackerel.

I could see from his expression how stupid I looked. I tugged the dress down a bit further and glanced down at the brown river. It's so wide here it's like a motorway, and it smells a little of the sea. I caught a shadowy reflection of myself in the water. A skinny girl in a sparkly gold dress, her limbs and throat exposed. She looked nothing like me.

'Yeah, you look all right,' said Elfie with a quick nod. 'I should be a stylist, me.'

Jimmy was still staring at me.

'I look stupid,' I said.

'You want me to say you look amazing?' said Elfie. 'I never took you for a fishing-for-compliments type.'

'No, I –'

'Flippin' 'eck! I swear you've got that body dysmorphic thing,' she went on.

'What?' I could feel Jimmy still looking at me.

'You know, body dysmorphic problem or disorder, or whatever. It's when you reckon you look rubbish in everything. That It-girl's got it, and her therapist made her wear a see-through dress on the red carpet as part of her treatment. I reckon me mam's Primani number should be a miracle cure for you, too.'

'I don't have body dys–' I hesitated, stumbling over the difficult word – 'dys-mor-phic disorder.'

'Yeah, that's what the It-girl said, too,' Elfie replied. 'Right before she started wrapping herself in cellophane and trying to chop off body parts.'

Jimmy wasn't looking at me any more. He was glancing off across the water, still flushed, his eyes blinking like mad.

'I look stupid,' I repeated, seeing my ghostly reflection in the water again. Me but not me.

'Oh, for effing Norah's sake! We're meant to look stupid!' said Elfie. 'We're pop stars!'

I stared at her for a moment, imagining myself sinking beneath the muddy brown water. Didn't Elfie say she once fell in and Jimmy dived in to save her?

'What if I don't want to be pop star?' I said quietly.

'Then go home,' she said with a shrug. 'Jimmy can sing with me.'

Jimmy looked back quickly, a horrified expression on his face. 'Elfie, I . . .'

'Reckon he'd look awesome in that dress. He's deffo got the legs for it.'

'Elfie!' Jimmy stared desperately at me, his mouth opening and closing like a fish on land, struggling for air.

'Bit of loo roll down his top to give him a bit of cleavage. Mind you,' she said, staring critically at my boobs, 'you could do with a couple of boxes of Kleenex an' all.'

I wrapped my hand quickly round my chest and felt my cheeks burning as Jimmy made a choking noise.

Just then, Alfie, who'd been tottering over the pebbles, fell into Elfie's legs with a giggle. She picked him up and cuddled him close, nibbling at his nose and ears as he wriggled and laughed some more.

'So, you gonna wear it or does swim boy here get to do his Mariah Carey impression?' she asked, burying her nose into Alfie's tummy and blowing a raspberry, making him shriek with laughter.

I said nothing. Alfie giggled and poked his finger into Elfie's grey-blue eye socket. I didn't dare look at Jimmy who had bent down and started fiddling with the MP3 player again.

'Yes,' I said, quietly. 'I do it.'

'Good,' she said, her voice light and breezy again, back into her storytelling mode. 'And don't go round telling anyone all that stuff I told you about me mam either. Half the stuff she does, I've had to sign the Official Secrets Act about, and the other half is subject to confidentiality agreements drawn up by various A-listers. It's all very hush-hush/need to know,' she said. She kissed Alfie on the cheek again and gave him a freckly smile. 'And I'm afraid, Agg-ness, you're simply not in the circle of trust.'

Rules of Talent TV No. 7:
Give 110% at the first audition

Jimmy

So it was the morning of the first audition and all Elfie had been going on about for the past two days was 'putting our heart and soul' into it and 'giving it one-hundred-and-ten per cent', even though clearly the whole idea was mad and never going to work. Mind you, I was used to that with Elfie's plans. The big difference with this one was that it was also going to land us in a whole load of trouble. Well, at least a whole load more trouble than we'd ever been in before.

I mean my and Elfie's dads basically hated Agnes's dad because of the strike. So when it came out we'd formed a pop group together and entered the North West equivalent of *American Idol*, it was going to cause no end of strife. Only, whenever I tried to suggest this to Elfie she just came back with stuff like, 'It's all under control,' and, 'It'll be worth it when we win.' And when I tried to point out that we might not win, she told me I needed to bring more positive energy to the project. 'Agnes is a star in the making and if you can't tell that, you need your ears testing,' she said. 'And your eyes an' all.'

And she was right about that. When Agnes sang, it was so beautiful it made shivers go up and down my spine. And when she put on Elfie's mam's gold dress, she looked like some kind of magical fairy creature or a water nymph. When I swam in the pool the morning of the auditions, I felt like I could hear her voice echoing under the water and it made me swim faster.

There's a big whiteboard on the wall up by the deep end and my dad had written on it my lap sequences for the day: *8 x butterfly, 8 x front crawl, 16 x breast stroke, 8 x back crawl.* That was what I saw each time I came up for air. That and the giant timer clock with massive hands that speed round the dial once every sixty seconds. And my dad, with his stopwatch and clipboard, watching me intently but never catching my eye, noting down every single lap time. Every single one.

But when I went under I could see flashes of gold, just ahead of me, constantly disappearing out of sight, and I swear I could hear her voice, pulling me along.

After I completed the last sequence I came up for air, my heart pounding. My dad came over to the poolside, got down on his haunches and talked me through the day's lap times. I didn't take all of it in. My head was still in the water, clouded with blue and flickering tiles. And for some reason, Agnes's face kept popping into my mind, mingling with the ripples.

'Good times today,' said my dad. 'But you still need to streamline those turns on the butterfly. You're losing time with every rotation.'

I felt kind of bad, because normally when I'm swimming if I think about anybody, it's Elfie. But that day all I could see was Agnes, her arms wrapped so tightly round her body it looked like they were knotted. I was pretty sure Elfie would have been mad at me if I told her – not that I would be stupid enough to do that, and not that she even knew I normally thought about her. But still, I felt funny about it.

When my dad had finished debriefing, I climbed

out and he passed me a towel which I wrapped round my neck. I was still out of breath and I could feel my body starting to sting, the way it always does after a session.

'Dad,' I said. 'Have you ever talked to any of the immos?'

'No,' he said bluntly.

I shrugged and ran the towel over my eyes. 'I just wondered, you know. No one talks to them at school so I just –'

I pulled myself up to my feet. Now I was out of the pool my body had gone back to being gangly and awkward.

'It's the way things are, son,' said my dad, noting something on his clipboard and not looking at me. 'I don't like it any more than you do but there's no point worrying about it. All you've got to worry about at the moment is shaving a few seconds off those lap times so you can impress the Olympic target squad inspectors at Nationals and get some funding, OK?'

He patted me on the back then. He doesn't do that very often. He's not a great one for hugs and stuff.

'OK,' I said.

'Now go and warm down, then get in that shower before your muscles tense up.'

I started to move off towards the showers then I turned round again and said, 'Dad?'

'Yes, son.'

'If I don't get the funding, what'll happen? You know, about paying for training and stuff.'

He didn't answer for a moment. Then he said, 'Don't you worry about that. We'll work it out.'

And that was the end of that discussion.

As soon as I got back, I went to call for Elfie. She was already dressed in full-on audition gear: four inch gladiator sandals, a purple playsuit covered in Playboy bunnies (which I'd once seen her mam wear to the supermarket) and purple, wet-look leggings. She's not as tall as her mam so the leggings sagged a bit round her ankles and she'd had to hold the playsuit up with a big pink plastic belt, but she still looked pretty amazing. She came out on to the doorstep, waving a pack of butties in one hand ('Be prepared. That's my motto,' she explained) and hoiking Alfie up on her hip with the other.

'How do I look?' she asked, doing a little shimmy.

'Um – good?' I replied.

'I was aiming for *dazzling*,' she said, puckering her brow. 'Or breathtaking. Or ravishing. Even awesome would do.'

'Sorry,' I mumbled. 'You look – um – great?'

'Effing Norah! Your vocabulary is even worse than the immo's!' she said with a glare. 'Come on, let's get a move on. It's audition day and we've a talent show to win.'

'But, Elfie –'

Elfie bounced out of the front door, handing Alfie to me and kicking open the buggy at the same time. Clearly she was on electric-bunny form and there was no stopping her.

The sun was shining for once and Alfie was singing in baby language as we made our way to the station. Elfie had taken off her gladiator shoes ('Bleedin' agony – don't know how them gladiators stood it.') and was walking barefoot along the grass verge.

'That's our song,' she announced suddenly.

'What is?' I'd been busy trying to work out if we were going to make it back on time for swim training that evening, and wondering what my dad would say if I pitched up late.

'What our kid's singing. It's our song, that.'

I listened. She was right: Alfie was singing a baby version of The Juliets' audition song. It sounded dead cute, coming out in his little baby voice.

Elfie laughed. 'Reckon he's spent so much time hanging out with us he's got it going round and round in his head all the time.'

I knew how Alfie felt.

'Maybe he should join the band,' laughed Elfie. 'That'd be sure to get us through to the next round. Baby singing genius! Should have thought of that meself.'

We rounded the corner and there was Agnes waiting for us outside the station. She looked up and almost immediately I could feel my face getting hot.

Elfie stopped and turned to me. 'Do a reccy and check no one's around,' she said. 'You never know who could be tailing us.'

'We're not in a spy movie, Elfie,' I said.

But she wasn't listening so I did as she said. When I gave the all clear, she marched up to Agnes, looked her up and down and said, 'So, you turned up then?'

'Yes,' said Agnes, her cheeks pink. 'I turn up.'

Elfie checked her out again and tutted loudly. 'You look a right mess though.'

Agnes bit her lip.

'Where's me mam's dress?'

'In my bag,' said Agnes.

'Well at least that's something,' said Elfie. 'But we need to give you a serious sixty-minute makeover if we're not going to get kicked out of the auditions by the fashion police! I hope you didn't tell your mam and dad where we're going?'

'No. I say we visit museums in Liverpool.'

Elfie snorted. 'That's a good one! My old man would have clocked I was lying straight off if I'd said that. He reckons I'm taking our Alfie to soft play.' She turned to me then. 'What did you tell your dad?'

'Just that I was with you.'

'Bet he loved that, right?'

I shrugged, remembering how he'd pulled a face and said, 'You don't have to do everything that girl tells you, remember?'

'Come on, let's get a wriggle on or we'll miss the train.' And, with that, Elfie marched into the station, leaving me and Agnes staring awkwardly at each other.

Elfie and Agnes couldn't be more different if they tried. For a start, Agnes is tiny. I mean, really small and skinny with no boobs or hips at all – like the waif models you see in magazines. And she's got this deep black hair and olive skin and a face like a baby animal with giant eyes – all black and velvety.

Elfie on the other hand is all curves, pale white freckly skin and light green eyes. Her hair is sort of reddish (although she calls it strawberry blonde) and her lips are just a bit too big for her face. She's probably what magazines would call sassy, or striking, but I reckon Agnes is what they'd call beautiful.

The other big difference between them is the clothes they wear. Elfie had been going more and more trampy in the wardrobe department since her mam did her latest disappearing act. In her short skirts and strappy tops, she reckoned she looked like a WAG, but that morning she just looked like a kid in her mam's high heels and clubbing cast-offs – which I suppose she was.

Agnes didn't seem to want to show an inch of skin. She was wearing a polo neck which went up so high it looked like she would've hidden her face in it if she could. Her sleeves were pulled right down to the tips of her fingers, too. It was like she wanted to be invisible.

Mind you, she didn't stay looking like that for long. Elfie made her change into the gold mini-dress in the bogs at Lime Street Station. Elfie reckoned that if we wanted to be famous we had to act like there were cameras on us at all times. But it had started chucking it down with rain which meant that we all got wet through and by the time we reached the auditions Agnes looked more like a drowned rat than a pop princess. Although she still managed to look sort of beautiful somehow whereas Elfie's hair had gone all frizzy and her gladiator sandals were broken.

Agnes had only been to Liverpool once before, but Elfie said there was no time to visit the Albert Docks or the Liver Building, or take the ferry cross the Mersey. This was not a sightseeing visit, or some kind of social event, she said; this was part of the plan, and strictly business.

So we stood getting soaked outside this big conference centre with hundreds of other auditionees (auditioners? I'm never sure which is the right word) for about two hours waiting to be let in. Elfie was wearing her dad's jacket over her head to stop her hair going even more frizzy, but I hadn't brought a coat and neither had Agnes, and her bare legs started to go blue in the cold.

'We look like we've coordinated the wet-look leggings!' said Elfie.

Agnes glanced down at her legs and said nothing. She was shivering and her lips looked a bruised purple colour. I wished I had a coat I could have lent her.

Then Elfie went off chasing Alfie round some bollards so it was just me and Agnes waiting in the queue. I could feel myself blinking away with the effort of trying not to look like I was staring at her in the tiny gold dress.

'School starts back next week,' I said awkwardly.

'Yes,' said Agnes, biting her lip and looking down.

'Guess you don't like school much?'

'No,' she said.

'I don't like it either, really.'

'Why?' She turned to me suddenly, fixing her black eyes on me in a way that made me start blinking all over again.

'Oh – um – no one really talks to me either,' I said. 'Except Elfie.'

'Why not?' she asked.

I hesitated, not sure how to explain. 'It's the swimming, I suppose,' I said. 'It makes me different, you know? And kids round here don't like anyone different.'

'I think it is the same in every place,' she said quietly.

'You think?' I looked up and caught her eye then.

Elfie had never bothered to ask Agnes about her family or where she came from or anything. And I'd wanted to but hadn't really known how. 'Where were you at school before?' I said. I could smell chlorine on my hair and I wondered if she could smell it, too.

'Germany for a small while,' she said. 'And before in Portugal. And before for a year in Switzerland. My dad work on contracts.'

'Wow!' I said, looking down at my feet again, remembering what my dad said about keeping them in a particular position in the water, using them like fins.

Agnes glanced over at Elfie who was splashing through puddles with Alfie. Neither of us said anything for a few minutes.

'Elfie says if we get through to the next round we'll probably have to skive off school to go,' I said after a while. 'Have you ever skived before?'

'Skived?' she asked, looking at me.

She has this thing about words, I've noticed. She likes all the weird ones, the ones you don't get in the dictionary. She's always asking Elfie what they mean, which really irritates Elfie.

'Skived – bunked – it means skipped school,' I said, blinking.

She smiled then, like I'd given her a present, and her whole face lit up. 'Oh,' she said. 'No, I haven't. You?'

'Only when I'm doing one of Elfie's plans,' I said.

'She has lot of plans?' Agnes asked. Her eyes were darker in the rain and her lashes had little drops of water on them, like beads.

I looked across to Elfie. She had caught Alfie and was tickling him so hard he was doubled over with laughter. The coat had slid off Elfie's head, but she seemed to have forgotten all about her hair going frizzy and she was smiling in that way she only ever does when she's with Alfie.

'Lots,' I said.

'Like this one?'

'No. All different.'

'Tell me,' she said.

'Oh,' I said, feeling myself go pink again. 'Well – um – one time we tried to make our own fireworks and ended up burning off Elfie's eyebrows. Another time we cut up her mam's old clothes to make bunting and hung it out along the street.'

Agnes let out a quick laugh and she suddenly looked like she does when she sings. Different somehow, lighter. 'Elfie does not like her mother?' she asked.

Elfie hadn't told Agnes about her mam going off but I figured she probably knew anyway. Everyone round here knows about Elfie's mam.

'It's complicated,' I said. We were both leaning against the wall of the conference centre, our four feet all pointing in the same direction. I read somewhere that your feet always point towards the person you're thinking of and at that moment all our twenty toes were pointing at Elfie.

'Once we swapped round the door numbers on everyone's houses in the close,' I said, to try and change the subject. 'Even Mrs Newsround never figured out who did it.'

Agnes smiled. 'Mrs Newsround. Who she?'

'Biggest gossip on the estate,' I said. 'Apart from Elfie that is.'

Agnes laughed again and this time I joined in and we both watched as Elfie released the squirming Alfie and then chased him as he ran off.

'Maybe she find another plan,' said Agnes, looking at me again. 'Forget this one?'

'Maybe,' I said, looking down again. Agnes's feet are much smaller than mine – about half the size. They had shifted, just a little, following Elfie's moving figure. 'But Elfie likes to see a plan through,' I continued. 'And she's always wanted to be a celeb. I think it's all those gossip mags her mam gets. Besides,' I added quickly, 'she really needs the money.'

'Money? I no understand,' said Agnes.

I wiggle my toes nervously. 'The prize money,' I said. 'She reckons it's the answer to all her problems.'

'Oh,' Agnes murmured.

'So I think we're both stuck here till we get kicked off the show.'

'Or her dad find out,' said Agnes.

'Yeah,' I said. 'Or that!'

Then Agnes went really quiet. I looked across at her. She was staring into space and her eyes looked sort of faraway.

'What's up?' I asked. 'Are you OK?'

She looked like she was about to say something but

then Elfie started legging it in our direction, shouting, 'Come on, losers. The doors are opening!' I turned round and saw that the crowds were starting to move. Then I looked back at Agnes.

'Are you sure you're OK?' I asked.

'Yes,' she said, with a small, sad smile. 'I am OK. Really.'

Agnes

Since I was a little girl, I have loved to sing. My dad says I could sing even before I could talk. I used to sing all the time – at home, in the street, at school. Then one day – I was maybe six years old – my teacher said there was going to be a concert and she would like me to be in it. It was when we still lived in Portugal, before my father started taking on all the overseas contract work.

I had to stand on a stage in front of a room full of parents. I remember that the lights were bright and hot and there was a baby crying at the back of the room. When the piano began to play I opened my mouth and no sound came out. I stood there, with the piano notes falling all around me, and for the first time ever I could not sing.

I cried and cried and my dad had to come up on to the stage and carry me down. He told me it did not matter. He said it over and over again. He said I was a little songbird, not a performing seal. That made me laugh and then I stopped crying.

I have never sung in public since.

When I agreed to sing with Elfie, I never thought it would really happen. I thought the competition idea was just another one of her – what does Jimmy call them? – tall tales. Everyone at school knows Elfie Baguley makes up stories and I thought this was just another of them.

But then we were outside the audition centre and I was going to have to sing. And Jimmy said Elfie really needed this. He said it was what was keeping her going. And I wanted to do it, because even though she was rude to me most of the time and kept reminding me that we could never be friends, I liked her. I wanted to do it, but in that moment, walking into the audition centre, I didn't know if I could.

Jimmy

We had to sign in at the reception desk. Elfie handed in our forms and the lady looked us up and down – we must have looked a right state, three soaking-wet kids and a grubby baby – and said, 'Where are your parents?'

'Oh, they couldn't make it,' said Elfie, super-confidently.

The woman stared at her. 'It states clearly on the application form that all under-sixteens need to be accompanied by a parent or guardian,' she said in a bored voice.

'Yes,' said Elfie, 'but these are exceptional circumstances, you see.' And she tipped her head to one side and launched into one of her stories. 'His parents are both in a coma following a tragic car accident involving a lollipop lady,' she said, rolling her eyes in my direction. 'And *her* parents had to fly back to Spain unexpectedly.'

'Portugal,' I cut in.

Elfie glared at me. 'Yeah, yeah, Portugal. They had to fly back cos her granny is dying of foot and mouth disease, and me mam is doing a sponsored knit with Elton John and that one from The Saturdays – the one with the short hair, you know?'

'And your dad?' asks the woman on reception, curling her lip like she doesn't believe a word of it.

Elfie assumes a sad expression, 'Sadly, he passed away when I was just a babe in arms, but I know he'd be so proud if he could see me now!'

'No parents, no audition,' said the receptionist drily.

'Ah, but you see, we have signed permission letters from all our parents – except my dear old daddy, of course – stating that we're allowed to take part.'

Elfie handed over the letters she'd written on the train ride over. I had to admit they were pretty good. She'd brought different pens and notepaper and written one with her left hand to make it look different, and one in capitals.

The receptionist glanced over them. 'Hmmm!' she said. 'This is really most irregular.'

'Look, love,' said Elfie, leaning over the desk and speaking to her in a confidential tone. 'Between you and me, we're not that good. We're just doing this cos she –' she pointed at Agnes, 'has only six months to live and it's her dream to enter *Pop to the Top*. There's no way we'll make it through to the next round so be a love and let us take part today, eh! To make a sick girl's dream come true.'

The receptionist stared at Agnes. 'She's really sick?' she asked, sounding unconvinced.

'Well she's hardly gonna look like that by choice, is she?' said Elfie.

'Elfie!' I hissed.

The receptionist sighed. 'Go on, then!'

Elfie whooped. My stomach sank. I must admit I'd been half hoping she wouldn't let us in.

'But only this once. And I need to keep hold of these letters,' she said.

Elfie nodded, still grinning.

'And if you get through to the next round,

you'll need to bring your parents, OK?'

'Of course,' said Elfie. Then, with a solemn expression, she added, 'If Agnes lives that long!'

'I can't believe you just did that,' I said as we made our way inside the conference centre and battled through hundreds of people to find a corner to sit in.

'You ain't heard nothin' yet,' said Elfie.

'What's that supposed to mean?'

'Just you wait and see.'

Alfie was crying for food again and Elfie was fretting about finding somewhere to plug in her hair straighteners.

I looked around. I could see a cameraman with a camera balanced lazily on one shoulder, chatting to a group of girls who were wearing even fewer clothes – and more make-up – than Elfie. He didn't look like he was doing much filming.

'They won't film us unless we get to the final rounds, will they?' I said nervously. 'And your hair looks fine, by the way.'

I glanced at Agnes but she didn't appear to be

listening. She'd gone really pale and she was even quieter than usual.

'My hair looks like it belongs to some dodgy seventies footballer,' said Elfie, peering into a tiny pocket mirror and pulling a face. 'And if we want to GET to the final rounds, Jimmy Wigmore, we need to get our faces known before then!' She turned to look at me like I'd just said the most stupid thing in the world. 'Don't you know anything about the rules of Talent TV?'

'Right,' I said. 'But then won't our parents see it?'

'Don't sweat it, Wigmore. They film weeks in advance,' Elfie declared. 'The strike will probably be over by the time it goes on air! Maybe the shaggy perm will be back in fashion, an' all.' She pulled another cross face and tugged a big lock of hair through her mam's second-best pair of electric-pink straighteners.

'Hey!' she said suddenly. 'The camera crew are coming in our direction.'

I glanced round to see the cameraman sauntering our way, talking into his mobile phone. My heart sank.

'Give Alfie a pinch or summat to make him

scream a bit louder!' squeaked Elfie.

'I can't pinch him,' I said, my ears getting hot. 'That's child abuse.'

'Kiss him then,' Elfie demanded. 'That ought to frighten the life out of him! Your big gob and ready-for-take-off ears looming in his face!'

'I . . .' I stood there, holding Alfie, my ears getting hotter and hotter, not knowing what to do.

'Oh, for effin' Norah's sake, I'll do it.'

I glanced at Agnes again but she was just staring straight in front of her, with the weird faraway look on her face.

Elfie picked Alfie up and started tickling him until he gave off a massive shriek that made the cameraman swivel his lens round in our direction.

'Just let me do the talking, OK?' said Elfie. She had straight hair on one side of her head and wild frizzy curls on the other and she was grinning like some crazy woman in the direction of the camera man.

I groaned. 'Fine,' I said.

Like anyone else was ever going to get a word in anyway!

Rules of Talent TV No. 8: Bring along a cute kid for the 'Aaah!' factor

Elfie

It was all going to kick off when my dad found out. That much was obvious. But if we won the competition and came home with the £25,000 then I figured he would probably forgive me. And Agnes could become a huge superstar, and Jimmy would be able to fund his Olympic dream. Everyone would be happy. Which meant this plan had to work.

So, I'd done my homework. Studied all the laws of Talent TV dead carefully. I'd looked up every contest winner for the past five years and checked out their strategy for success. There were the gobby ones, the shy ones, the overcoming adversity ones, the ordinary-lad/lass-like-you-and-me ones and the who'd-have thought-its. There were some the judges loved, some they hated, some with silver spoons in their gobs, some who wanted to make something of their lives. And a few of them who actually had talent.

The cute kid factor was the sure-fire winner though. The *I'm-just-doing-this-to-make-a-better-life-for-my-kid* contestants melted the judges' hearts every time – and our Alfie is just about as cute as they come.

But for maximum impact, I needed to tinker with our story. And when I say tinker . . . I basically mean lie. I figured this was the moment for me to put my legendary storytelling talents to good use and with £25,000 on the table, it wasn't the time to fret about getting a bit artistic with the truth.

I did feel bad about Jimmy though. He's my best mate, sort of like my brother and my knight in chlorinated armour all rolled into one, and I didn't want to hurt him. I knew he wasn't going to like it but I was doing it for him as well as me, so I figured he'd forgive me in the end. Like he always did.

I figured I might as well put my plan into action straight away, so when I saw the cameraman coming

I tickled Alfie till he screamed and shrieked with laughter. The *I want this so badly it hurt*s girls and *this has always been our dream* boybands must have been well annoyed when the kid in nappies had a better set of vocal chords than all of them put together. But I can't help that, can I? And everyone knows it's all about playing the game.

Anyway, the cameraman started filming us: Alfie squealing, me throwing him up in the air. Me giving him a bottle and changing his nappy. Me looking young and a bit sad, yet somehow full of hope. Least that's how I was supposed to look.

Then they got the presenter guy from the local news programme (who isn't half as good looking as he seems on TV) to ask me loads of questions and I could see Jimmy's eyes popping out of his head as I answered. But I kept on going anyway, because it was all part of my plan.

'I want to show all the other teenage mams like me that you can still follow your dream when you have a baby,' I said, looking straight into the camera and crossing my fingers behind my back.

Next to me, Jimmy nearly choked on his Hula Hoops.

Ignoring him, I glanced down at Alfie and tried to look teary eyed. 'And I want *my* baby boy to be proud of his mam one day.'

Jimmy gulped like he was coming up for air. 'His what?'

I kicked him sharply in the ankle, wondering if it might have been a good idea to tell him about the back story I'd invented for us, after all.

'And what about Alfie's father?' asked the presenter. 'Is he still on the scene?'

I turned to Jimmy, who'd gone so red I was worried he might actually pass out. Then I took a deep breath, crossed my fingers really tightly and said, 'Yeah, this is Jimmy. And I *think* he's the father.'

Jimmy made a kind of strangled sound, halfway between a scream and gagging.

'When you say, you "think" he's the father . . .?' The presenter glanced at Jimmy.

'I can't be sure,' I said. 'But Jimmy's sticking by me.'

The presenter turned to the camera crew and I

took Jimmy's hand in mine and whispered, 'Don't forget to breathe!'

'What're you doing, Elfie?' he hissed back.

'Just roll with it,' I whispered. Then I turned back to the presenter who was trying to look sympathetic (although I could tell he was chuffed to bits cos this was going to make class telly) and said, 'Only the thing is, he's in love with my singing partner, Agnes.'

From the expression on Jimmy's face I reckon his heart (or gills, or whatever) was about to come flying out of his chest. The presenter looked as if he was gonna wet himself with excitement.

'Really?' he said and the camera swung round to focus on Agnes. She still had her weird 'rabbit in headlights' expression on, but I have to admit that she was looking pretty stunning now she'd dried out a bit.

'Yeah, it's a crazy love triangle,' I said, putting on my sad face again. 'But we're trying to make the best of it for the sake of the baby.'

'How do you feel about all this, Jimmy?' the presented asked as the cameraman zoomed in close on Jimmy's face.

Jimmy was staring desperately at Agnes. 'Um – I – um . . .'

'Oh, you know, he's torn between love and duty,' I explained quickly, before he could put his foot in it. 'We all are. You'll probably be able to see the rippling tensions in our performance. It can get pretty electric with all those passions bubbling underneath, you know!'

And I knew from the look on the presenter's face that I'd nailed it, but I also wondered if Jimmy was ever going to forgive me.

Jimmy

I've never been great at telling lies. I change colour like a traffic light and go all clammy and I never get away with it. So when Elfie told the TV crew that I was the baby's dad, I thought they'd take one look at my red ears and work out straight away that she was making it up. I just sat there, struggling to breathe and hoping it was all a bad dream.

After the interview was over, we were sent to wait outside the audition room. Alfie was happy thanks to another pack of cheesy Wotsits. He kept running up and down the corridor, squeaking and talking to himself in baby language. Agnes was staring at the door to the audition room like she was in some kind of trance. And I was just concentrating on trying to breathe normally.

'How could you say that, Elfie?' I asked for about the fourth time.

'Which bit exactly?' Elfie whispered, putting a finger to her lips and looking round to check no one was listening.

'All of it!' I hissed back.

I felt like I'd been through ten rounds with the World Heavyweight Champion and every time I thought about that awful interview it was like being punched all over again.

'I'm dead sorry. Honest I am,' she said, and she did look like she meant it. I just couldn't figure out why she would have said all that stuff in the first place.

'But it worked, didn't it? That presenter will be in

there now, briefing the judges to let us through to the next round. Talent shows depend on stories like ours.'

'But none of it was true, Elfie!' I groaned.

'Please don't be mad,' Elfie pleaded, her cocky expression melting away. 'I'm sorry. You know I am. And I'll make it up to you. I promise.'

'How?' I asked.

'When we win you won't have to worry about getting that funding to pay for your training,' she said enthusiastically. 'You'll thank me for this when you're standing on an Olympic podium collecting your gold medal.'

I wondered if this was how Elfie's dad felt each time her mam announced she was leaving.

'Some of it might be true for all you know!'

'Not the bit about me being Alfie's dad!'

'But the rest could be true. How do you know I'm not Alfie's mam?'

'Because I was there when your mam's waters broke on the floor of Lidl,' I said loudly.

'That's true, I s'pose,' she said, wrinkling up her nose. 'But you could have a secret crush on Agnes.

You always go red whenever you look at her.'

'I don't,' I said, my voice rising again.

'OK, keep your swimming trunks on,' said Elfie. 'I'm just saying.'

'But soon the judges are going to figure it out,' I said.

'Ssssh!' said Elfie again, glancing round at the producer girl with the clipboard standing behind us.

'There's no way you're going to win once they find out you've fed them a pack of lies,' I went on.

'That's where you're wrong,' she whispered, her eyes bright. 'The more outrageous the lies, the better. The public love a bit of scandal and controversy. They'll probably vote for us even more when they find out.'

'But the public don't even get to vote till the grand final,' I reminded her.

'OK, the judges will keep putting us through cos they know we'll improve the ratings!' I groaned, but Elfie went on, 'And even if we don't win, we'll still be able to sell our story to *The Liverpool Echo*. I wonder what they pay for a *Pop to the Top* losers' story?'

I stared at her, feeling sick, but knowing it was too late to argue with her. 'What about Agnes?' I asked.

We both looked over to Agnes. Her hair was dry now and hung over her bare shoulders in glossy black curls. The bright red lipstick Elfie smeared over her had rubbed off but her lips were still stained like she'd been eating a cherry ice lolly. Her face was white as a sheet and her eyes looked black and terrified, but in the gold dress she looked like a catwalk model or a pop star. A very nervous pop star.

'Well, if she plays her cards right – and doesn't throw up as soon as we get in there,' said Elfie, 'we might just be able to make her into a star!'

Agnes

Elfie Baguley is good at telling stories. When she tells them, her eyes go wide and her nose puckers a little. And she looks at you sideways, tilting her head slightly to one side and eyeing you from an angle.

I think it's because she's being creative. My dad

once told me that when you are being creative, you use the left side of your brain more – or perhaps it is the right. I don't remember. Either way, it's the tilt of Elfie's head that is always a giveaway. But the presenter didn't know that; he seemed to believe her whole story.

So we got bumped to the head of the queue and about fifteen minutes later we were told we were next to audition. By that time I was so nervous I could hardly breathe and my head had gone dizzy. I was only half listening to what Elfie and Jimmy were saying because I was concentrating really hard on not being sick.

'It was just to keep the public hooked,' Elfie was still busy explaining to Jimmy, who was sitting, staring at his feet, looking like he'd been punched over and over in the stomach. 'A bit of teen pregnancy goes a long way at prime time. And as for a love triangle . . .'

Jimmy groaned. He hadn't looked me in the eye once since Elfie had told the presenter he was in love with me, and every time Elfie mentioned it he went bright red and moaned like it was the most embarrassing thing ever.

I looked down at my feet, the moths buzzing manically in my stomach. In Elfie's mum's shoes and with my toenails painted bright red, they didn't look like my feet at all.

Suddenly, the door of the audition room opened and the producer with the clipboard turned to me and Elfie and said, 'It's your turn now. Good luck.'

And I thought I was actually going to be sick then, because my stomach lurched and the moths fizzed their way up into my chest and I had to swallow and swallow to stop myself retching.

'Come on, partner,' said Elfie brightly, looping her arm through mine. She felt hot and she smelled of Alfie and cheesy Wotsits.

I was shaking.

'Are you OK?' she said, giving me a funny look. 'You're all goosebumpy.'

'I . . .'

'Now is not the time for cold feet, sister,' Elfie was going on. 'We've got a show to win here!'

I looked up and caught Jimmy's eye for the first time since Elfie's interview. His ears went pink but he said, 'You'll be great. You're dead good.'

Elfie gave him one of her looks.

'Both of you are,' he added quickly.

'Exactly,' said Elfie. 'We rock. And you scrub up pretty well with a bit of bling,' she said to me. 'Don't bottle it now. Come on.'

My legs had turned to jelly so Elfie had to drag me into the audition room. Just before the doors closed, I glanced back and saw Jimmy, with Alfie in his arms, watching us with a worried expression on his face.

The audition room was really just a big board room, with a space cleared for the contestants to perform in front of a massive black and gold *Pop to the Top* banner. The judges sat on a row of chairs behind a large table, holding clipboards and staring at us with bored expressions. Elfie had shown me all their faces in one of her celeb magazines so I recognised the head judge – the local pop legend who sponsored the competition. And sitting on his right was the girl who'd come second a couple of years ago, the one

Elfie called 'The Tabloid Princess'.

'So, why do you want to win *Pop to the Top*?' she asked in a high-pitched nasal voice, shaking her blonde curls and pouting.

Elfie turned on a stage-school sparkly grin and said, 'Because we want to be stars!' Then she added, 'Just like you!'

The third judge was an orange-skinned man with thinning purple hair. Elfie had told me he was a disgraced local radio DJ who was convicted of shoplifting women's underwear ('Everyone calls him "The Lingerie Lizard",' she said). 'And what makes you think you've got what it takes?' he asked drily.

'Easy,' said Elfie with a grin. 'She's got the voice of an angel and the looks of a young supermodel, and I've got the bubbly personality and tragic past! Between us we've got the whole package.'

'Right,' drawled judge number four ('D-list former soap star, ex darts' player's wife and plastic surgery addict, AKA "The Facelift",' – Elfie's description). 'And what about you, Agnes? Why did you decide to enter the competition?'

'Singing is all she's ever wanted to do,' said Elfie, still in her super-bright voice.

I felt as if the moths were fluttering in and out of my line of sight, black shadows passing over my eyes. I knew I couldn't speak even if I wanted to.

'Hmm!' It was the head judge ('The Legend', Elfie called him) who spoke. Everyone else fell silent and turned to look at him. Elfie said he was massive all over the world in the eighties. Now he does loads of stuff for charities and nurturing local talent. His record company was offering the recording contract and the cash prize was from his own personal fortune. 'Hmm,' he said again. He was looking at us curiously, like he was rapidly making some calculation in his brain. 'And what's the band called?'

'The Juliets,' Elfie replied.

I was finding it hard to breathe, moth wings clogging my throat.

'Why?' asked The Legend. And, as he looked at me, I swear I saw his eyes flicker and narrow. I closed my eyes and breathed deeply, trying to pretend I was somewhere else.

'Ah,' Elfie was saying. 'Now that is a whole other story.'

Jimmy

Me and Alfie had to wait outside with the presenter and the skinny producer girl with the clipboard superglued to her chest. Oh, and a bored-looking cameraman with a tattoo of Kylie Minogue on his neck who filmed us while we watched the audition on the monitor.

Alfie had cheered up and was toddling up and down the corridor, so he didn't hear his sister claiming to be his mam for the second time in the space of half an hour. Me, I had to listen to the whole saga all over again. I'd started to feel kind of numb now. I should still have been mad at Elfie but I knew she was doing all this for her dad, and for Alfie. I just wished she could have done it without making me look like a total divvy on TV.

Then I glanced at the time on the monitor and

groaned. If they didn't hurry up I wasn't going to make swim training on time and I'd promised my dad I would never be late again. This day just kept getting worse and worse.

The producer was also watching the monitor, wide-eyed, still clutching her clipboard. 'This is definitely going to make the cut,' she said in a squeaky voice.

'You think they'll show all this on telly?' I said.

'Too right they will,' said the presenter, who always seemed to speak like he was on TV even when he wasn't being filmed. 'We couldn't have scripted this one better. And believe me, we've had to resort to a bit of creative scriptwriting on occasions.'

'You make some of the auditions up?'

'Just embellish some of the really rubbish ones,' he said, giving me a wink. 'For the comedy value, you know.'

'He's only joking,' cut in the producer, giggling nervously. 'Obviously!'

'Course I am,' the presenter said, winking again. 'But this,' he indicated at the screen, 'this is totally class. This will make it straight to the top of the pile for the highlights show – no editing required.'

I imagined my dad turning on the TV and seeing us. He was definitely going to kill me. That was if he hadn't already murdered me for missing training.

On the monitor, the head judge – the one Elfie called The Legend – was telling them to sing. Then the camera turned to Agnes who'd gone so pale she looked like you could walk right through her. She was staring blankly at the camera. I wondered if she was going to bottle it, and I wondered what Elfie would say if she did.

Then Alfie spotted his sister on the monitor and started pointing and squealing, 'Effie! Effie!'

'He calls his mum by her name?' said the presenter, glancing curiously in Alfie's direction.

'Um –' I hesitated and glanced at the monitor, where Elfie was busy making up more tall tales about Alfie's parentage to fill in the silence. 'Thing is, Alfie doesn't – um – he doesn't know Elfie is his mam.'

'Really?' said the producer, looking up from her clipboard.

'Yeah – um . . .' Heat was flooding my face. Like I

say, I'm no good at lying. I felt like I was turning into Elfie as I said, 'Her family decided it was easier – for all of them, you know – if her mam sort of said he was hers.'

'Really!' repeated the presenter with a big grin.

'Yeah, only – um – only then Elfie's mam left and so now it's a big muddle,' I finished quickly, hoping Elfie wasn't going to kill me.

'You don't say,' said the presenter, raising a perfectly plucked eyebrow. And he looked like he was about to start asking me a whole load more questions, but just then the backing track to Elfie and Agnes' song started up and we all turned to look and I was saved from putting my foot in it even more.

I'd listened to them perform so often that I knew something was wrong right away. The lyrics came in and only Elfie started singing – Agnes just stood there with this terrified expression on her face. Elfie was glaring at her and trying to hold the vocal but not really managing it and Agnes was just staring into space, her lips slightly parted, the sequinned dress glittering and sparkling under the lights.

'She's not going to be sick, is she?' asked the presenter.

Agnes was getting paler and paler by the moment. Her black eyes were huge and dark, catching the gold reflections from her dress.

The camera panned across to the judges. The Lingerie Lizard coughed and shifted uncomfortably in his seat. The Facelift attempted to raise her eyebrows – without much success – then whispered something to The Tabloid Princess who let out a loud giggle.

Elfie was trying to keep the lyrics going but her voice sounded thin and reedy against the blaring backing track. And still Agnes didn't sing.

The Legend sat there with his arms folded, looking unimpressed.

'Come on, Agnes,' I muttered. I knew how she felt. I feel like that sometimes before a big swimming race. Like I've forgotten how to swim, how to breathe even because I'm so paralysed with fear. Once I swim the first stroke and my head is under the water I'm OK, but that moment, standing on the edge, staring into the blue, is the worst moment of all. 'Sing!' I murmured. 'You can do it.'

The camera panned back to Agnes and Elfie again. Elfie was singing bravely with a plastic grin stuck on her face but she kept glancing at Agnes and giving her desperate looks.

Then suddenly The Legend waved his hand and the music stopped. A couple of notes later, Elfie's singing also ground to a halt.

'OK,' said The Legend with a sigh. 'I'm guessing that was supposed to be a duet?'

Elfie nodded and glared at Agnes.

'But only one of you appeared to be singing.'

The Tabloid Princess snorted loudly. She shook her blonde plastic-looking curls and for a second she reminded me of Elfie's mam.

'I'm feeling kind so I'm going to ask if you'd like to try again?' said The Legend.

'Yes, please,' Elfie nodded, suddenly looking young and a bit silly in her mam's super-sexy clothes.

'And you?' The Legend looked at Agnes.

'You don't look too good to be honest, honey!'

said The Facelift in a syrupy voice.

'Look who's talking!' squeaked The Tabloid Princess, then she gave another snort of laughter.

The Facelift (who is fifty if she's a day and pretending to be twenty-seven, according to Elfie) turned to give The Tabloid Princess a death stare as the Lingerie Lizard muttered, 'Mi-aow!'

'Ladies, please!' said The Legend. He turned back to Agnes. 'Do you want to get some air?'

Agnes nodded.

'OK,' the Legend sighed. Five minutes then you come back and sing. This is last-chance saloon.'

As Agnes and Elfie bundled out of the audition room, I glanced down at my watch. There was no way I was going to make it back for training at this rate, and I felt sick at the thought of what my dad was going to say.

Agnes leaned against the wall beside me and closed her eyes.

'What happened in there?' Elfie was saying, waving her arms around like she was in some kind of soap opera. 'And please don't say you forgot the words!'

Agnes said nothing. She just took a shaky breath.

'Give her a minute,' I said quietly.

'We've got to go back in there and wow the judges in –' Elfie glanced at her watch, even though she wasn't wearing one '– four minutes, fifteen seconds! We don't have a minute,' she said crossly.

'I'm sorry,' Agnes murmured.

'You will be if we don't make it to the second round,' Elfie muttered. But, although she was trying to act all tough, I knew Elfie well enough to see she was rattled. 'Is she actually OK or what?' she whispered to me.

I shrugged. 'I dunno.'

I tried to remember the stuff my dad said to me before races. His pep-talk patter, he called it. 'You can do it,' I said, looking right at Agnes, even though I could feel the heat spreading from my ears all over my face. 'You've trained hard for this. You know exactly what to do.' That was what my dad always said. 'Just start to sing and let your voice do the work for you.'

'You think?' She looked at me anxiously.

'My dad reckons you can do anything you set your

mind to,' I said, sounding more certain than I felt.

Elfie nodded, frowning. 'Keep going,' she whispered.

'And you've got an amazing voice,' I added, blinking nervously. I wasn't used to looking her straight in the eye.

'Yeah, and an amazing singing partner,' Elfie chipped in. 'Not to mention you totally flippin' promised me you'd do this. So there's no way you're backing out now! You owe me a finger if you do, remember?'

'Ok, time to go back in,' said the producer girl, holding the door open. 'The judges are ready for you.'

Agnes breathed out, a long shuddering sigh.

'You can do it,' I said. 'Just let the singing take over.'

'Thanks,' said Agnes with a tiny smile. I noticed that she'd been biting her lip so hard it had started to bleed.

Elfie stared at her impatiently. 'Come on then, or you'll have one less digit,' she said.

'Give her a hug,' I whispered.

'You what?'

'A hug!' I said.

Elfie sighed dramatically. 'If I must!' She put her arm round Agnes and pulled her into an awkward hug. 'Honestly, the things I do for my art!'

Agnes looked startled and a nervous little laugh bubbled from her lips.

'Show time,' said the producer, looking impatient.

'Good luck!' I said as they were bundled back into the audition room.

'Who needs luck with a talent like ours,' Elfie shouted back. She'd obviously got her mojo back but I wasn't so sure about Agnes. The Legend had said this was it. No more second chances. And I was pretty certain Elfie would want to chop off more than Agnes's finger if she let her down this time.

The doors closed behind them and I watched the scene unfold on the monitor.

'Hello again,' said Elfie brightly as they stood in front of the judges.

The Legend raised an eyebrow and stared at her. 'So, are you ready to wow us this time?'

'Absolutely!' said Elfie with a grin.

The Tabloid Princess giggled. Elfie said she had the most annoying laugh in the world and I was starting to agree.

The Legend narrowed his eyes then nodded slowly. There was a long silence as they waited for the backing track to come on. Agnes clutched a fistful of Elfie's mam's gold dress and twisted it in her fingers. She had her eyes tightly closed.

Then the first notes of the music started up. Elfie glanced nervously at Agnes. She might have been trying to act all cool, but I could see how much she wanted this to work out. We were all watching Agnes: me, Elfie, the judges, the presenter, the producer, the cameraman. She stood there, swaying slightly in her gold dress for a moment as the first notes washed over her. Then she took a deep breath, opened her eyes . . . and started to sing.

Elfie broke into a relieved grin (like she'd planned the whole false start thing herself) beamed at the judges, did a thumbs up at the camera and then launched into her usual 'la-la-la'-ing. Elfie is clever enough to know that, when it comes to the vocals, it's best to let Agnes take centre stage, so she just did a few harmony bits and a few 'shoo-be-doos' while Agnes carried the song.

Next to me, the producer had gone totally quiet and the presenter's mouth actually dropped open with surprise, which I always thought only happened in cartoons. The cameraman raised an eyebrow and made Kylie on his neck give a little wiggle. And The Legend stopped scribbling in his notepad and just stared.

If you'd been there, you'd have known why. Cos even though I'd watched them rehearse the song dozens of times under the bridge, I was still blown away when Agnes started to sing. It's not just that she has this amazing voice – so big you can't imagine how it comes out of a skinny little thing like her. It's that when she sings, she actually *stops* looking like a little kid wearing a dress two sizes too big and she stops looking like she's going to be sick or pass out with stage fright. Her beautiful voice sort of lights her up and makes her shine. Like a star.

'Wow! She's good,' breathed the producer, making

a note on her clipboard.

'This just gets better and better!' whispered the presenter. 'You know, if she keeps singing like that, your girlfriends might just have a real shot in this competition.'

'They're not my girlfriends,' I said hastily.

'Whatever!' he said, not even listening. 'These two could go all the way.'

Rules of Talent TV No. 9:
Divide the judging panel

Elfie

Most reality TV viewers think that if you want to do well, you've got to get the judges on your side. But the *real* junkies know that to go all the way, you have to *divide* the panel. Why? Because nothing guarantees massive viewing figures like judge warfare.

It's a risky game, of course, but if you can just get one member of the panel to really loathe you, then you're pretty much guaranteed the support of the others – not to mention the public sympathy vote. And it helps if the judge you choose to irritate is someone the public loves to hate. So I'd read up about each judge and worked out my plan carefully.

After Agnes did her singing-like-an-angel bit – I really thought she was going to bottle it again, but she delivered the goods in the end – it was my turn to do my stuff.

'OK, thanks, girls,' said The Legend. He turned to the other members of the panel. 'So, what did we think?'

The Tabloid Princess giggled. She sort of reminded me of me mam but the gossip mags all loved her so I figured it wasn't a good idea to get her back up. 'You remind me so much of myself when I was your age!'

'How long ago was that, darling?' sniped The Facelift.

The Legend laughed but The Tabloid Princess just gave The Facelift a look like she was going to punch her. 'Not as long ago as it was for you, *darling*!' Then she turned to us. 'I don't think you realise how good you are,' she said, pointing at Agnes. 'You sing like a young Whitney Houston! And you –' this was to me – 'You've got so much personality. You need to work on your vocals but you've got something. You both have. So I'm going to say –' She hesitated, just for a moment, then shook her shiny curls again and said, 'Yes.'

I whooped and planted a kiss on Agnes's cheek. Everything was going according to plan!

Then it was The Facelift's turn. She was the one

I'd earmarked as public enemy number one. and she was still looking mad about The Tabloid Princess's comment, so I figured it shouldn't be too difficult to get her really narked. 'I agree with some of that,' she said slowly in her Wigan-via-LA accent (although she's probably never even been to Disneyland, let alone Hollywood). 'You've got the voice. And you've got the personality. But you're both very young. And you already have a lot of commitments.'

'The kid won't get in the way!' I said quickly.

'Well, maybe he should!'

'What's that supposed to mean?' I said.

'It means that being a good mother should come before anything else.'

I took a deep breath and put my plan into action. 'Like you know anything about being a good mam?' I muttered, just loud enough for the microphone to pick it up. Then I tossed my hair and waited for the fireworks.

The Facelift glared and there was a sharp intake of breath from the judging panel. Everyone knows The Facelift's son is a junkie and her daughter once pulled a moonie at the darts' championship finals.

The Legend smiled his lazy smile. 'So is that a yes or a no from you?' he asked The Facelift.

'I'm afraid it's a no from me,' said The Facelift sourly.

'Surprise, surprise,' I muttered, looking directly into the camera and giving a kooky grin.

'And what about you?' said The Legend, turning to The Lingerie Lizard.

The Lingerie Lizard smiled his smarmy grin. 'Two hundred per cent yes from me, little ladies!'

'OK,' said The Legend. It all hung on his vote now, which was exactly what I'd been hoping for. Spin out that drama as long as possible, I reckoned.

'Here's what I think.' He paused and ran a hand over his chin. The Facelift was shooting me daggers and The Tabloid Princess was smiling her fake smile. The Lingerie Lizard just looked half asleep.

'I think you've got something and I think local people will like you,' said The Legend. 'Elfie, you need to work on your attitude and your vocals. And Agnes, you need to believe in yourself, and you need to get rid of that hideous dress.'

The Facelift laughed.

'But . . .' He paused again. 'But I think you've got potential so I'm going to say . . .' He paused, stringing the moment out, 'Yes!'

I gave another whoop, leapt in the air and landed on Agnes with such force that we both staggered backwards, stumbling to the ground (not intentional, but also good TV!).

'Congratulations, girls. I'll see you in the next round!' said the Legend.

Agnes

I was sick afterwards. I ran straight to the girls' toilets and retched over the toilet bowl. Then I closed my eyes and felt my brain slowly clear.

Afterwards, I stared at my reflection in the water. I looked like one of the Iron Men on the beach, my face elongated in the ripples just like their bodies on the ebbing and flowing tides.

I was still in the cubicle when Elfie came in. I could hear her jumping up on to the sink and telling Jimmy he might as well come in because he's 'practically a girl anyway'.

I stared at the graffiti on the toilet door. The phrases 'Jubber loves Cathy P 4 Eva' and 'The Legend sucks!' were repeated over and over, the words filling almost every blank space so they started to look more like patterns.

'They loved the whole love-triangle thing!' Elfie was saying.

'Don't you think you went a bit overboard?' said Jimmy.

'No way! It'll make great TV. The whole stage fright bit was genius an' all,' she yelled in my direction. 'They totally lapped that up!'

I didn't say anything but Elfie didn't seem to need an answer because she went straight on. 'I mean, I nearly had a heart attack when you were standing there with your gob shut looking like you'd just seen a ghost.'

'Sorry,' I whispered, leaning on the toilet bowl to pull myself up to my feet.

'But it was pretty skill when you did start singing. You should have seen the looks on the judges' faces, Jimmy.'

'I did,' I heard Jimmy saying.

'Really?'

'I was watching the whole thing on the monitor outside.'

'Cool! Then you saw how I totally peed off The Facelift, too. That rocked! Seriously, the way she acts you'd think this was *American Idol* and she was some A-lister.'

I hesitated for a moment and breathed in deeply before pushing open the cubicle door. Elfie was perched on the sink and Jimmy was hovering by the doorway looking red and self-conscious. He glanced at me and then looked away.

'Bleedin' hell! What happened to you?' said Elfie.

I caught sight of myself in the mirror. There were thick dark smudges over my eyes and black tear marks streaked down my cheeks. My hair had vomit in it.

'I must clean this,' I said, grabbing my hair and running it up under a tap.

'What happened? Did you stick your head down the toilet or what?'

'I not feel very well,' I said. I grabbed a paper towel and rubbed at my face as hard as I could. The colour didn't shift.

'You need make-up remover,' said Elfie. Her make-up was smudged, too, and her lipgloss had all rubbed off, but she didn't seem to notice or care.

'Have you got?' I said. 'Make-up remover?'

'Nope. So, was the whole stage fright thing for real or just a genius stunt?' she asked. 'Cos I really wish I'd come up with that one meself.'

'It was real,' I heard Jimmy say quietly. I glanced at him. He was watching me closely in the mirror.

Elfie was grinning from ear to ear. 'Cool! For a moment there I thought you were the queen of spin, sister,' she said. 'Still, I guess it'll be more realistic if it's not a put-on job. The public can always tell when someone's faking summat like that.'

I ran another paper towel under the tap, squirted some soap on it then tried again. This time the sodden paper disintegrated as I wiped my eyes and the soap stung.

'Are you OK?' asked Jimmy.

I looked up to the mirror and he was still watching me.

'You were amazing in there,' he said quietly.

'All right, you two. Don't go getting all pally on me,' Elfie said sharply, glancing from him to me. 'She might be the next Beyonce Knowles for all I care but she's still an immo and a scab and this is purely a business arrangement, so don't either of you forget it.'

Jimmy immediately went bright red.

'Anyway, what about me?' Elfie demanded. 'I reckon I rocked it in there, an' all!'

'You were great too, Elfie,' said Jimmy, dutifully.

'I was, wasn't I!' She grinned. 'I love it when a plan comes together!'

Jimmy caught my eye in the mirror, raised his eyebrows and gave the smallest of smiles. I tried to smile back.

'Now can we go, Elfie,' said Jimmy. 'Or my dad is gonna be well mad at me!'

Elfie

The night before the audition, I had this dream where me mam came back to the house wearing white gloves and a housecoat. She had those cleaning ladies from the TV with her and they all went round the house tut-tutting about the state everything's got into and running their white gloves over every surface.

It was a stupid dream because me mam never did any housework, not even in the rare times when she was pretending to be a 'proper mam'. She said it was because of her nail-art (Cillit Bang plays havoc with her vinyl extensions apparently), and also because only boring people have clean houses and if there was one thing me mam never was, it was boring.

And when we got back from the audition, there she was, perched on the garden wall outside our house, swinging her legs and sucking on a cigarette like it was a lolly. I stopped dead. I had that feeling, like there's a ticking time bomb in my stomach about to go off, which I get every time she does one of her comeback acts.

That day she looked like she'd raided The Facelift's 1980s wardrobe: shiny black leggings and four-inch thigh-high red boots topped off with a cropped stonewashed denim jacket (which I know used to be my dad's back when stonewash was cool the first time round). She didn't have her suitcase with her, and she hadn't let herself into the house though, which were both good signs, I reckoned.

'Is she . . .' Jimmy hesitated. 'Is she back?'

I just shrugged, 'I hope not. Better go find out.'

'Do you want me to come with you?' asked Jimmy.

'No,' I said, 'It's not like I'm scared of her or anything!' My stomach lurched a bit when I said that.

'OK. I'll just wait here then,' he said.

'What about your swim training?' He looked sort of distracted and he'd been checking his watch the whole way home.

He glanced over at his house. 'I'm late already,' he said.

'Won't your dad be waiting for you then?'

'Probably,' he said. 'But he's going to be mad either way so another five minutes won't hurt. And if

I stand on the corner, he won't see me.'

'OK,' I said, 'Whatever.' I tried to sound like it made no difference but I was secretly really glad – and I reckon we both knew it.

I grabbed the buggy – Alfie was still asleep – and, with my head up and my best 'Sod you!' expression, I started walking towards the house. The last thing I wanted to do was make her think I actually cared.

When she caught sight of me, me mam jumped up and stamped out her cigarette under the heel of her left boot. 'Elfie, darling!' she squealed. I marched straight past without even looking at her. 'Wait!' She teetered after me on her platform heels. 'I need to talk to you.'

I was trying to find the front door key in my pocket. But I could smell her coming towards me – all cheap perfume and cigarettes.

'I need to see you, darling,' she was saying. 'To explain. Just to talk. I need to see you, and Alfie.'

I jammed the key into the lock and didn't turn round.

'Elfie, Elfie, don't be like this,' she said. She was

right behind me now. I could even smell her hairspray and the sickly scent of fake tan.

I forced open the door and tried to yank the buggy up over the doorstep, tipping it on its side in the process.

'You've got to forgive me, Elfie,' she said, grabbing my arm. 'I'm a *love* addict!'

I stared at her for a second before pulling my arm free. Then I shoved the buggy into the hallway and closed the door. I didn't want Alfie waking up and seeing her like this.

'Love addiction?' I said, turning to face her again. 'Is that what you're calling it?'

'Yeah. I've been watching this show on cable. "Am I a Love Addict?" it's called,' she said. 'It's made me understand meself and why I do the things I do.'

'Because you're a selfish cow?'

She sighed dramatically. 'You are so like your father.'

'I hope so,' I muttered.

'What the pair of you don't realise is that craving

love and affirmation can be a kind of addiction,' she went on.

'So, why can't you just take up drugs or alcohol like a normal mam?'

'I don't expect someone like you to understand,' she said, sighing again. I glanced across the road where I could see Mrs Newsround peering through her net curtains. She'd be out pretending to clean her windows in a minute. Jimmy stood waiting on the corner, just out of sight of his house where his dad was probably pacing up and down fretting about not getting his chlorine fix. A couple of the biker kids were hovering behind Jimmy, pulling fish faces behind his back.

'I've got really low self-esteem,' me mam was going on. 'That's why I crave love wherever I can find it.'

'Not so hot at giving it out, though, are you,' I said.

I looked down and noticed she'd had her nails done again. Deep purple talons, each embossed with a single pink jewel.

'I see now that I need to invest in those I love,' she said.

On the other side of the door, Alfie had woken and was starting to whimper. Me mam stared at me: I stared back. Mrs Newsround was out on her doorstep, in her apron and slippers, looking round for summat to pretend to do. *That was quick*, I thought.

'My baby wants to see me,' said me mam with a flick of her new hairdo.

'Actually, he wants me,' I said. 'He's already forgotten about you, and I'm doing my best to do the same.'

She stared at me, false eyelashes flickering beneath the weight of layers of silver sparkle. 'I'm not coming back this time, Elfie,' she said.

'Good,' I replied quickly, feeling my stomach do another flip. 'What are you doing here then?'

'I came to tell you that Marco and I are getting married and I'm converting to Catholicism.'

My stomach lurched again. I knew she wanted me to ask who Marco was, only I wasn't going to give her the satisfaction. 'I thought Catholics didn't believe in divorce?' I said quickly.

'Marco's going to write to the Pope.'

I rolled my eyes. I'd stopped believing me mam's lines around the time I stopped believing in the tooth fairy and Father Christmas.

From behind the door, I could still hear Alfie grizzling and calling for his mam. I wasn't sure if he meant me or her. Over on the corner, one of the biker kids was doing an impression of Jimmy swimming, mouth opening and closing like a fish, his arms doing breaststroke as he rode along on his bike. Jimmy just ignored him and kept staring in my direction.

Me mam shoved a Marlboro Light between her glossy red lips and lit it. 'Marco says the Pope will grant an annulment on the grounds that I was "psychologically incapable of taking on the obligation of marriage",' she said.

I snorted again. 'Can me and Alfie divorce you on the grounds that you are psychologically incapable of taking on the obligation of motherhood then?'

Alfie had stopped calling and was just whimpering again.

'Motherhood is a lifelong commitment. I can see that now,' she said, inhaling quickly, her red lips pursed around the white tube, the colour bleeding angrily outwards.

'Yeah, kids are for life, not just for Christmas. Didn't you hear?'

'I know I've hurt you very badly, Elfie,' she said, blowing out smoke and placing her talons on my arm. 'But I've changed. I'm ready to be a proper mother. Marco and I want you to come and live with us and be a family.'

I took a deep breath. 'Yeah? And what about Dad?' I said. 'What do you think he'll do when he finds out you're shacked up with an immo?'

I eyeballed her and she eyeballed me right back. And I wished for about the ten millionth time that me mam were plain and wishy-washy – like Jimmy's mam — because things might have been different then. Or maybe not. Maybe she'd have been the same no matter what.

'That term is offensive and racist, Elfie,' she said, jabbing the cigarette between her lips again.

'So, it's true then? You are seeing an immo? Is he a scab an' all?'

She just exhaled more smoke and checked out her nails.

'Why don't you just cut out dad's heart with a spoon and eat it. It would be easier on him,' I said. I could feel myself shaking.

'The heart wants what it wants, Elfie.'

'Well, my heart doesn't want you anywhere in my life,' I said.

She looked for a moment as if she was about to slap me. I almost wanted her to. 'You really can be a heartless little cow, you know that?' she said. 'You need to learn to let a bit of love in, Elfie,' she said.

'And you need to give a bit back,' I said, shoving my way back into the house and slamming the door behind me.

It should have made me feel good, getting in the last word, but it didn't.

She stayed outside for a while. I know because I watched her through the net curtains. She lit a cigarette and reapplied her lipstick, then she just sat on the wall for a bit before heading off out of the close.

And the whole time she was there, Jimmy was waiting on the corner. Even though I'd made up all that stuff about him at the auditions, he still waited until she'd gone before he went in. That's the thing about Jimmy Wigmore: he couldn't be much more different to me mam if he tried. He always keeps his promises – even when they get him into trouble.

After me mam had disappeared round the corner, I got Alfie out of his buggy and he tottered over and grabbed my legs, looking up at me with his little angel face. 'Mam?' he said. And I still didn't know if he meant me or not but I picked him up and kissed his soft little tummy.

Then I held him tight so our faces were close to each other and I could smell the baby shampoo and feel his wet little tongue on my nose. 'Don't worry, little man,' I told him. 'Elfie's gonna win the competition and everything will be OK.'

He giggled as I closed my eyes and he planted baby kisses on my eyelids.

Jimmy

My dad doesn't get mad often and when he does, he doesn't get all shouty and loud. He goes really quiet and doesn't say much and just sort of radiates disappointment, which is so much worse than shouting.

It was so late by the time Elfie's mam had gone that I'd totally missed training and my dad wasn't speaking to me he was so angry. Me and him and my mam ate dinner in silence with him glowering at me across the table. And then, out of nowhere, just when I was expecting him to shout at me, he did something much worse: he said, 'I'm thinking of breaking the strike.'

My mam looked up, her eyes bright with alarm. 'Why?' she said quickly.

'You know full well why.'

'It's only money, Phil,' said my mam. 'We can get through this.'

'How?' said Dad, still looking at her. She wouldn't meet his eye. 'We've got bills mounting up and hardly enough to buy groceries, let alone training costs for Jimmy. There are Nationals coming up and then the European Youth Championships next April. How are we even going to pay travel expenses?'

'We'll manage,' said Mam, laying down her knife and fork carefully, her voice tight and strained. 'You said if he does well at Nationals he could get sponsorship.'

'And how's he meant to do that if we can't afford to put proper meals in front of him?'

'He's doing fine,' she said, her voice breaking on the last word.

'I'm fine, Dad,' I repeated.

'No one asked you, son,' he snapped, without even turning his head. 'If he can place in the top three and maybe get a sponsorship deal then I can rejoin the strike but until then . . .'

'Until then what?' I said.

My dad didn't reply.

Mum hesitated. Her face was pale and blotchy and I noticed her hands were quivering. 'You know what will happen if you cross the picket lines,' she said.

'You've seen how they treat the scabs.' Again, her voice quivered as she pronounced the final word.

'Right now I'm more concerned about the bailiffs than I am about Clive Baguley and his cronies,' said my dad.

'Think of our Jimmy,' said my mam quietly. 'He's back at school next week. The other kids'll make his life hell if you cross the line.'

'Who do you think I'm doing this for?' said my dad, still refusing to look at me. 'This is our Jimmy's big chance. I'm not going to blow that. Not for Clive Baguley or a few playground bullies. Not a chance.'

Neither of them said anything for a minute. My mam reached across the table but my dad looked down at his hand and didn't reach out to take hers.

'I don't want you crossing the line for me, Dad,' I said.

'As long as I'm your coach, you'll do as you're told and leave the decisions to me,' he said. It was the first time he'd looked at me all evening and he sounded angrier than I'd ever heard him before.

'But, Dad –'

'We're running ourselves into debt to pay for your swimming and you don't even bother to turn up to training,' he spluttered.

'I said I was sorry, Dad.'

'Your mam was worried sick about you. No phone call even to say you were running late.'

'I don't have a phone,' I said quietly.

He didn't say anything to that. He sniffed loudly then said, 'Where were you anyway?'

I stared down at my unfinished plate of food. 'I can't tell you.'

'What do you mean you can't tell me? Your mam and me were out of our minds worrying about you.'

'I –' I hesitated. 'I just can't tell you. I promised . . .'

He raised his eyebrows and glared. 'Let me guess. You promised Elfie Baguley, right?'

I nodded.

'How many times do I have to tell you that girl is trouble?'

I didn't say anything. There was no need to: he'd been telling me Elfie was a bad influence since the day she moved to the estate.

We all sat there for about a minute, quiet. Eventually, my dad sighed. I looked up and his face had changed. He wasn't glaring and he didn't seem mad any more, just sort of sad. 'Look, son, he said, looking back down at his hands. 'You've got a real chance to get out of here. Out of all this. Get yourself a better life. And me and your mam, we'll do anything – anything – to make sure you have the chances you deserve. Do you get that?'

'Yes, Dad.'

'There's little enough money coming in while I'm on strike but I swear we'll always find enough for your swimming, one way or another.'

'Thanks, Dad.'

'All I ask in return is a bit of commitment, OK?'

'OK,' I said. 'But don't go crossing the line, Dad.'

My mam looked at my dad expectantly. Then after a silence that seemed to stretch forever, he got up and pushed away his untouched plate of food. 'I'll not do anything yet,' he said. 'But I'm not making any promises, you hear me. No promises.'

Second Round

Agnes

The holiday was over and the sun had finally started shining. 'Indian summer,' Elfie called it. 'Typical. It rains all through the holidays then the minute we have to get back in the flippin' classroom, England decides to have a heat wave.'

The phrase 'Indian Summer' made me think of colourful saris, incense, ladies lavishly painted with henna tattoes. And it made me think of home – the hot sand under my feet, the sun sparkling on the waves, orange sunsets and the smell of hot tarmac. But it didn't seem like India to me here, with the flat white marshes, the brown river, the blue white skies and the eight towers looming like giants over the estate.

School had started again and it was worse than ever: the same hissed abuse everywhere I went, the same angry stares and my stuff going missing all the time. But now there were other things too: a desk behind me slamming viciously into mine, a fist in my stomach in the girls' toilets, a flask of acid thrown over my books, melting them away to a pulpy nothing.

Elfie thought this was because all the strikers' families were really feeling the pinch now (this was another one of Elfie's phrases). 'Look around you and see how many kids are still wearing last year's school shoes with the soles stuck back on, and trousers two inches short cos their mams can't afford new,' she said after somebody Tipp-Ex-ed the word scab all over my school blazer. 'Half the kids in our year are probably eating cornflakes for tea and daren't leave a bathroom window open in case the bailiffs come visiting. And they all reckon it's your fault. Which it is, by the way.'

She made Jimmy promise not to talk to me – or even look at me – at school. Due to the current climate, she said, we had to tighten our security measures. No one must find out about the plan.

'This isn't the front line in Afghanistan, Elfie,' said Jimmy.

'If you ask me, there's not much difference between Widnes and Helmet Province, or whatever that place is called,' Elfie replied, her face barely visible behind a giant pair of pink sunglasses.

'Helmand,' said Jimmy quietly. He gave me an

apologetic glance but he didn't argue with her any more after that.

But he didn't completely ignore me in school. Every now and again, when nobody was looking, he'd glance over and smile. And two days after that, when Kirby Winstanley threw my fountain pen into the boys' urinals after English, Jimmy turned up after school with a replacement his pocket.

It was sunny again that day – Elfie's Indian summer still holding – and I was the first one down by the bridge. Elfie had gone down to the picket line to get Alfie from her dad like she did every day, and Jimmy was late. I was sitting by the river bank, dangling my feet in the water and I didn't even hear Jimmy coming till he sat beside me.

'Here,' he said, ears pink, handing me the pen. 'It's not as good as the one you had but . . .'

I looked at the pen. It was bit chewed at the end. 'Thanks,' I said. 'But it is yours?'

He shrugged. 'I don't use it much. I don't get much time for homework. With the swimming, you know.'

'Right,' I said.

Jimmy glanced round to see if Elfie was coming but there was no sign of her. 'What's the water like?' he asked, nodding at my feet.

'Cold,' I said.

'Good, I'm baking.' He scrambled to get his shoes off. His feet seemed even longer now they were bare and he had patches of eczema around his toes. He stretched out his legs and dipped his feet into the water, shivering as he did so.

'Me and Elfie learned to swim in here,' he said. 'It's where I realised how much I like the water.'

I looked at him sideways and said, 'Do you still enjoy it then? The swimming?'

'Yeah,' he said. But then his face clouded and he kicked his feet, causing brown ripples to spread in all directions across the water. 'Most of the time I do, anyway. My dad gets pretty intense about it sometimes.'

'Intense?' I hadn't heard the word before.

'Stressed – um – sort of pushy,' he said, blinking a bit too much and not really looking at me. 'But only cos he wants me to do well.'

'Like Elfie?' I said. 'She is intense too. About *Pop to the Top*.'

He laughed then. Really laughed. I didn't hear Jimmy laugh much and when he did it made his face look very young suddenly and his blue eyes really twinkled. 'Yeah, Elfie is definitely intense,' he said. 'Only I never thought of my dad being like Elfie before.'

We both sat in silence for a bit, neither of us knowing quite what to say, both of us watching the water running over our feet. 'I'm sorry,' he said eventually.

'Why?'I asked.

'Because I should have had a go at Kirby Winstanley for what she did today,' he said. 'With your pen.'

'It doesn't matter,' I said. My feet looked a ghostly white below the brown waves and so did Jimmy's. Almost like they didn't really belong to us.

'Yes it does,' he said quickly. 'I hate it when I see people treat you like that.'

I curled my arms round my body and pulled my

knees up, my toes barely skimming the surface of the water now. 'I don't mind really,' I said.

'I do,' said Jimmy.

I wrapped my arms tighter round myself so my fingers were touching behind my back. Jimmy was staring out across the brown river, over towards the soap factory which belched out steam in the distance. Everything was quiet for a moment, apart from the sound the water made.

That was until Elfie turned up, Alfie in tow, the buggy lurching over the bumpy ground. 'Come on, losers!' she shouted. 'No time for sitting round. We've got a show to win!'

I turned to Jimmy and said quietly so Elfie didn't hear, 'Thanks for the pen.'

'Come on, peeps!' Elfie bellowed. 'Let's get this party started!'

Jimmy looked up and for a moment he was looking right at me. Then he leaned quickly forwards and whispered, 'I wouldn't let anyone do anything really bad, you know that?'

He pulled away too quickly for me to answer, his

face bright, blotchy red and his eyes blinking like mad. And I didn't say anything.

'Right,' said Elfie. 'I've figured out our Plan B for the second round auditions.'

'Plan B?' said Jimmy.

'Yeah, you've always gotta have a Plan B, right? You can't just repeat what you did in the first audition. That's Talent TV suicide, that is.'

'Is it?' said Jimmy.

'Yeah, you wanna give the viewers something new, something they weren't expecting,' said Elfie with a grin.

'And are you gonna tell us what it is this time?' said Jimmy.

'No,' said Elfie.

'Course not,' said Jimmy.

'I don't want to spoil the surprise for you,' said Elfie cheerily. 'I'm dead nice like that, but let's just say it's going to make the first audition look pretty tame!'

Rules of Talent TV No. 10:
Work your audition wardrobe

Elfie

'Explain to me again why I have to go to the second round auditions?' Jimmy said. It was a Friday and I'd persuaded him to bunk off school with me to look after Alfie. I tried to skive at least once a week so me dad didn't have to take him down the picket line every day cos I figured it's tough being hard-as-nails with a kid in tow. Course I didn't tell me dad that's why I did it, I just said I was ill or whatever. Mostly I got Jimmy to keep me company and we hung out on the marshes so we didn't get caught. But it was four o'clock and school was out so we'd gone into town. We were in the bargain clothes shop, wandering among the rails of itty-bitty clothes looking for stuff me and Agnes could wear to the second round auditions.

'We could save a train fare if I stayed back and

looked after Alfie,' Jimmy was saying. 'And I wouldn't have to miss training.'

'Yeah, but Alfie is our human-interest appeal,' I said, my eyes scanning the racks. Me mam had been round again and taken nearly all the rest of her clothes, so we needed loads of new stuff if I was going to make Agnes look half decent for the next auditions.

'Why can't you take him on your own, then?' Jimmy went on. 'You're supposed to be a struggling single mam, aren't you?'

'Because I don't want to be upstaged by my own kid brother – or my own kid, or whatever he's supposed to be. That's why!' I fingered a spangly chiffon halter-neck top with a butterfly on the front and wondered if I'd be able to persuade Agnes to wear it. For someone who'd look good in a bin bag she was dead fussy about clothes and put her nose up at most of the stuff I suggested.

'Couldn't some backstage person hold him for five minutes while you sing?' said Jimmy.

'You backing out on me, Jimmy Wigmore?' I said, turning on him. 'Cos I thought you were part of the band – our roadie, or groupie, or manager or whatever.'

'Yeah, I am, but –'

'But what?' I said, quickly grabbing the spangly number and seeing if it would fit up my sleeve, enjoying the horrified look on Jimmy's face as he watched me do it.

'Elfie!' hissed Jimmy. 'What are you doing?'

'I'm sorting out our audition wardrobe, that's what,' I said, wriggling madly as I tried to make sure the top was hidden (which was harder than you might think because all the sequins kept snagging).

'Elfie! You can't!' He made a grab for the wisps of chiffon that were still poking out from my sleeve.

I raised my arm high above my head. 'What's the big deal?' I said. 'It's not like I'm holding up the store with a gun.'

'No, but –' His light green eyes were wide with concern. 'Elfie!'

I stared at him until he met my eye. It was quite funny seeing him get so worked up so I whipped round as quick as I could and marched towards the exit.

'Elfie, this is stupid,' Jimmy said, following me, but he struggled to keep up because he was steering the tatty old buggy round the overflowing racks of clothes.

'Keep walking,' I said, sailing out of the shop and giving the massive security guard by the exit a big grin. 'And don't look back!'

'Elfie!' Jimmy hissed, nearly knocking over a rail of feathered crop tops as he tore after me.

'Now, run!' I said, as we came out on to the grimy high street.

I legged it off like a lunatic in the direction of the bus station with Jimmy following me. I was pushing past people and I nearly knocked over Kirby and Pinkie who were hanging round outside by the bus stop. I could hear the security guard shouting after us and Kirby yelling, 'You seriously need a sports bra, Elfie Baguley!' as I wove in and out of the shoppers. Jimmy was going, 'Sorry!' and 'Excuse me!' and 'Bloody Hell, Elfie!' behind me.

I was running so fast I nearly crashed right into Agnes. I came skidding to a halt just in front of her and then Jimmy smashed into the back of my legs.

'Ow!' I yelled, turning on him crossly. 'That hurt!'

'Sorry!' he said, breathless.

Then I looked at Agnes who had gone pale as milk. I probably would've said 'hi' only then I caught sight of Kirby and Pinkie walking in our direction. So I scrunched up my nose and said, 'Excuse me,' in my politest tea-with-the-Queen voice, before starting to elbow my way past.

'Oi, Elfie Baguley!' came a voice from behind. I groaned and turned round to see Kirby standing there in the remains of her school uniform (she'd ditched the tie and hitched up her skirt) with her hands on her hips, staring at Agnes. 'You're not gonna let the anorexic immo get in your way like that, are you?'

I glanced at Agnes. 'You what?' I said.

'That scratty cow shouldn't be allowed to walk on the same side of the street as proper locals like us,' Kirby said, marching right up to Agnes and eyeballing her.

It was like all the blood had drained from Agnes's face. Her wide eyes looked far away, like they did when she had stage fright. And I was wondering why my life always had to be like a soap opera.

I glanced at Jimmy, who didn't say anything. He was deliberately not looking at Agnes or at me either and his aeroplane ears were the colour of cherryade.

Then Kirby made a swipe for Agnes's school bag, grabbed it and held it high in the air. Agnes gave a little gasp and glanced quickly at me, then at Jimmy who stood rooted to the spot.

'Here, catch!' yelled Kirby, lobbing the bag in my direction. Agnes's pencil case came flying out along with a hairbrush and some books which fell with a clatter on to the pavement. I caught the bag and held it for a second.

'Elfie!' said Agnes, turning her big black eyes on me, like a little lost puppy dog.

And I felt bad. Honest I did. 'Specially when I saw Agnes's face go all blotchy white and red and her eyes were all twinkly like she was going to cry. And I nearly – nearly – told Kirby Winstanley where to stuff it right there and then. Only I didn't want to risk blowing our cover and I figured there was no point getting all goody-goody about it if it meant risking the dream. Cos how would that help any of us? No, I decided we all had to keep our heads down and our eyes on the prize (if it's even possible to do both things at once). We could sort all the other stuff out later.

'Elfie!' said Jimmy, in a warning sort of voice.

'You want to play, too, fish-boy?' asked Kirby. 'I heard Dolphins were good at catch.'

I glanced at Agnes again. Her eyes were brimming with tears.

'Chuck it here, Elfie,' Pinkie called.

I figured if I was going to play along I might as well make up my own rules so I lobbed the bag as hard as I could in her direction, making sure it caught Pinkie square in the stomach. She doubled over in pain.

'Nice one!' Kirby said with a laugh.

'What'd you do that for, Elfie Baguley?' yelled Pinkie, her hands clutching her belly.

'Sorry,' I said, 'Shoulder injury. I had a glittering career ahead of me as one of those butch netball players who play for England, but then I hurt my shoulder in a freak fishing accident and now I'll never throw properly again. Good job you've got plenty of padding on your stomach, eh?'

Pinkie opened her mouth to say something but nothing came out. Kirby laughed even louder.

'You coming, Jimmy?' I said.

Agnes looked up suddenly. Jimmy was staring at her.

'Er . . . yeah.' But he was still looking at Agnes and blinking a hundred times a minute like he does when he's nervous.

I got the feeling he was about to do summat stupid so I said, 'Don't want that security guard catching us, right?'

'Oh – yeah – right,' he said, but he still didn't move.

'See you around, immo,' I said, grabbing Jimmy's arm and practically dragging him off with me.

And Agnes just stood there, rooted to the spot, saying nothing.

I bundled the two of us into the girls' loos by the bus station: the ones that stink of cigarettes and have lipstick smeared all over the plastic mirrors. I let go of

Jimmy's arm and he stared at me; I don't think I've ever seen him looking so mad before.

'That was a really crap thing to do, Elfie,' he exploded, red-faced, his eyes bright and unblinking now.

'Chill out, mall cop,' I laughed. 'I didn't take anything.'

'What?' I could see his face reflected in the scratched plastic. Both versions looked confused.

'Look,' I said, shaking out the sleeves to show him there was nothing there. 'I ditched the top before I legged it. I was just winding you up. You can give me a full body search if you want.'

He looked confused for a moment. 'You could have got us arrested!' he said.

'But I didn't.'

'Why did you run then?'

'Cos it was funny!' I grinned. 'Seriously. You should have seen your face!'

He didn't look like he thought it was very funny but he looks sweet when he's cross. A bit like Alfie when he's angry. 'Anyway, that wasn't what I meant,' he said. 'That's not why I'm mad.'

'What then? Come on, you can't be mad at me when I didn't even take anything. It was only a joke.'

'Agnes,' he said. 'You just – you were –'

'Spit it out!' I said.

He stopped blinking and looked right at me. 'You were well out of order back there.' He sounded properly angry now and the colour had drained out of his face so that he looked pale and mad. I wondered, for the first time ever, if there was anything I could ever do that was so bad Jimmy Wigmore wouldn't want to be my friend any more.

'It's an undercover operation,' I said, trying to put on my best 'Whatever' face. 'Blanking the immo was always part of the plan, you knew that.'

'Don't call her that!'

'You knew the deal: purely business, nothing more. So you can't go all Jimminy Cricket on me now.'

Jimmy looked hard at me for a moment and I got a funny feeling in my tummy. I wondered if I'd pushed him too far. Then he said, 'You need to say sorry to her.'

I scrunched up my nose and stuck my chin in the air. 'And when was the last time you saw me say sorry to anyone?' I asked. 'You know I don't do apologies.'

'You have to, Elfie.'

'Maybe,' I said, wrinkling up my nose and trying to look unbothered. 'If I promise to say sorry will you stop acting like a teacher and chill out?'

Jimmy looked at me for a moment. 'I s'pose. If you promise.'

'Pinkie promise,' I said. 'Now, if shoplifting is banned, we need to check out if your mam's got any secret sex-kitten gear hidden at the back of her wardrobe. Come on!'

Agnes

After Jimmy and Elfie went off and left me in the middle of the street I just stood there for ages holding my bag. I didn't even pick up my stuff which was scattered all over the pavement.

I was thinking about Elfie. It wasn't that I wanted

to be like her. Or that I wanted people to notice me, the way they noticed her. Or even that I wanted Jimmy Wigmore to look at me – just sometimes – the way he looked at Elfie Baguley. It was the way she'd almost stared right through me that bothered me: like she didn't even know me. No one could ever stare through Elfie like that. And the way she'd said, 'See you around, immo,' and then gone off without even a backward glance. I shouldn't have been surprised because she'd insisted from the start that we couldn't ever be friends. But I thought she was just saying that.

And now I didn't know what to believe.

Rules of Talent TV No. 11:
Keep your eyes on the prize

Elfie

I did feel bad about Agnes but we had to keep our eyes on the prize if we wanted to win this thing. I wasn't sure Jimmy saw it that way though. Even after I'd promised to say sorry, he was still weirdly quiet and talking even less than usual (and for Jimmy Wigmore that's saying something).

'What's eating you now, fish face?'

After we raided Jimmy's mam's wardrobe (which he was not happy about and which was a total waste of time anyway because she has the most boring clothes in the world!) we made our way back across the marshes to the bridge. Jimmy just walked along, staring at his shoes like he wasn't even listening to what I was saying.

'Come on. What's up?'

'Nothing,' he said.

I've known Jimmy Wigmore long enough to know when he's lying. 'Is this about me going through your mam's underwear drawer?'

'No,' said Jimmy, flushing red, just like he had when I'd dangled one of his mam's tatty old bras in front of his face.

'Is it cos I said her wardrobe needed one of those ten-years-younger makeovers?'

'No,' said Jimmy.

'Please don't tell me it's still about the immo?'

He gave me a look.

'All right, all right! Is this about Agg-ness?' I said it wrong deliberately to annoy him but he didn't even bother to correct me like he usually does.

'No,' he said again, even quieter this time.

'Come on,' I said, skipping in front of him so he had to look at me. 'No use trying to keep secrets from me. You know I'll get it out of you if something's up.'

'Nothing's up,' I said.

'You never were a very good liar, Jimmy Wigmore.'

He looked up then and stared at the sky. It was flat and white today, and full of noisy seagulls circling over the estuary. 'I think my dad is going to break the strike,' he said.

'Whooah!' I said, kicking at the salty white earth with my toe. 'Has he got a death wish, or summat?'

'I know,' he said. 'And it's all my fault.'

'How do you figure that?'

'It's expensive, all my training,' he said, looking up, his face creased with worry. 'And now he's not earning any money, him and my mam are struggling to afford it.'

'Really?' I said, pulling a face. 'Surely all you need is a pair of trunks and some goggles.'

'The only Olympic-sized pool is seven miles away, and all those bus fares add up,' said Jimmy, miserably. 'Then there's club fees and pool hire and travel to all the swim meets and my kit and all the special stuff I'm supposed to eat.'

'Yeah, but –' I started to say. Only I didn't get to finish because Jimmy Wigmore actually interrupted me (I knew he must be properly upset because he never – I mean, NEVER – interrupts me!).

'People think my dad is some kind of freeloader,

hoping to cash in on me if I make it to the top,' he said. 'But it's costing him a fortune.'

'Yeah, but when you make it big, he'll be laughing,' I said. 'You'll be minted and you'll buy your old man a massive mansion and see him all right.'

Jimmy shook his head. 'Not many swimmers make a lot of money from what they do,' he said. 'Even if they make it to the top.'

'Are you for real?' I said. 'Why's your old man making you do it then?'

'He knows I love it. And it's not about the money for him. It's about the pride,' said Jimmy. His feet were covered in white dust. They looked like massive space boots sprinkled in moon dust. 'He says he wants me to achieve something great with my life because he didn't.'

'Well, he's never going to see that happen if he turns scab, cos he'll be dead!' I said, looking up at him. I always have to look up at him these days. I swear he grows overnight sometimes. 'Your dad'll get beaten to a pulp by the strikers if he crosses that line.'

'Yeah,' he said, staring up at the sky again. 'I know.'

'So you've got to talk him out of it,' I said.

'I know, but how?'

'I don't know,' I glanced over in the direction of the river, my mind racing. Jimmy Wigmore was always there for me when crap stuff was happening, and it was my turn to help him. 'You could tell him you won't swim if he crosses the line.'

Jimmy grimaced.

'No! Seriously,' I said. And the more I thought about it the more I figured this was actually pretty inspired. 'He's so obsessed with you being this swim champ. If you tell him you're quitting he'll deffo sit up and take notice.'

He shrugged and said, 'I can't.' And he might be about ten feet tall but right then with his big sad eyes, he looked about eight years old.

'Why not?' I asked.

He shrugged. 'I s'pose it's like your dad and the strike,' he said. 'My swimming is sort of . . .' he hesitated, '. . . what keeps him together.'

'What are you, a tube of superglue or what?'

'He used to joke about me winning gold in 2016

and being Merseyside's next big hope,' said Jimmy glumly. 'Only since the strike started, he's just got – I dunno – more serious about it. Like it's all that matters.'

'Which is exactly why this is the perfect plan,' I insisted.

Jimmy didn't say anything.

'Plus, if your family gets blacklisted, I'll have to find me another band manager,' I added. 'Which will be, like, a total pain!'

'I'm more worried about my dad getting beaten up, or me being kicked to death at school,' he said quietly.

'I suppose there is that and all but if we win *Pop to the Top* you'll be able to use your share of the prize money to fund your training,' I said.

'If,' said Jimmy, unconvinced. He stared out over the water while I racked my brains for another way to try and cheer him up. Then suddenly it all came together in my head. A way to make sure we made it to the semi-finals, and sort out Jimmy's money worries, all in one go. I don't know why I hadn't thought of it before because it was genius.

'I've got it!' I said, looking up at the eight towers – the cause of all our problems, if you ask me. Well, nearly all. 'I know exactly what we need to figure all this out.'

'What?' he said in a flat voice.

The eight towers belched out smoke into the white sky.

'Plan C!' I grinned.

Jimmy

We spent about an hour waiting for Agnes under the bridge. Elfie wouldn't tell me what Plan C was. She hadn't even told me what Plan B was yet and she reckoned this was even more top secret. She said it relied on the element of surprise and anyway, it was so brilliant it would blow my mind if she told me.

After a while it was pretty obvious Agnes wasn't coming and Elfie wasn't happy about it. Eventually, she stood up, patted the dust off her bum and announced that it was too early in the band's career to split up over artistic differences. Then she marched us both over to Agnes's house for a showdown.

The sky had cleared by the time we got to the immo houses, and the sun was out. 'What if someone sees us?' I said, glancing around anxiously. We hadn't been over to Agnes's house since that first day, cos Elfie reckoned it was too risky. ('Mrs Newsround has her spies everywhere!' she said).

'Then we'll just have to throw a brick through Agnes's window and run, won't we!' said Elfie.

'We can't do that!'

'Serve her right for sacking off rehearsal, I reckon, and at least it won't blow our cover,' said Elfie pounding on the door.

Agnes opened the door wearing a pair of tracksuit bottoms and what looked like her dad's shirt. She had her arms wrapped round her waist and looked so thin they seemed to go round her twice.

'Trying on outfits for the finals?' said Elfie, looking her up and down.

'What you want?' said Agnes, not looking her in the eye.

'You were supposed to be at rehearsal an hour ago,' said Elfie with a little toss of her head. 'We're not going to scoop the twenty-five grand prize if we start slacking off, you know. You're good but not that good.'

Agnes didn't say anything. I tried to catch her eye but it was like she was deliberately not looking at me either.

'So, where were you?'

Agnes shrugged.

'Is this just because of what happened in town?' said Elfie impatiently.

Still no response.

'I think it probably is,' I said quietly.

'Yeah, I realised that, you divvy!' snapped Elfie. She had her hands on her hips and was staring at Agnes, who was twisting her fingers round her wrist nervously.

'Look, kiddo. I'm not doing this just so we can play at pop stars and sing into our hairbrushes, right?'

said Elfie. 'I'm risking breaking me dad's heart singing with you, but I'm doing it so that we can win that money and get me dad out of debt – and out of me mam's evil clutches for good.'

Agnes still didn't say anything. Elfie had never really talked about her mam in front of Agnes before. And she hated talking about her mam full stop so I knew she must be really serious now.

'So, that's why I had to do the whole blanking you thing,' Elfie went on, her face a bit flushed now. 'Because this is too important to mess up. OK?'

I stared at Elfie and nodded in Agnes's direction.

'What?' she said.

'You promised to say sorry,' I muttered.

'OK, I'm sorry,' she said super-quickly. 'Whatever!'

Agnes twisted her lips.

'I give up!' said Elfie, throwing her hands into the air. 'You talk to her, Jimmy,' she said, turning to me.

'What am I supposed to say?' I hissed.

'How should I know?' she said. 'But you're the band manager – it's your job to sort out artistic differences, isn't it. So, sort it.'

'Elfie!'

But she wasn't listening. 'Alfie needs a nap,' she said, grabbing the buggy and wheeling it off down the path. 'Call me when she's ready to sing again.'

'I don't have a phone,' I called after her.

'Not my problem.'

'And neither do you!'

'Like I said, your problem not mine!'

'Elfie!' I yelled again as she turned off into the close. But she made a big 'W' sign with her hands over her head, and didn't look back. And me and Agnes were left staring at each other not knowing what to say. For the second time that day.

Agnes

I told Jimmy he'd better come in before somebody saw him. He muttered something I didn't understand, then took a step forwards, tripped up over his giant shoes and went flying straight into me. He stared down at me, his eyes blinking really fast and I stared up at him, so tall his head nearly touched the ceiling. Then he pulled away really quickly.

'Sorry,' he said, blinking madly and standing up very, very straight.

'You go upstairs,' I said. 'I make some tea.'

I showed Jimmy the way to my bedroom then I went to make us both a cup of tea. When I came up, he was standing in the middle of the room and he looked so out of place amongst the pink stuff and the fairy lights and the butterflies on the wall that I nearly laughed.

'Nice room,' he said, and brushed one of the butterflies out of his face.

'Um, you want sit down?' I asked, passing him the mug.

He sat down on the floor with his back against my wardrobe. There were photos all over the wardrobe door, pictures I'd stuck there to remind me of home: of sand and sun shining on blue water, me smiling with friends, my skin browner than it is now, of our home on the cliffs, of the lighthouse I can see from my bedroom window. Jimmy glanced at them and then turned away quickly – like he shouldn't have been looking.

I went to sit on the bed, curling my limbs up to make myself as small as possible. There were only a few metres of floor between us but it felt like miles.

'It feels like we're in detention,' Jimmy said. He was staring really, really hard at the carpet and didn't look at me as he spoke.

'Detention?' I asked.

'You know. When you're in trouble at school?'

'Right,' I said, storing the word up in my mind for later.

'So is that where you live – when you're not here?' he asked, twisting round and pointing at the photos.

I nodded.

'It looks nice,' he said, looking back at the carpet. 'Do you miss it?'

'Every day,' I said.

'Reckon anyone'd miss a place like that,' he said. Then there was a long pause. I could see the eight towers through the window behind him, smoke gushing out into the pale blue sky.

'You were really good last week – at the audition, you know,' Jimmy said after a while.

'Thank you.' I could feel myself colouring and I wondered if my ears went pink like Jimmy's did.

'Did you, like, do any singing, back home? You know, before you came here.'

I shook my head. 'I get – I don't know the word in English. *Medo da Plateia*. Afraid of the –' I hesitated – 'Stage? Stages?'

'Stage fright?' he said.

'Yes.' I nodded quickly. 'Stage frightened.'

'Yeah, I could kind of see that,' he said. 'I thought you were going to bottle it at one point.'

I caught his eye when he said 'bottle it'. He was watching me, like he'd thrown the new phrase in on purpose and was waiting for my reaction.

'Bottle it?' I asked.

'Oh, it means, not do it, because you were too frightened, you know?' He nodded as he said it.

'Yes. That's it. I think I nearly . . . bottle it.'

'Good job you didn't,' he said. 'I reckon Elfie would have gone mental!'

'Yes,' I said. 'She would go – how you say? – apes?'

Jimmy laughed and for a moment I wondered if I'd got it wrong. 'Yeah, she would have gone totally ape!' he said, and we both grinned.

I sipped on my tea. I'd put sugar in it and I'd made it way stronger than my mum makes it. It tasted sweet and tarry.

'You know, Elfie is kind of used to people doing what she wants,' Jimmy said. 'But she's OK, really.'

'She is?' I said.

'Yeah, I mean, she was way out of order today. With your bag and stuff. And she knows that. That's why she came over. She's no good at saying sorry, but she is really.'

'That was her way of saying so?' I said, remembering Elfie's cross face, the puckered-up freckles and stormy green eyes.

'I did say she wasn't very good at it,' he said. He tailed off then, like he didn't know what to say next.

'You know her a long time?' I asked.

'Since we were little kids,' he said.

'And –' I hesitated, biting my lip. 'You . . . like her?'

Jimmy dropped his eyes. 'Um . . . yeah, I suppose.' Then he added quickly, 'Just as a friend, you know.'

'Why?' I asked.

'What do you mean?'

'Why you like her?' I got the feeling nobody had ever asked him that before, because he didn't answer right away and he looked like he was thinking really hard for a minute. Eventually he said, 'Because she can be cool and funny. And she's a good friend. And she's not as tough as she makes out. She's having a hard time, that's all.'

'Because of the strike?'

'Yeah, and other stuff,' he said. He looked at the pictures on the wall again, frowning and pushing his hair back off his face so that the eczema around his eyes was more visible.

'What other stuff?'

'They haven't got any money. I mean, nobody round here has really, but it's worse cos her mam spends everything and then clears off.' He looked awkward, like he thought he shouldn't be saying all this.

'She wants her mum to come back?'

Jimmy sort of shrugged. 'Not exactly! Elfie's mam is – I dunno – she's a bit unreliable. Elfie reckons she's no good for Alfie. She wants her dad to ditch her and find a new mam. Sort of.'

'Right,' I said.

'You know how she is,' he said with an awkward grin. 'She never does stuff like anyone else.'

I bit my lip and half smiled back. 'What her dad do if he find out she sing with me?'

'Oh, he'll kill her!' he said, his blue eyes meeting mine.

'Kill her?'

'Not literally,' he said. 'I mean, he'll be mad, yeah, but he won't actually kill her.' I was staring at him and it seemed to make him nervous. He looked away and said, 'It's just something we say, you know . . . an expression.'

'An expression. Right.'

Then I curled up my toes, bit my lip and said quickly, 'Would you like her to be – how you say? – your girlfriend?'

He seemed to lurch a bit more upright. 'No!' he said.

'Would you like to . . .' I could taste blood on my lip, warm and tinny. Would you like to kiss her?'

'No way!' he said again, a bit too loud and a bit too quick.

And he looked at me and I looked at him and the room seemed too bright suddenly. But then he looked away and so did I. I stared at the pictures behind his head, of me looking younger and happier and the sun shining on the red-gold sands.

'So, you'll keep singing, yeah?' Jimmy managed to say, although his voice sounded a bit weird and croaky.

I nodded.

'Good. Elfie will be dead chuffed.' Then he added, 'She won't admit it, but she likes you really, you know.'

Jimmy

I stared out the window and tried really hard not to think about how that corner of Agnes's lip that she

217

kept biting looked red and swollen, and how I wanted to run my finger over it.

'I used to think giants built the towers when I was little,' I said. I don't know why I said it. It just sort of came out, all in a rush.

Agnes gave a funny sort of little nod.

I could feel myself getting all hot and bothered but for some reason I just kept on talking. 'And I used to say I was going to work at the plant when I grew up, cos I wanted to climb to the top of the big towers every morning and look down on all the little houses below.' I stopped then, and glanced quickly at Agnes who was biting her lip again.

'I think I be frightened so high up,' she said.

'Me too,' I said, glancing back out at the towers again, watching the patterns the belching smoke made against the grey sky. 'And anyway, my dad said I could do something better with my life than work at the plant. That I should set my ambitions higher than he had.'

I'd never thought of my dad and Elfie having anything in common before but it occurred to me then that they did. Because they both wanted to build a better life for the people they loved. I reckon that's one reason why, when Agnes said she'd rejoin the band, I got this strange funny leaping feeling in my tummy. Cos I knew Elfie would be made up.

'It would have been . . . weird without you,' I said, still not looking at her, still staring out of the window.

'Weird?' she said, lifting her voice at the end so you know it's a question.

'We'd have missed you,' I said, feeling my ears go hotter than ever. I blinked and focused really hard on the eight towers. 'I'd have missed you.'

'I would miss you too,' she said.

And I felt the leap in my tummy again. Like winning a race. Or beating a personal best. Only better. Much better. Except this time, it felt like I was betraying Elfie.

Elfie

'Your mam wants you to go and live with her.

'What?'

Me dad was in the kitchen when I got back from Agnes's house. He was putting a load of washing in the machine, but he had whites and colours all mixed up. He looked different from how he does down the picket line. Older, and tireder.

'She reckons she's discussed it with you,' he said.

'But I haven't even spoken to her,' I said quickly.

'She's probably right,' he said, tugging at a sachet of washing powder which refused to open. 'She can look after you and Alfie better than I'm doing.'

'This is me mam we're talking about!' A panicky feeling started jumping round in my chest. Like a bouncing bean of fear. 'We're better off without her.'

'You're fourteen,' he said, trying to yank the sachet open with his teeth. 'You shouldn't be saddled with a baby to look after half the time.'

'But I don't mind, Dad.'

'I appreciate that, but it's not right, Elfie.'

My dad sighed and glared at the washing powder sachet, looking defeated.

I've always been jealous of kids with proper mams. The sort who wear supermarket jeans and flowery tops; who actually turn up to parents' evenings and read bedtime stories and bake cakes and help you with your homework. The sort of mams who don't spend the child benefit on fake designer shoes, or flirt with the doctor, or leave you in the beer garden for three hours in the rain while they get drunk.

Only *my* mam reckons those mams – the normal ones – are jealous of her. She reckons it's better to have what it takes to make workmen and teenage boys whistle than to be able to make fairy cakes.

'Apparently your mam's got some new man,' me dad went on. He didn't look at me as he said it.

'Nothing stays secret round here for long, does it!' I muttered.

'Not with Mrs Newsround living right next door,' he said with a sad sort of grin.

And I wondered if our friendly neighbourhood news agency had told him that me mam's new man was an immo.

'She always comes back to you,' I said quickly. 'Cos no one else will put up with her.'

He didn't answer that. He just stood there, staring

at the half-opened powder sachet. And right then, I wanted to punch me mam for how much she'd hurt him.

'Anyway, school called,' he said, with a sigh. 'They say you've not been doing any homework; failing tests. And I know you've been pulling sickies to help me with Alfie.'

'I haven't,' I protested. 'I've just been poorly a lot.'

He raised an eyebrow and said, 'You shouldn't be missing out on your education.'

And I wanted to tell him that I'd been working on stuff that was way more important than my education too. Only I couldn't.

'It's my fault. I shouldn't have let you do so much,' he said quietly.

'Yeah, but when the strike's over –'

'If this bleedin' strike ever comes to end, I'll still be up to my eyes in debt,' he said.

'We'll manage. We always do,' I said, the bean of fear bouncing harder in my chest. 'Everything'll be OK.'

I wanted to grab him, shake him, remind him he was the hero of the picket lines, that he couldn't let me mam defeat him so easily.

He grabbed a knife and dug it into the sachet and sent washing powder flying over the room. Then he paused, took a long breath, closed his eyes. 'I just wonder if it'd be better for all of us if Alfie was with his mother.'

'She'll have to get him off me first,' I said loudly.

My dad sighed and rubbed his hands over his eyes. 'I'm not sure I've got the stomach for another fight, Elfie love.'

'But I've got a plan, Dad!' I said quickly. He still didn't look at me. The bean of fear was getting bigger, making me feel sick. 'Just wait. Give it a bit more time. I've got a plan to make some money so it'll all be OK.'

He laughed – only it didn't really sound like a laugh. 'One of your plans, eh?'

'Seriously, this one is solid, Dad,' I said. 'It'll all work out.'

But it was like he wasn't listening; like he'd already

made up his mind because he said, 'Thanks, Elfie, but I think we need something more concrete to rely on than one of your madcap plans.'

Rules of Talent TV No. 12: Surprise the judges at the second-round auditions

Jimmy

The morning of the second auditions my dad talked to me all the way to the pool. Normally we don't speak much on the bus. I stare out of the window, watching the early risers trudging to work and the occasional drunk staggering home in the half light. My dad usually just looks over my training logs and scribbles stuff down. But that morning he couldn't seem to stop: he went on about training schedules, tactics for the trials, diet plans. That's how I knew something was wrong.

I couldn't find my rhythm in the pool. My brain just wouldn't shut off and let my body do what it normally does. I couldn't stop thinking about Elfie and Agnes, and about what would happen if my dad turned scab. Elfie said she had a plan to stop him but she said it needed time and I figured my dad was running out of both. He kept shouting at me from the edge that my timings were all off and my stroke pattern was uneven and each time I plunged back into the blue, all I could hear was his voice, echoing through the water like some kind of whale call. 'Scab! Scab! Scab!' it seemed to chant.

On the journey home he was silent, which I think was worse than the talking. I'd put in my worst lap times for weeks. 'I'm sorry, Dad,' I said when we were waiting in the bus terminus, waiting to catch the local bus that ran right past the estate. It was raining hard and the roof was leaking, so a stream of cold water was splashing down on to the concrete to my right. Elfie's Indian summer seemed to have come to an abrupt end.

He looked up. 'What for?' he said.

'The training session,' I said. 'I was terrible.'

'Oh, that,' he said. Then he looked down again. 'Never mind, son. We all have off days.'

'I'll do better tomorrow,' I said. The water drummed on the pavement, catching my dad's shoes, but he didn't even seem to notice.

'I know you will, son,' he said. Then he looked at me. 'I know you've got what it takes. That's why I'm doing this. You know that, don't you?'

'Doing what?' I looked up, even more anxious suddenly. I really, really hoped he didn't mean what I thought he meant.

But just then the bus drew in and my dad climbed on board without answering. He went and sat down at the back and stared wordlessly out of the window all the way home. And I sat next to him with a bad feeling in the pit of my stomach that didn't go away for the rest of the day.

The second round of auditions was in the Empire Theatre, which is right next to Liverpool Lime Street station. It's a proper big old theatre with twinkly lights at the entrance and red velvet seats inside.

We only just made it on time cos I got back late from training and then me and Elfie had to pretend like we were going to school before legging it round to the station by the back streets so no one would see us skiving. We arrived hot, sweaty and out of breath just as the train was being called over the loudspeaker. There was no sign of Agnes.

'If she's bailed I'm gonna kill her!' said Elfie.

But then I caught sight of her, at the far end of the platform, half hidden by a pillar.

'Geez!' said Elfie. 'Who is so skinny they can actually hide behind a flippin' pole? That girl seriously needs to get some curves.'

I just looked over and smiled. Agnes smiled back. The weird feeling in my stomach was still there but it didn't feel so bad then.

On the train, Elfie spent ages slapping make-up all over Agnes and telling her how we had to surprise the judges at the second audition, although she didn't explain exactly how ('Plan B,' she said, tapping her nose). Then she sent Agnes off to the toilet to put on a little pink dress she'd found stuffed at the back of my mam's wardrobe last week. When Agnes came out she looked amazing. The dress had an old-fashioned look to it that sort of suited Agnes and it wasn't as trashy as some of the stuff Elfie's mam wears. I remembered seeing a picture of my mam in that dress when she was much younger. She was laughing with my dad in the picture and holding me when I was just a baby. It looked different on Agnes cos it was a bit too big for her, but it still looked really nice.

'It is OK?' she asked.

'Yeah!' said Elfie in a bored sort of voice. 'You look all right, I s'pose.'

Then Agnes looked at me and I just sort of nodded.

There must have been about a hundred other acts there who'd also got through from the open auditions: solo singers, girl bands, boy bands, ensemble groups and a couple of other pop duos (none as good as us, though, Elfie reckoned). We all had to sit in the stalls whilst the same producer girl who'd been at the last auditions told us what was going to happen.

'Only twenty-four acts will make it through to the next round,' she said, clutching her clipboard nervously. 'So, sadly, for many of you, today will be the end of your *Pop to the Top* journey.'

'Not for us,' Elfie whispered. 'Not after I unleash Plan B.'

'I thought we were on Plan C?'

'Plan B today and then on to Plan C if we make it to the semis,' said Elfie.

'But . . .' Elfie had said Plan C would stop my dad crossing the picket line and I don't know why I even thought it would work, but it was the only hope I had.

'Have faith,' said Elfie. 'The best-laid plans take a little time.'

'We'll call you all up on to the stage to perform and you'll just get one chance to impress,' the producer was saying. 'No second chances today, everybody!'

'Miss Stage Fright better not have another one of her weird-outs then!' Elfie said, glancing at Agnes who had gone pale just like last time.

'So, good luck everybody!' said the producer. 'And may the best acts win!'

Everyone clapped and then the cameras started panning over the auditorium where we were all sitting in the audience, which made everyone go into overdrive pretending to be nice to each other. The posh student with the voice like an opera singer stopped doing vocal warm-ups and started getting pally with a group of hip-hop boys, while some middle-aged woman with big hair was telling a younger girl about how she got off with The Lingerie Lizard in 1987. 'So he's bound to put me through to the next round,' I heard her say. 'For old time's sake, y'know!'

We plonked ourselves down on the floor of the gangway behind the back row so that Alfie could crawl up and down the aisles. Next to us the seven scantily clad members of a girl band were flirting with every sound man/camera guy/tea boy in sight. A couple of them checked us out and giggled.

Elfie glared at them. 'I wonder why we didn't get the Spanish Inquisition at reception this time?' she said, eyes still narrowed in the direction of the girl band.

'Maybe they've forgotten about the whole parental permission issue,' I suggested.

'Maybe,' she said, sounding unconvinced. Then she grinned. 'But don't worry, cos if they do ask, I've got that one sorted, an' all.'

'Right,' I said.

She frowned again. 'What's up with you today, anyhow? You've been in a funny mood all morning.

You and her.' She gestured at Agnes. 'She looks like she's about to go off into her whole, "I'm about to die of stage fright!" thing again any second, and you're as jumpy as a frog on Red Bull.'

I thought again about what my dad had said that morning, but I just shrugged.

'I suppose you're stressing about bunking off school,' she said.

'And getting back late for swimming practice,' I added.

'You care way too much about education, if you ask me,' said Elfie. 'It's not like Olympic athletes need any GCSEs, is it?'

'I've just got to be back by five o'clock, OK. I totally promised my dad I wouldn't miss another session . . .'

'Chill!' Elfie said. 'We'll get you back before you turn into a pumpkin. I promised, didn't I?'

'You never pinkie promised,' said Agnes quietly.

Me and Elfie both glanced over at her in surprise. She hadn't looked like she'd even been listening.

Elfie pulled a face. 'That's because I'm not about

to lose one of my digits to make sure he makes it for his chlorine marinade, OK? Anyway, I don't need to promise because there's no way it's gonna take that long.'

I looked around, unconvinced. 'There are loads of acts here. It'll take ages to get through them all.'

'Then I'll get us bumped to the head of the queue again,' Elfie said.

My heart sank. 'How?'

'It's all part of Plan B,' said Elfie.

'So does this involve telling the judges I'm actually like your brother, or a girl in disguise, or on the run from the police or something?'

'Nope!' she said. 'Don't fret, Jimmy Wigmore. The truth will set you free.'

Rules of Talent TV No. 13 (unlucky for some!):
Know when to tell the truth

Elfie

If I say so myself, Plan B was total genius. And dead simple too. Surprise the judges by coming clean, that was my new strategy. Well, nearly clean. I had to keep a little something up my sleeve for the next rounds, of course. No point using all your lifelines at once.

The idea was to crank up the sympathy vote with a few nuggets of real-life tragedy. I figured we'd nailed the first auditions with my genius teen-mam-love-triangle back story, but you can't keep flogging old material. Plus I'd decided it was a crying shame not to make use of my totally tragic existence, the one time it might actually be an advantage.

Luckily, Alfie was in a good mood again, all smiley and cute.

'So, how old were you when you had Alfie?' asked

the presenter guy in a loud whisper. We were doing one of those in-the-wings interview things while we hung around waiting for our turn.

'Twelve,' I whispered back, quickly doing the maths in my head and hoping it don't make me sound too trampy.

'Wow, that must have been tough!' said the presenter with a fake expression of sympathy.

'Yeah, you could say I was robbed of my childhood!' I said, trying to look wide-eyed and tragic.

'But Jimmy tells us that your parents agreed to raise the baby for you at first – is that right?'

I glanced at Jimmy who just shrugged. 'Summat like that,' I said. 'Only me mam's pretty hot on big promises, not so good on delivery. You know, the sort that does a disappearing act the minute the going gets tough.'

'That's heartbreaking!' the presenter said, nodding his head.

'Not really,' I said, brightly, hoping they'd show this bit. I looked straight into the camera and said, 'We're doing just fine without her actually.'

'I notice that none of you have brought your parents along with you today,' he said.

'That's true,' I said. I looked up at the camera and put my serious-but-likeable face back on and launched Plan B. 'You see, basically, our families hate each other.'

'Really?' said the presenter, eyes widening with interest again.

Jimmy was looking totally alarmed but I ignored him and turned back to the presenter. 'Yeah. They don't even know we're doing the show.'

'They don't know you're here?' The presenter said, barely able to keep the excitement out of his voice.

'No,' I said solemnly. 'In fact, we're not even supposed to see each other.'

Jimmy made a kind of choking noise.

'At least me and Jimmy aren't supposed to see Agnes. And his dad don't approve of me much neither.'

'Elfie!' said Jimmy.

I just silently mouthed the words, 'Plan B.'

'Why do they hate each other so much?' the presenter was asking.

'Oh, it's all to do with the strike, you know. Scabs versus strikers – a load of boring politics, basically.'

Jimmy was looking a bit like he did the time Kirby Winstanley nicked Agnes's bag. Only worse.

'But how did you get this far without parental permission?' asked the presenter.

'Oh, that,' I said. I glanced around to check the producer girl wasn't listening then leaned in and said in a whisper loud enough for the cameras to pick up, 'I lied and then faked their signatures.'

Jimmy groaned quietly as the presenter let out a long, low whistle. 'Wow!' he said. 'So, um, what do you plan to do now?'

'Well, I figured it was time to come clean and throw myself on the mercy of the judges,' I said, trying to look dead wholesome and honest. 'I just couldn't stand the lying and deceit any more.'

'Right,' said the presenter, putting on a serious and concerned expression. 'And what will happen if your parents do find out?'

'Oh, they'll go mad!' I said. 'Won't they, Agnes?'

Camera swings to Agnes, who is pale as – I don't

know – Snow White or summat, although she didn't seem to be listening. She was just staring blank eyed at the stage.

'Don't mind her,' I said. 'She gets pre-performance jitters. She'll get over it. My dad on the other hand . . .'

'What will he do?'

'Basically, he might try and kill her – or me. But it's a risk we have to take to follow our dream.'

The presenter whistled again. I glanced at Jimmy who had gone the colour of a tomato and was staring at me so hard I thought his eyes might pop out.

'And maybe – just maybe – if we're allowed to stay in the competition and we end up going all the way, the fighting will finally stop and the two families will unite behind us,' I said, with what was supposed to be a hopeful-but-anxious sort of face. I'd been rehearsing this and I reckoned it sounded pretty good.

'Wow!' said the presenter, trying to look like a serious journalist reporting on a war zone or summat.

Then he got a message through on his earpiece and he turned away for a moment.

'Bloody hell, Elfie!' Jimmy whispered, his voice

cracking. 'Your dad's going to go mental.'

'Yeah, he probably won't be best pleased,' I said.

'And you told them we'd faked the permission slips. Are you trying to get us kicked off the show?'

'Maybe.' I shrugged. 'I figure it's either that or we get catapulted straight into the semis. Calculated risk, you know.'

'But that stuff you said about the strike . . .'

'Can't make an omelette without breaking a few eggs,' I said.

Jimmy

Elfie is so good at making stuff up, I figured she wouldn't bother telling the TV people the actual *truth*. I mean, she was always going on about how the truth was usually flipping rubbish whereas stories got to be as exciting as you wanted them to be. But suddenly she seemed to have changed her mind. Or gone *out* of her mind, more like. Because Plan B seemed to me like the worst plan ever in the history of Elfie's plans. If we didn't get kicked off for faking our parents' signatures, then there was no way we'd survive the fallout from our families if any of this ever got on to the TV.

It was bad enough her spinning a load of rubbish about us, but this was so much worse. I knew what my dad would say, and what her dad would say too, when they saw it – that we were making light of a cause they were fighting for. And I knew we were going to be in serious, serious trouble.

The whole thing took ages, of course. And even though Elfie's coming-clean routine got us bumped up the schedule (she was right about one thing at least), there were sound checks and lighting checks and camera-angle checks and make-up girls dusting the judges and loads of other stuff before Elfie and Agnes could do their audition. They had to stand in the middle of the stage while all this was going on and Agnes was looking more and more like she was going to be sick. Her black eyes were as wide as saucers in her pale, pale face.

I was standing in the wings holding Alfie who had fallen asleep in my arms and was starting to get really heavy. I couldn't look at my watch cos of holding him but I knew it was getting later and later and, as the time slipped away, so did the chance of me making it back on time for training.

Then, finally, the onstage cameras started to roll and the producer said, 'Oops! Silly me!' and tiptoed theatrically off the stage with her clipboard. The giant spotlight focused on Elfie and Agnes and the audience went quiet.

'So, ladies,' said The Legend in his gravelly voice. 'You still look like a mismatch to me.'

'But when we sing, we're in perfect harmony!' Elfie replied with her brightest, fakest smile.

The audience laughed.

'We'll see about that!' said The Legend, raising an eyebrow. 'And I've just been told that neither of your families knows you're here today. Is that right?'

I glanced at the presenter who just kind of shrugged, but Elfie looked like she'd been expecting this and she nodded, still smiling.

'And that you forged your parents' signatures on the parental consent forms?'

'Yes, sirree!' said Elfie.

I felt the knot in my stomach tighten. The presenter standing next to me turned to the camera and pulled a concerned expression.

'You know I should kick you off the show right now, don't you?' said The Legend.

'Yes,' said Elfie. 'But I figure you won't.'

'Really? And why is that?'

'Because the way I see it, shows like this need human interest stories.'

The Legend raised an eyebrow.

'And cos none of your other contestants have half as much talent as my Spanish amigo here,' she said, jabbing Agnes in the ribs.

'Isn't she Portuguese?' whispered the producer. She'd scanned her notes with a confused expression.

'That may be true, but we can't allow you to perform without parental permission,' The Legend said in his slow drawl.

'I agree,' said Elfie in her best grown-up sensible voice. 'So, why not say that if we get through to the next round, then we'll tell them. And if not, we won't.

No point starting World War Three if we're about to get kicked off anyway, right?'

'World War Three!' The Legend raised an eyebrow.

'That's right,' said Elfie. 'Lives could be lost.'

I groaned. I knew how much my dad would hate this. And hers too. But there was no stopping Elfie now and it just got worse and worse.

'So what were you planning to do when the programme went on air?' asked The Lingerie Lizard, who sounded a bit drunk today.

'I thought maybe the producers might be able to give us new identities,' said Elfie. 'You know, like on a witness protection programme?'

The audience laughed again. The presenter turned to the camera and did a thumbs up and a stupid grin.

'And how did you plan to combine that sort of anonymity with the celebrity that comes with a successful pop career?' enquired The Facelift, acidly.

That got another laugh.

'She's priceless, isn't she?' the presenter whispered loudly to me.

'You have no idea,' I said under my breath.

'OK, I've heard enough,' said The Legend.

'So, are you gonna let us sing or what?' said Elfie.

'I'm not happy about this, let me tell you, young lady,' said The Legend, sounding like our headmaster or something. 'I'm going to let you sing, but if . . .' he paused, '. . . if you get through to the next round, you won't just need parental permission. I want to personally hear it coming from their mouths. Do you understand?'

'Loud and clear!' said Elfie, doing a little salute.

The knot in my stomach pulled tighter than ever.

'All right,' said The Legend with a sigh. 'Let's hear you sing.'

I looked at Agnes. In all the fuss nobody had been paying any attention to her and she'd gone pale as death. As the intro to the backing track started, she turned and looked over to where I was standing in the wings.

I caught her eye and smiled and nodded and she held my gaze for a long moment and then she turned away like she hadn't even seen me. And then she opened her mouth and sang.

Agnes had a way of making a song seem like it was brand sparkling new. Like you were hearing it for the first time ever; like it had been written specially for you. And as she stood there in my mam's old pink dress, The Legend narrowed his eyes and stroked his chin, The Tabloid Princess leaned forwards and blinked till her eyes filled with tears and even The Lingerie Lizard nodded his head appreciatively. Only The Facelift looked unimpressed.

Meanwhile, Elfie went into full-on pop-diva mode, throwing her head back and then leaning over her microphone like she was trying to snog it. She was kind of cool in her own way, but it didn't really fit with Agnes. It was almost like they were singing different songs.

Still, at the end, the audience went wild. They kept clapping for ages. Elfie was jumping up and down looking well excited. Agnes turned and smiled in my direction and I gave her the thumbs up.

Finally, the cheering died down and The Legend leaned back and put a pen to his mouth. 'OK, I'm gonna say something controversial here,' he said at last.

The audience fell silent. The cameraman closed in on Agnes and Elfie. Elfie had stopped skipping around and was trying to look all tough and cocky but I could see her fingers were trembling. And even though I was holding Alfie I crossed my fingers as tight as I could, cos although I knew my life would be so much easier if they got sent home, I also knew how much Elfie needed this.

'I think you –' The Legend pointed at Agnes – 'have all the makings of a huge star.'

Massive cheer from the audience.

'But I think you –' pointing at Elfie – 'are holding her back.'

Gasp from the audience. The cameraman moved from Agnes's face to Elfie's as she wrinkled up her nose and flushed pink. My stomach did an awful lurch.

'I'm sorry, Elfie,' said The Legend.

Elfie just shrugged and bit her lip like Agnes does.

'I like you. I really do,' he went on. 'And I think you've done your friend a favour, because I doubt she would ever have got on that stage if it wasn't for you. But a two-piece girl band just isn't working for me and I think Agnes could have a real shot at the big prize if she went for it as a soloist.'

Another flurry from the audience.

Elfie sniffed loudly. 'Fine,' she said, breezily, 'You're welcome to your opinion!' She did her sideways head thing and tried to look cross and not bothered at the same time. Only it didn't quite work and she just ended up looking a bit lost.

'Well, I totally disagree,' drawled The Lingerie Lizard in his slurred voice. His hair was a more vivid shade of purple today and it clashed with his leathery orange skin. 'I think they make a good team.'

'Me too!' squeaked The Tabloid Princess, shaking her blonde curls and looking more like a Barbie doll than ever.

I could have hugged them. But Elfie was still looking like she does when her mam launches into one of her star turns. And I sort of wanted to rescue her.

'What about you?' The Legend turned to The Facelift, who was staring at Elfie. Elfie stared right back – like it was a blinking contest or something.

'I agree with you,' drawled The Facelift. The audience booed. 'Only one of you has the vocal talent to get through, and it's not the one dressed like a floozy.'

My stomach contracted again as Elfie's face went a deeper shade of pink. The audience booed again, but there was an edge of laughter too. The presenter turned to the camera and said, 'Ouch!'

Elfie had said it worked to their advantage if one of the judges didn't like them, and getting The Facelift riled was part of her master plan, but I wasn't quite sure this was what she'd intended. Still, she put on a sickly sweet expression and said, 'But I just want to look like you!'

The audience laughed again, louder this time. The Facelift glowered.

I glanced across to the other side of the stage where the producer was hopping from foot to foot and smiling nervously.

'Are you going to let her speak to me like that?' said The Facelift, turning to The Legend.

'Is he?' the presenter asked the camera.

But The Legend just waved a dismissive hand in her direction.

'I think we all need to calm down for a moment,' he said. 'Right now, all I'm suggesting is that Elfie lets Agnes audition again, this time as a soloist.'

I glanced at Agnes to try and work out what she made of all this, but her face was blank and she was running her fingers nervously down the pink fabric of the dress.

'Then we'll consider them both as separate acts,' The Legend went on. 'The Juliets versus Agnes. The strongest goes through. And we'll let the audience decide.'

There was a murmur of excitement from the audience. Elfie coloured again and tossed her hair crossly.

'I'll give you girls a moment to think about it, OK?'

As the audience erupted into animated chatter, the presenter turned to me and said, 'So, what do you think they'll do, Jimmy?'

I looked over at Elfie who was tapping her foot and staring at her nails.

'Um – well – Elfie usually does the thing you least expect,' I said.

'And Agnes?'

I glanced at Agnes again. She was virtually transparent now, and she was biting her lip really hard. I wondered if it was bleeding.

'I don't know,' I said quietly.

And right then, just as I predicted, Elfie did the thing no one was expecting. She turned to Agnes, shrugged, and said loudly, 'Sure. Go for it. Don't worry about me.'

Agnes

Everyone was staring at me. Everyone was waiting for me to say something. It was like the dreams I have when I open my mouth to speak and nothing comes out; as if I'd forgotten all the words, or they'd dried and shrivelled up like a pile of yellow leaves or papery moths' wings. I felt like I was going to be sick, or faint, or both.

The Legend was saying, 'So, Agnes, what are you going to do? Do you want to sing on your own or not?'

Elfie was whispering, loud enough for the microphones to pick it up, 'This is your moment! Go for it!'

And the audience was buzzing and backstage all the technicians and people were talking excitedly.

But mostly all I could hear was a kind of pounding in my ears, the rhythmic underwater sound of my heartbeat magnified a hundred times over. The same sound Jimmy must hear when he is swimming, I thought. And when I closed my eyes I could see myriad colours dancing in front of them. I thought of the Iron Men on the beach, silent, staring, unable to speak even when the water submerged them completely. Unable to cry out for help as they drowned nightly, daily, with each and every high tide.

I opened my eyes and glanced desperately at Jimmy, who was standing in the wings next to the presenter. But he wasn't looking at me any more, he was looking at Elfie.

Just like he is always looking at Elfie.

Jimmy

I felt kind of proud of Elfie when she told Agnes to sing on her own. Because this totally was not part of the plan. And even if she was putting on the nice act for the cameras, I knew it couldn't have been easy for her to see her dream of stardom go out of the window.

'Do you have a song you can sing on your own?' asked The Legend.

Agnes didn't respond. She looked like she'd totally frozen on stage. I wished I could remember the word she'd told me, the Portuguese word for stage fright – *medo de* something. The cameras were all focused on her, and Elfie and the audience was hushed, waiting. The judges were all looking at them too. Beside me in the wings, the presenter was trying to look sincere and concerned.

Agnes still didn't answer.

'Yes, she has,' Elfie said suddenly. 'She knows both parts to the other one we practised.'

Agnes's face flared from white to bright red as Elfie nudged her. And I felt even more proud of Elfie than ever.

'Then it's decision time,' said The Legend. 'Do you want to audition again, Agnes? Without Elfie this time?'

Agnes closed her eyes and clutched the fabric of my mam's dress, tugging nervously at the hem.

'This could be one of the most important decisions of your life,' said the Facelift. 'As a duet you are OK. But as a soloist you could go all the way.'

Agnes still didn't answer. She looked like she might dissolve in the middle of the stage.

'Yes or no, Agnes?' said The Legend.

Agnes opened her eyes and looked at Elfie, who nodded violently, looking like she really meant it. The producer hugged her clipboard to her chest; the presenter put a supportive arm round me; the audience started to get restless again. A cry of: 'Go for it, Agnes!' went up, followed by a few whoops and yells. Then a single voice in the audience started a slow chant of: 'Agg-ness! Say yes!' A few other voices joined in: 'Agg-ness! Say yes!'

The chant grew louder and more insistent. I looked at the panel of judges: The Lingerie Lizard had an inane grin on his face; The Tabloid Princess was leaning forwards, nodding encouragingly at Agnes. And The Legend just sat there with his arms folded, smiling to himself.

'Agg-ness! Say yes! Agg-ness! Say yes!'

Finally, The Legend turned to the audience and gestured them to be quiet. The chanting petered out. The Legend faced Agnes again and said, 'For the last time, would you like to audition alone, Agnes?'

For a moment there was almost total silence. No one in the whole theatre stirred. Then Alfie wriggled in my arms and let out a sudden cry.

The sound seemed to jolt Agnes out of her trance. She gave a little shudder, closed her eyes, took a deep breath and then opened them again.

'No,' she said clearly.

There were shocked murmurs from the audience

as Alfie let out another cry and started trying to pull himself out of my arms. The producer was miming theatrical 'shhh!' sounds from the wings opposite but nobody else seemed to be taking too much notice.

'No?' said The Legend. This obviously wasn't the answer he was expecting.

'I will not sing without Elfie,' Agnes whispered. She said it so quietly The Legend had to lean forwards to actually hear her.

Elfie was shaking her head and I thought I could see the hint of tears welling up in her eyes, but she sniffed them back angrily. Alfie was starting to get frantic, struggling in my arms, crying, 'Effie! Effie!' in the direction of his sister.

'You're turning this chance down?' said The Legend, eyebrows raised nearly to his hairline. 'Even if I say this could be the end of the road for the pair of you?'

'She is my friend,' said Agnes, swallowing hard, her voice coming out a little more confidently this time.

Elfie sniffed again, even louder this time.

And that's when Alfie wriggled free from my

arms and ran on stage towards his sister/on-screen teen mam.

Elfie turned and scooped him up in her arms as he cried, 'Mammy!' Then she pulled Agnes into the embrace as the audience burst into spontaneous applause, whooping and cheering.

Rules of Talent TV No. 14: Practise your 'waiting for the judges' verdict' face

Agnes

They divided us into two groups and sent us off to different rooms to await the judges' verdict. It was me and Elfie and about twenty other acts, in this big room with white walls and orange strip lighting. They let Jimmy and Alfie in with us, too. Jimmy kept glancing at his watch and looking more and more anxious as the time went past.

I was still feeling sick and dizzy and my head was full of the moths' wings and the papery leaves. I stared at the pattern of swirling circles on the carpet while Elfie chattered away, checking out the other acts who'd been picked for our room, trying to work out which group had made it through to the next round.

'What about us?' I said quietly.

Elfie and Jimmy both turned to me in surprise.

Elfie raised an eyebrow. 'Oh! So, you can talk now, can you?'

I felt myself blushing. I was the first time I'd spoken since I came off stage. 'Yes.'

'So what was that back there? Panic attack? Heart failure? Or did you have some kind of stroke?'

'Elfie!' said Jimmy.

'And don't think I fell for the whole "friend" line, either,' she went on. 'It was dead obvious the only reason you didn't go solo was cos you didn't have the bottle to sing without me.'

I said nothing – just stared at the swirling circles on the carpet.

'And everyone knows that sparkling personality always counts for way more than the vocal talent anyway,' she went on, her head tipped to one side, staring at me.

'I think she was trying to be nice, Elfie,' muttered Jimmy.

Elfie straightened her head and stared at me with narrowed eyes. I stared back. I could taste blood in my mouth and suddenly I wanted to cry.

'Whatever!' Elfie said, with a talk-to-the-hand gesture and another toss of her head. 'I just hope you're not regretting your decision, cos what I did up there today was truly heroic and self-sacrificing, you know.'

'I thought you'd be well mad,' said Jimmy. 'When the judges said – you know . . .'

Elfie gave her hair another little shake and pouted her lips. 'Well, you don't know everything, do you, Jimmy Wigmore,' said Elfie. 'Maybe I'm a nicer person than you think.'

Jimmy turned to me then and I thought I could see a twinkle in his eye. I suppressed a giggle and he looked away quickly as Elfie went on with her predictions about who was through to the next round. 'So, we've got Handsome Student, Lap-Dancer Girl Band and Girl-Who-Used-To-Be-A-Guy. They're pretty good. But we've also got Miss Fat Chip-Shop Girl 2011 who may have lost ten stone in order to follow her dream but is still way too lardy to make it to the finals.'

'Sssh!' Jimmy said, glancing anxiously at the large girl in the giant gold hot pants behind us. He was sitting on the floor, rolling Cheerios along the carpet to Alfie. Alfie was giggling like mad and screeching each time he caught one.

'Big Hair Lady can't sing, but she makes good TV,' Elfie went on, ignoring him. 'And the same goes for that twin boy band from Wigan who are a blatant rip-off of last year's Talentless Triplets.'

'Being twins isn't exactly something you can copy, Elfie,' Jimmy said.

'Whatever, multiple births are so last year,' Elfie said dismissively.

'You think this is the rejects group then?' Jimmy asked, rolling a sugary yellow hoop right into Alfie's outstretched hand.

'What are you talking about?' said Elfie, who didn't seem to have noticed his worried expression – or was deliberately ignoring it. 'Big Hair and Wigan's IVF Boys are dead certs. The producers would be mad to axe them. No, I reckon we're the "it's good news" group.'

'Really?' Jimmy pretended to eat a Cheerio before rolling it as hard as he could across the floor, sending Alfie toddling after it in fits of giggles. He glanced at his watch and I saw a frown pucker his brow. It was already gone three.

'Will you stop clock-watching!' Elfie snapped. 'We'll make it back on time.'

Jimmy just shrugged. I could tell he didn't believe her but he knew there was no point in saying so.

'And, yeah!' Elfie went on. 'The judges know that when it comes to the public vote in the final, Miss Weight-Loss will get the fat-lovers' sympathy-vote, and Girl-Who-Used-To-Be-A-Guy will probably out herself and get the trannies onside,' said Elfie. 'So I reckon we're in!'

She said this in a confident voice, like she wasn't bothered either way, but her eyes were still bright and there were little spots of colour in her cheeks and she wouldn't look either of us in the eye. Then she leaped up and went to rescue Alfie who was climbing under a stack of chairs trying to reach a Cheerio. Jimmy watched her for a minute then leaned back and glanced over to where I was sitting. Neither of us said anything for a bit.

'You know, I reckon if you'd sung on your own you

could have won this whole show,' he said eventually. 'The final and everything.'

I watched Elfie scoop up her brother and start tickling him. 'But you say she need this,' I said quietly. 'To keep her . . . together?'

'Yeah, she does so it was dead nice of you,' he said. 'She knows that, too. Even if she doesn't say so. She just doesn't like people knowing she cares.'

'Because of her mum?' I asked.

'Exactly,' he said, nodding. He wasn't blinking as much as normal and I could see the lovely blue colour of his eyes. 'She figures if people know she cares then they can hurt her.'

He looked up quickly then and gave a wonky smile that made his ears go pink. Then he glanced at his watch again. It was nearly half past three.

'Will you miss your training?' I asked.

He nodded glumly. 'Probably.'

'I'm sorry,' I said.

'It's not your fault. I could have gone home and left you, but –' he paused and looked down at his feet. 'But I didn't want to.'

Elfie returned with a giggling Alfie in her arms and at that moment the door opened and in came the judges.

Elfie grabbed my hand and held it tight. It felt warm and sticky. 'Here goes,' she whispered. And for some reason my mind went back to the Iron Men on the beach. Cos for a moment it felt like we were statues – me and Elfie and Jimmy – all three of us, staring out to sea. Waiting.

Elfie

Of course they strung it out. That's what they do, isn't it? The cameraman spent ages sweeping his lens across the room, capturing the various acts competing to show just how much they all wanted this. The chubby one from Lap-Dancer Girl Band actually started crying and all her lap-dancing mates clustered round and held her tight, Big Hair Lady did some kind of yogic breathing, Girl-Who-Used-To Be-A-Guy whispered into his/her rosary beads, and the IVF

Boys did a Siamese river dance to show how excited-slash-nervous they were.

Meanwhile the judges just stood there and said nothing. The Legend had this little smile playing on his lips, The Lingerie Lizard was nodding his head like one of those dogs you get in the back of a car and The Tabloid Princess was doing her best to look misty-eyed and sweet. The Facelift tried – and failed – to morph her botox features into an expression that looked like she actually cared.

I'd worked on my 'waiting for the judges' verdict' face at home in case we made it on to the TV. I didn't want to overdo it and look totally fake and tragic, but then I didn't want it to look like I was too cocky either. So I'd perfected a wide-eyed hopeful face – modelled on Agnes who does the whole Bambi thing brilliantly. Oh, and I didn't put my hand over my face either, cos that always looks like you're trying to hide summat (I read that in one of me mam's mags). So, I had my hands by my side, eyes all big – only they eked it out so long I started to worry my face was going to stick like that and I'd end up looking like the immo forever.

I noticed Jimmy was giving Agnes another one of his looks. He thinks I haven't noticed all the little glances and secret smiles he keeps sending in her direction, but I'm not blind. It's been happening more and more recently and I'm not sure I like it. So when she smiled back – the little hussy – I coughed loudly and they both looked down at their feet again.

It was The Tabloid Princess who got to break the news. 'OK, everybody,' she said, e-flippin'-ventually. 'You've all worked your socks off today and you can be dead proud of how far you've come. But –'

She smiled and took a deep breath. All six members of Lap-Dancer Girl Band sobbed in unison (bet they rehearsed that). I tried to hold my 'waiting for the judges' verdict' face but I kept thinking about how Jimmy had looked at Agnes and it kept slipping into a scowl.

'I've got to tell you that –' The Tabloid Princess was looking even more sparkly than usual in a sequinned dress with a sort of tiara thing in her blonde curls and her skin covered in body glitter. Even her lips were sparkling with some kind of diamante lipgloss which I knew me mam would just love.

Another long pause. Girl-Who-Used-To-Be-A-Guy put her arm around Big Hair Lady. The IVF Boys emitted little squeaks. I grabbed Agnes's hand and squeezed it, only then I caught her stealing another look at Jimmy, so I squeezed even harder.

'– you're all through to the semi-finals!'

Jimmy

The room went wild!

Everyone started jumping up and down and screaming and hugging each other and mobbing The Tabloid Princess. Next to us, Lap-Dancer Girl Band collapsed in a squealing heap on top of each other, and Big Hair Lady was kissing Girl-Who-Used-To-Be-A-Guy full on the lips.

Elfie grabbed Alfie and started throwing him up in the air which made him shriek with delight. I turned shyly to Agnes and said, 'Well done.'

And we stood there looking at each other while the

room erupted around us. She's about a foot smaller than me and I was just wondering if I should give her a hug and how I'd even go about it if I did, when suddenly Elfie flew at us both, nearly knocking Agnes over, screaming, 'We did it!'

And then she did something that took me completely by surprise. She grabbed me and kissed me full on the lips.

I had my eyes wide open. I could taste tea-bag cigarettes and raspberry lipgloss. Alfie was crushed between us, squirming and giggling. And as her lips crashed against mine my eyes locked with Agnes who just stood there, staring. And I don't know what was weirder: the fact that Elfie Baguley was kissing me, or the fact that I sort of wanted her to stop.

Rules of Talent TV No. 15: Never ignore the 'Emotional Roller Coaster' theory

Elfie

So, the 'Emotional Roller Coaster' theory. Basically, it goes like this: you're doing really well, and everything seems to be going right for you and then it goes belly up because the public start to think you're smug, or stop voting for you because they reckon you're safe, or whatever. Basically, when you're at the top of the roller coaster, the only way is down.

The best thing you can do if you're at the top is to have a bit of a bad week: lose your voice or have to take your dog to be put down or split up with your boyfriend or sprain your ankle or summat. Cos you need to get off the top yourself before somebody pushes you off the edge.

I guess I should have known, because of the Emotional Roller Coaster theory, that summat was gonna go wrong. Me and Agnes had been doing too well, so the gods of Talent TV needed to throw some horse poo our way.

There was a police car parked outside the house when we got back home. Me and Jimmy that is; Agnes had walked home the other way cos I said we still couldn't risk being spotted together. Jimmy hadn't spoken a word to me the whole journey home. I wasn't sure if it was because of the kiss or the fact that I'd made him miss swim training again or what, but he seemed really mad at me.

I was about to make a joke about Jimmy's dad calling the bizzies cos he'd bailed out on practice, when this female police officer stepped out of the car and said, 'Elfie Baguley?'

'Yeah, that's me,' I said.

'Your dad's been arrested,' said the police lady in a bored voice, like it was no big deal, like this sort of thing happened every day. 'I need you to come with me down to the station.'

'Why? What's he done?' I asked. I glanced at Jimmy

but he wasn't looking at me. He was staring over in the direction of his house with the weirdest look on his face.

'If you'd like to come with me,' said the policewoman impatiently.

'Tell me what he's supposed to have done first,' I said.

She sighed and glanced at her watch. 'He's been involved in a fight down at the picket line.'

'What? Who with?' In the buggy, Alfie stirred, wriggling like he knew something was up, even in his sleep.

'I don't know the details,' said the lady cop, opening the door of the police car and pointing inside. 'If you come with me, you can ask him yourself.'

I glanced at Jimmy again, but he was still staring across the road, his face white as a sheet. I looked over too. His whole house was covered in graffiti.

'Oh, no,' I said. 'That's all we need.'

Jimmy

The front of our house had red paint all over it. It was like someone had taken a massive can of paint and chucked the whole lot against the walls. They'd even painted *Scab* on the patio in giant bleeding letters.

There was rubbish, too, bin bags full, emptied all over the doorstep and shoved through the letter box.

All the way home I'd been worrying about my dad being mad at me for missing training, and about Elfie kissing me and Agnes seeing her do it. But suddenly none of that seemed to matter. Cos my dad had only gone and done the worst thing possible. He'd crossed the line.

After Elfie and Alfie went off in the police car, I let myself in the front door and went into the sitting room. My mam was sitting on the sofa, curtains closed, TV on with the sound off. Her face was red with tears. She started when I opened the door.

'It's OK, Mam,' I said. 'It's only me.'

She let out a little sob. 'Oh, Jimmy, love,' she said.

So I went and sat on the sofa next to her and wrapped my arms round her, like she used to do to me when I was a kid. She tipped her head on to my chest and I could feel her shuddering quietly. Her light brown hair was soft against my chin and her skin glowed blue in the flickering light of the TV.

'Where's Dad?' I said.

'Out looking for you,' she replied.

My heart sank. I'd expected him to be mad at me but this was even worse.

'Why?'

'When you didn't turn up for practice, he was worried. He thought something might have happened to you. You know, because of him . . .' She swallowed, like she didn't even want to say it. 'Because of him crossing the line.'

'Where's he gone?' I asked.

'I don't know,' she said.

I could see images from the picket line on the silent TV screen. There was a running headline beneath: *Violence erupts at local plant as strikers and scabs come to blows.*

'He did this for you, you know,' she said.

'I know,' I said. Only I really wished he hadn't.

Elfie

My dad was sitting in this little interview room down the police station – just like ones you see on the telly. He had this massive black eye and a seriously big cut across his face and he was looking totally gutted.

I sat down opposite him while the lady cop who'd picked me up stood in the corner of the room, pretending not to listen in.

'Does it hurt?' I asked.

'Not so much,' he said, with a small smile.

'What happened, Dad?'

'Scabs,' he said simply.

I thought of the graffiti outside Jimmy's house, the giant red painted letters. 'Who?' I asked.

'Does it matter?'

I shrugged. 'What happens now, then?' I said,

trying to sound like it was all no big deal even though we both knew it was.

'We've called social services,' the police woman said. 'Someone should be here shortly.'

'What?'

My dad looked down at his hands.

'Your dad's not going anywhere tonight,' she said. 'So we need to make arrangements for you and the baby.'

'I don't understand.'

Dad kept staring at his hands. I noticed that the knuckles on his right fingers were swollen and bruised.

'Your mam's on her way,' the policewoman said.

'I'm not going with her, Dad!' I said. 'And neither is Alfie, so don't even think about it.'

Alfie had fallen back to sleep in my arms in the police car. His face was covered in chocolate and his clothes smelt of wee but there was a smile on his face. Like he was dreaming of nice stuff. The thought of me mam getting her hands on him made me so mad I wanted to cry.

'They'll take you into care otherwise,' said me dad,

his voice cracked and low, still not looking up.

'Fine,' I said. 'Anything's better than going with her.'

'Elfie . . .'

'I want to talk to that social worker,' I said loudly. 'Soon as she gets here. I want to see her, you hear?'

'Elfie!'

'Don't worry, Dad,' I said, although the panic was making my voice a bit squeaky. 'I'll sort it out. Only I'm not going anywhere with that woman. And neither is Alfie.' I was talking too fast, my voice too high-pitched. 'I'll come up with a plan. You'll see.'

'Elfie, this is hardly the time . . .'

But I wasn't listening. If I ever needed a plan it was now. Only everything was moving dead fast suddenly and five minutes later I was being bundled out into reception by this social worker lady called Jenny. She must have weighed in at about 25 tonnes, and she was wearing a massive purple cardigan and huge earrings in the shape of green elephants and she said she'd come to make arrangements for me, whatever that meant. She wouldn't listen to a word I had to say.

And standing in reception with a massive fake grin

on her face, acting like she'd just won 'Mother of the Year', was me mam. She'd died her hair again, brunette this time, and her lips were blood red (always match your lipstick to your knickers, she once told me). She was dressed like she was going clubbing.

'Darling!' she said, rushing forwards.

I took a step back, holding Alfie tight to me, fear fluttering in my tummy.

Jenny the social worker was standing behind me, smelling of sickly sweet perfume and stale cigarettes.

'I'd rather spend a night in the cells,' I said, but my voice sounded wobbly, not as strong as I wanted it to.

'My baby!' said me mam, reaching out towards Alfie. 'I've missed him so much.'

'Don't touch him,' I said, taking another step back. 'He's sleeping. He needs his sleep.'

'You've obviously done a wonderful job looking after him, darling,' she said, reaching out to stroke his face. She'd had her nails done again, green and gold, each encrusted with a little pink jewel.

'I said get your hands off him. I swear if you lay a finger on him I'll scream!' I was on top of the rollercoaster looking down. I felt dizzy, unstable.

'Your mam won't touch him,' said Jenny the Elephant, gently. 'But perhaps she can just look at him?'

I didn't reply. I glanced over to the reception desk, and there was Agnes's dad. I recognised him from the photos at her house, only now he had a massive black eye and a cut on his lip.

He glanced over and caught my eye. 'That's all I need!' I said under my breath. It was just typical of the way this day was going that the man me dad had got in a punch-up with was the father of my immo pop partner.

'You must have missed your baby, Mrs Baguley,' Jenny the Elephant was saying to me mam.

'I've missed both of my children,' she said. Her eye make-up looked smudgy and even her lipstick was a little uneven.

The drunk in the corner of the waiting room twitched and swore loudly.

'Well, we haven't missed you,' I said. 'We're doing just fine without you.'

I glanced at Jenny who was shaking her head so that the elephants in her ears waggled crazily.

'Don't think you can force me to go with her, cos you can't,' I said.

'No one's going to force you to do anything, Elfie,' she said.

I looked up to see Agnes's dad watching me. My face felt hot and my eyes were burning, but there was no way I was going to let any of them see me cry.

'Your mam can just take your brother for now and we'll look into other arrangements for you.'

'No,' I said, my voice high, panicked. 'She can't take Alfie. We go together.'

'It's the best thing for him in the circumstances,' said Jenny.

'But he needs me to look after him.' I glanced round the room. Everyone was watching now: the duty officer behind the desk, the drunk in the corner with drool coming out of his mouth, Agnes's dad.

'And you've done a wonderful job,' said Jenny, taking a step towards me, arms out. 'But now it's time to let your mum take over.'

I was gripping Alfie so tightly that he started to stir in my arms. And then Jenny tried to take him from me and I backed up till I was right against the wall. Alfie was awake properly now and had started to whimper, and me mam kept going, 'Alfie, darling,' only he took one look at her bright red lips and her mad brown hair and started to scream at the top of his voice.

'We need to stay together,' I said.

'Alfie needs to be properly looked after,' said Jenny.

'You can't do this!' I yelled at me mam. 'Not after you walked out on him. On all of us. You can't do this.'

That was when it all started getting weird; everything seemed to go really quickly and really slowly at the same time. I felt like I was being held down underwater and my ears were ringing and I couldn't breathe. The drunk man in the corner put his hands over his ears and started to shout obscenities. The duty officer looked away as Jenny the Elephant tried again to pull Alfie out of my arms and that's when I realised that it was me who was shouting louder than any of them. I was shouting, 'No, no, please don't take him, please don't take him!' and I was holding him so tight I was hurting us both. Jenny was saying, 'Just give him to me, Elfie. Don't make a scene,' and then I couldn't hold on to him any more and she had him and she was taking him off me.

And Alfie screamed, thrashing wildly. 'Effie! Effie!' he was shouting, and I was shouting, 'Alfie!' and me mam was reaching out to take him off Jenny the Elephant with her green and gold jewel-encrusted fingers. And all I was thinking was that I couldn't let her take him. I just couldn't.

It took two police officers to hold me off: the duty officer and the policewoman who'd been in with me dad. Alfie reached out for me, sobbing and screeching, 'Effie!' as they carried him out of the door. I tried to run after them, to chase the car down the street, only the police officers blocked my way. I think I bit one of them. The policewoman called me a silly cow afterwards.

After about ten minutes, Jenny the Elephant came back and told me to wait while she made some phone calls. I wasn't shouting any more. I was sitting on a plastic chair in the waiting room and I wasn't even crying, although I was suddenly so cold I was shaking. And as she spoke I noticed that one of her little green elephant earrings was missing. I wondered if she knew where it was and if she'd picked it up and put it in her purse, or if Alfie had yanked it out. But I didn't ask. I didn't say anything.

After a while she went away and I was left in the waiting room, holding Alfie's little scrap of blankie, the one he can't sleep without. And I knew then that I was down at the bottom of the roller coaster and I had no idea how I was ever going to get back up again.

Jimmy

My dad turned up just after midnight. He was still holding my swimming bag. When he saw me and my mam in the sitting room he didn't say anything, just hung up my bag and slowly took off his shoes.

'I'm sorry, Dad,' I said.

'What for?' His back stiffened but he didn't turn round.

'For missing training again.'

'No need to apologise to me, son,' he said. His voice was faintly slurred, like he'd been drinking, only my dad never normally drinks. He says we need to save every penny for my training. 'I'm just glad you're safe, that's all,' he said.

'Dad, I had to be somewhere for someone.'

'Right. Well I hope this someone was worth it,' he said, turning round and looking at me with a lop-sided smile.

An image of Agnes flicked into my mind, of her singing in my mam's pink dress. And then I remembered the scared look on Elfie's face as she'd climbed into the police car. 'She was,' I said. 'She is.'

I thought he was going to shout at me but he just said, 'I wouldn't have thought you were Elfie Baguley's type.' He was looking beyond me at the TV. They were showing footage from the picket line on the twenty-four-hour news channel.

'She just – needed a favour.'

'Any road, I don't s'pose Clive Baguley will let his girl hang out with you after this.' He looked at me suddenly, the smile gone from his face. 'Not now your dad's a scab.'

My mam gave a little sob and buried her face in her hands.

I looked down but I could still feel him staring at me. I wonder where he went looking for me. Did he go across the marshes? Down by the bridge?

'Do I expect too much of you?' he asked quietly.

'No, it's not that.'

'I drive you too hard?'

'No.' I looked up. He was staring right at me. Just staring.

'You want me to give you a break?'

'No,' I said, looking back down at my feet: swimmer's feet, Elfie calls them, flipper feet. Right then I wished I was in the pool, submerged in the blue, cut off from everything but the sound of my own heartbeat and the whale call of pain echoing off my limbs.

'Cos you know I crossed that line today so that you

can have a chance to make something of your life?'

'I know. I'm really grateful, Dad.'

I opened my eyes, thought of the bleeding red letters and of Elfie saying, 'Our families hate each other. They'd kill us if they knew we were together.'

'I won't miss training again,' I said.

'Even if Elfie Baguley needs another favour?'

I hesitated. I thought of Elfie and Agnes. Elfie kissing me. Agnes's wide black eyes looking at me in surprise.

'Well?'

'OK,' I said.

'Promise?'

I hesitated again, glanced down at my little finger. Then I said, 'I promise.'

Elfie

'Are you OK?'

I was sitting on the metal bench next to the broken water cooler. I was cold and grubby and my arms ached without Alfie. The scrap of blankie lay limp on my lap. My tummy felt raw, like it had been gashed open.

Agnes's father was standing over me, holding a cup of tea.

'She took him,' I said quietly.

'Yes. I saw,' he replied. 'Here.' He held out the plastic mug.

'How do I know you've not spiked it?' I said, sniffing loudly.

'I just put sugar in, nothing else,' he said. 'It will make you feel better.'

'Thanks.' I took it off him and took a slurp of the warm sweet liquid, staring at the grubby blankie.

He sat down next to me and didn't say anything.

'Did me dad do that?' I asked, pointing to the bruising around his left eye socket.

'Your father is Clive Baguley?'

I nodded.

'Then, yes,' he said simply. He had a stronger accent that Agnes. 'He did.'

'Did you deck him one back?' I asked.

'I should have done.' He half-smiled and I took another slurp of the tea and wondered what my dad would think if he could see me talking to the enemy.

'Who did then?' I asked.

'Maybe one of the scabs he was yelling at,' he said. I looked at his shoes which were smart and polished.

'If you're going to get political, I'm going to have to stop drinking your tea,' I said, sniffing and taking in his neatly creased trousers and expensive looking leather jacket.

'Fair enough,' he said. He reached into his pocket, pulled out a handkerchief and passed it to me, nodding his head. 'So, what happens to you now?'

'They arrest me dad and I go into care, probably,' I said, blowing my nose loudly.

'Care?'

'Like foster home, I 'spect.' I sniffed again and handed him back the dirty hankie. 'Do you have them in Spain or Portugal or wherever?'

He took it off me with an amused smile and tucked it back into his pocket. 'Yes,' he said. 'We do have them – in Portugal.'

I didn't bother to respond.

'Elfie is an unusual name, yes?' he said.

'You know anyone else stupid enough to call their kid after a flippin' gnome?' I said.

'No.' He looked at me closely and said, 'Then I think perhaps you know my daughter.'

I couldn't see any point in denying it so I shrugged and said, 'Yeah? Maybe.'

'And does your father know you are friends with my daughter?' he asked.

'Don't be soft!' I laughed a bit too loud. The drunk in the corner, who had gone to sleep, stirred and twitched. 'Course he don't know. He'd kill me if he found out.'

'Really?'

'You have no idea.' I sniffed again and he handed me back his hankie. 'You're not going to tell him are you?'

'Not if you do not want me to.'

Neither of us said anything for about a minute. I stared down at my tea again. It was grey and watery and I could see my face reflected in it – my eyes swollen and black with make-up. I looked small and a million miles away.

'So,' he said eventually. 'How are you going to get your brother back?'

I shrugged again and looked down so he couldn't see I was about to cry.

'Would it help if I drop charges against your father?' he said.

'Why?' I looked up quickly. 'Are you going to?'

'Would you stop seeing my daughter if I did?' he asked. He was looking right at me and he had the same eyes as Agnes, and the same way of looking at me, too. Like he knew summat I didn't.

I couldn't work out if he was testing me or what so I figured I might as well tell the truth. 'No,' I said with a loud sniff. 'She's my mate.'

'I see.'

'And mates stick with each other. No matter what,' I said. 'So, what you gonna do about that then?'

'Hmm . . .' He looked hard at me. 'I haven't decided.'

We sat in silence for a bit, neither of us saying

anything much, me drinking tea and sniffing into his hankie, and him staring down at his shiny polished shoes. And then one of the police officers called him into a room to give a statement. I held out his hankie, which was damp and crumpled.

'Keep it,' he said.

'OK,' I nodded. 'Thanks.'

'Thank you for being a friend to my Agnes,' he said with a tilt of his head.

Then he was gone and I was all on my own again. And I couldn't believe that only a few hours ago I'd been jumping for joy and snogging Jimmy Wigmore, and now I was sitting in a police station holding Agnes's dad's hankie and Alfie was gone and me dad was in trouble and it felt like it was all over.

And I was all out of plans.

Semi-Finals

Rules of Talent TV No. 16: Practice makes perfect

Jimmy

My dad made me train extra hard the next morning. I had to practise race starts over and over until my head was spinning and my muscles screamed in agony.

'Flawless techniques win races,' my dad said when I asked for a break. 'Winning comes down to performing the drill. If you execute techniques and strategies like clockwork and swim smart, you'll be first across the line. You need to focus on being technically perfect.'

So I kept ploughing up and down the pool while my dad yelled instructions from the edge.

'Don't start too deep . . . don't breathe on the first stroke . . . accelerate inside the flags . . . then snappy flip turn, streamline and kick off . . . Breathe two down, one up . . . and remember your zones.'

I repeated the mantra over and over and over in my head. It helped shut all the other thoughts out.

I think that was why he was doing it, too, cos when we'd finally finished that drill he got me working on sprint finishes. 'Accelerate inside the flags . . . don't breathe the last four metres . . . reach out and touch the wall underwater with no extra stroke.' Over and over and over again. But no matter how often I did it or how hard I tried, it was never quite good enough for him. Never quite right.

He didn't speak the whole journey home and when we got back it was like the entire estate had been waiting for us. As we walked along our road, all the front doors started opening and people came out and stood on their steps and stared, faces cold, arms folded, saying nothing. Just staring.

'Keep walking, son,' said my dad. It was the first thing he'd said to me since we left the pool and it was like he'd been expecting this. He was looking straight ahead and his face was set.

I could see Mrs Newsround standing on her doorstep, arms tight across her massive chest. Further down, Mrs Tyzack and all her little ginger kids, and

Mr Winstanley, Kirby's dad, glowering and red faced. Clive Baguley was the last to come out. One eye was welded shut and there was still blood on the collar of his shirt. Elfie was behind him, looking down, not at me. Her arms were empty. No Alfie.

'Just keep walking. Go straight home,' said my dad.

'Dad!' I said, panicking now.

'I'm going to work,' he said simply.

Then the whispering started. The word, 'Scab!' hissed from a doorway. Then from another and another. It got louder as more voices joined in, like a slow hand clap: 'Scab! Scab! Scab!' It reminded me of the audition when the audience was chanting for Agnes. Only these voices were harsh, hostile, angry. Nobody moved, nobody shouted anything or threw anything. They all just kept up the chant.

'Go inside,' said my dad when we reached our house.

'But –'

'Just do as I say,' he snapped. So I stopped and he kept walking.

'Scab! Scab! Scab!' The chant went on until he'd

walked all the way down the road and turned the corner.

Elfie

I couldn't sleep without Alfie. I'd gotten so used to his grubby baby smell, the way he flings his body out like a starfish in the night, the snotty kisses, his little fingers poking up my nose to wake me up. Now that he'd gone, the bed felt cold and too big somehow. I wrapped my arms round my pillow and I could smell him in it, but it didn't feel the same.

I asked me dad the next morning when he would be coming back but he just said, 'I don't know, Elfie.'

And then there was the whole thing with Jimmy's dad and I remembered that I'd promised Jimmy I'd stop his dad turning scab, only now it was too late for that an' all.

I couldn't face school so I bunked off and went down to the bridge. Jimmy had obviously decided he was safer not showing his face in the classroom too because by the time I arrived, he was already there. He was sitting on the rock-studded concrete, back up against the arch of the bridge, throwing pebbles into the water. He didn't even look up when he heard me. He just kept picking up pebbles and skimming them across the surface of the river.

Someone else must have been down here last night because there were the remains of a fire and cans were strewn everywhere. And whoever it was had managed to graffiti all along the underside of the arch, nearly halfway out into the river. "Spoz Rules!" it said, over and over again in bright metallic spray paint.

'All right?' I said.

Jimmy looked up. His eyes were all red and puffy. He looked away again and ducked his head down. I figured he was allowed to be in a weird mood so I didn't have a go at him. I was still feeling pretty rubbish myself but I decided one of us had to try and be upbeat and I figured I owed him one for all the times he'd tried to cheer me up after me mam went AWOL.

'How do you reckon they did it?' I said, pointing to the graffiti.

He glanced up and shrugged.

I plonked myself down next to him, shifting my bum to get comfy on the stones. It felt like ages since it had just been the two of us.

'Reckon we should have another go, an' all,' I said. 'Get a real can of spray paint and see if we can get all the way across this time.'

'That's kids' stuff,' he replied, picking up another pebble and weighing it in his hand. 'Like pretending to be pop stars.'

I glanced at him again but he just kept staring at the pebble. He didn't seem like himself at all. It was as if somebody had flipped a switch in him. Like he was all burning up inside, and older somehow.

'Yeah. Only we're not pretending, are we? ' I said. 'We're the real deal.'

'Maybe,' he said, tracing his finger over the smooth surface of the pebble.

'Agnes could make it,' I said, serious now. 'I mean, she's really good.'

'And what about you?' Jimmy looked up and squinted at me from behind his hair.

'After we win, I'll quit the band I s'pose,' I said. 'I don't want to be the one holding her back.'

Jimmy kept staring at me. A cold wind came scudding across the river, sending the water dancing in little waves and carrying the smell of suds from the soap factory. 'You'd do that for her?' he asked.

I shrugged. 'It's like your dad, innit?' I said. 'Making a sacrifice so someone you care about can realise their talent. Personally, I think that's kind of cool.'

Jimmy lifted his arm and sent the pebble skimming out across the water. One, two, three, four, five bounces before it disappeared. He obviously didn't want to talk about his dad. The sun suddenly appeared from behind the white clouds, making the ripples on the water sparkle. 'I thought you said you didn't care about Agnes.'

'I don't,' I said. 'But she's helping me out. I'm doing the same for her.'

'Right,' said Jimmy, launching another stone. Then

he looked around anxiously. 'Hey,' he said. 'Where's Alfie?'

I looked down. 'I haven't got him today,' I said, trying to sound unbothered, although I knew there was no way he'd buy it. Whenever I skived school, I always brought Alfie along with me.

'Why?'

I shrugged and pretended to inspect my chipped nail varnish. The smell of burned soap flakes made me think of Alfie's little vests after me dad had washed them. It made my eyes sting only I didn't want Jimmy to think I was crying.

'Has your mam . . .?' His voice no longer sounded hard and I could feel him looking at me with anxious eyes.

I raised my eyebrows and kept my eyes on my nails.

'How?' he asked softly.

'Social Services,' I said quickly. 'They wanted me to go with her an' all.'

'Why didn't you?'

'Cos I refused, didn't I.'

'But they let your dad go?'

'Yeah. The charges got dropped,' I said. 'So I got to go home with him.'

'That was good, at least?' Jimmy said, but it sounded like a question.

'It was too late by then.' I turned over my hands and stared at the palms. They were covered in half-moons, deep crescents where I'd dug my nails into my skin last night. 'Me mam'd already taken Alfie.'

Jimmy kept staring at me but he looked less angry now. 'Guess we're both having a cruddy day then.'

'Yup,' I said. I stuffed my hands into the pockets of me dad's coat. I still had Alfie's bit of blankie in there and I ran my fingers over the satin lining, soft as Alfie's skin. But then I felt the other thing in there too – the thing I'd picked up at the police station which I figured was going to change our luck. I smiled. 'Which is exactly why we've got to go to Plan C.'

Jimmy sighed. 'Things are bad enough already, Elfie.'

But I'd been thinking about this on the way here. And I figured I'd promised Jimmy I'd sort it out with his dad and I still figured Plan C might work. And

I needed a plan today more than ever.

'Look, I need to get Alfie back and we both need to make some money, right?' I said.

'Right, but . . .'

'So the only way any of that is going to happen is if we make the most of our tragic situation. And that's where Plan C comes in.'

'But, Elfie . . .'

'Look, the way I see it, we're in so much trouble already we might as well crank things up another gear,' I said. 'I mean, it's a bummer about your dad turning scab and me mam getting Alfie, but it means we've not got anything to lose any more.'

Jimmy grimaced but said nothing.

'Nothing like a few dips in the roller coaster to grab the public sympathy vote,' I said. I knew I was talking a bit fast and sounding a bit crazy but I didn't care.

'I don't see how that's going to get Alfie back,' Jimmy said, looking tired and confused.

'They start showing the auditions on TV next week, right?'

Jimmy nodded, his forehead creased in worry. 'Every

night after the local news. Five minutes or whatever. Then it's really going to kick off,' he said flatly.

'Exactly,' I said. 'Only the way I see it, we've just got to turn this thing round to get everyone behind us – bring harmony to a divided community through the power of song, and all that.'

'And how are we going to do that exactly?' said Jimmy.

'A media campaign!' I said triumphantly. 'Basically, we sell our story to the tabloids.'

'What?' Jimmy looked like was about to explode. 'Elfie, you can't . . .'

'We've already got the makings of a great front pager, we just need to add a few more ingredients and, *Bingo!* They'll be lining up for an interview and then we can cash in. Make some dosh to pay for your training, get your dad back on the picket line, pay for a lawyer to get our Alfie back . . .'

'But . . .'

'Don't stress, Jimmy Wigmore. I've got it all worked out.'

'But, Elfie . . .'

'I haven't exactly ironed out all the details yet,' I said. Another gust of wind brought a fresh flurry of the soap powder smell with it, making me ache all over again for Alfie. 'But I'm sure it'll work!'

'Right,' said Jimmy. Only he didn't sound much like he believed me. And, to be honest, I wasn't really sure I believed me either.

Agnes

I could see them from far off: two figures leaning against the underside of the bridge. Jimmy was hunched over and Elfie was waving her arms around, opening and closing her mouth like a puppet. The wind was blowing west so I couldn't hear what she was saying but I could see she was dressed differently to usual: she looked like she'd raided her dad's wardrobe this morning, instead of her mum's. She was wearing a pair of massive jeans – so big that they sagged round her ankles and had to be held up with a giant belt. And she still had her dad's jacket on, the same one she always wore. I couldn't see Alfie anywhere either.

Elfie was the first to see me. She stopped talking, pulled up her chin and gave me a long, cool look.

'Hello,' I said.

'Hi,' said Elfie, scrunching up her nose so all her freckles melted together.

Jimmy just sort of nodded.

'Alfie is not here?' I said, scrambling down the bank to join them. It had started to rain – long, slow drops, like teardrops, although weirdly the sun was still shining.

'Don't look like it, does it!' said Elfie.

'Where is he?'

'He's with me mam.'

'Oh,' I said. 'I thought . . .'

But she didn't let me finish. 'Whatever!' she said with a sweep of her hand. 'Is your dad OK? You know, after my old man decked him?'

'Decked?'

'It means thumped, hit,' said Jimmy.

'Right,' I said.

'So, is he?' asked Elfie.

I looked back at her. Under her dad's jacket she was wearing a Buzz Lightyear T-shirt that was so tight it looked like it could be one of Alfie's. She looked totally different, and I wondered if that was the point. She didn't want to look like her mum any more.

'Yes.'

'Good,' said Elfie with a shrug and a little shake of her hair. 'Cos he's all right, your dad.'

My dad had told me about seeing Elfie down at the police station, and about what she'd said about being my friend. 'She's one of a kind, your Elfie, isn't she?' he had said. 'Plenty of fireworks when she's around, I imagine. *Fogos de artificio*, you know!'

And I had thought of fireworks bursting up into the air and blooming, like flowers, like a swarm of butterflies, a riot of colour. And then falling, falling, falling. And scattering into nothing.

'Yes,' I had said. 'She is one of a kind.'

I glanced over at Jimmy. He looked terrible. The eczema round his eyes was inflamed and it made him look like he'd been crying.

'Oh, don't mind him,' said Elfie, seeing the

direction of my gaze. 'His dad decided to turn scab, that's all.'

I stared at Jimmy but he avoided my eye.

'That's all?' he said. His voice sounded hoarse and almost bitter. Not like Jimmy at all.

'Well, it's not like anyone died!' said Elfie.

I stared at Jimmy some more. I could feel his sadness flooding through me and I wanted to touch him, put my fingers on his face, the way my dad does when I'm upset.

'I'm sorry,' I murmured.

Jimmy looked up and gave a little nod but didn't quite meet my eye.

'It's not like it's your fault,' Elfie cut in, crossly. 'Except in the sense that you immos are responsible for the whole strike starting in the first place, I s'pose. But look on the bright side, you two are on the same team now. You can be outcasts together. You should be grateful I'm still talking to you both really. I'm like a double agent, crossing enemy lines, risking life and limb to help Agnes realise her dream of singing stardom.'

'I thought it was *your* dream,' said Jimmy.

'Whatever, you know what I mean,' said Elfie. 'Now, we need to fill Agnes in on the shiny new Plan C so we can get this baby into production!'

And then Elfie started explaining all about her latest plan. But I wasn't really listening. I was looking at Jimmy who was staring out at the water like his world had come to an end.

Jimmy

Elfie reckoned the success of her plan depended on the element of surprise.

'Our best chance of grabbing the headlines is if nobody finds out until the programme actually goes on air,' she said, after she and Agnes had practised their new song a couple of times. Elfie had insisted on something poppy and upbeat which didn't really suit Agnes's voice, but there was no telling her that. I knew she was doing it to cheer me up, but she was even more manic than usual and there was a kind of crazy edge to her this morning that I knew was because of Alfie.

'Don't you think we'd be in less trouble if we just told our families about the show now?' I said.

'No way! If this thing is going to work, we need to create a few fireworks.'

'Fireworks?' asked Agnes.

'Trouble!' said Elfie. 'Big trouble. The more explosive the better.'

Agnes didn't say anything.

'Are you sure about this, Elfie?' I didn't have the energy for a fight, but for once I didn't really care if Elfie got mad at me either.

'Have you ever known one of my plans to backfire?'

'Um – yes,' I said.

It had started raining properly now. The sun was still shining on the river although it was puckered with raindrops, so there was probably a rainbow somewhere.

'Anyway, I'll leave you two outcasts to mingle while I slip home and plan strategy and styling,' said Elfie. 'Can't risk being seen together at this crucial stage in proceedings. Ta-ta for now!' And then she ran out into the rain and was gone.

I glanced at Agnes. She was standing just inside the shelter of the bridge, shivering. I thought of the pictures of her on the beach, bathed in sunshine, and I figured she wasn't used to English weather.

'You cold?'

She nodded.

'Here, have this.' I took off my jacket and passed it to her. She wrapped it round her shoulders and it came down nearly to her knees. She looked funny in it and I smiled. It felt like it was the first time I'd smiled in ages.

'So,' I said. 'Your dad and Elfie?'

'They met at police –' she hesitated, like she was searching for the word – 'station?'

'That must have been weird,' I said.

'I wish I could have see it,' she said. And she grinned then, and so did I.

'I'm sorry about your dad,' she said.

I looked down at my feet, and blinked hard. All morning, I'd had the chant going through my head:

'Scab! Scab! Scab!' And I could still see the look on my dad's face as he walked down the road, staring straight ahead.

'What happen now?' Agnes asked.

I carried on staring at my feet, lifting one foot then the other off the ground. 'Same as you,' I said. 'Nobody will talk to me, I guess.'

'I talk to you,' she said. 'If you want.'

I looked up. 'Thanks,' I said.

We were both leaning against the incline of the bridge and staring down at the ground. Her feet looked about half the size of mine and even with my head bent she was still about a foot shorter than I was. I don't know if she realised I was trying not to cry but if she did, she didn't say anything.

Eventually I said, 'Did you tell your dad? You know, about the competition?

She shook her head.

The rain had stopped but the river looked swollen with it. I imagined diving through the glittering surface and swimming down to its black murky depths.

'What do you think will happen?' I said. 'You know, when everyone finds out.'

Agnes shrugged. '*Fogos de artificio*,' she said. She looked up at me and sort of smiled. 'Fireworks!'

Her arm was right next to mine and our feet were centimetres apart.

'Yeah,' I said. 'That sounds about right. Fireworks.'

She hesitated, just for an instant, then she stood up on tiptoes and kissed me on the lips.

And I could see the fireworks, exploding underwater.

I always thought the first girl I kissed would be Elfie. Not that she'd be my girlfriend or anything. I suppose I just thought one day she'd say, 'Do you want to then?' and we'd kiss and then afterwards she'd tell me I was rubbish at it and there was no way she was ever kissing me again. I never thought any other girl would want to kiss me. Or that I'd want to kiss anyone else.

And I suppose Elfie did kiss me – sort of – at the auditions. But it didn't feel like a real kiss. More of an assault – a crashing of lips, slightly painful and wet. But when Agnes kissed me her lips tasted of apples and they were warmer than I would have thought and her hair smelt like cherries. And it felt like a real kiss, my first real kiss, and I didn't want it to stop.

Only it did.

'Who're you tonguing, fish-boy?'

I looked up. Kirby and Pinkie were standing at the foot of the bridge and staring at us. Suddenly the fireworks fizzled and I felt like I'd been plunged into icy cold water – too cold to breathe.

'I – um – no one,' I said. My ears were on fire already and my voice came out as a whisper.

Kirby sniggered. 'You trying to say you weren't just sticking your tongue down her throat, or that she's a nobody?'

'Neither – I mean . . .' I said, stumbling over my words. 'I mean – I wasn't – it wasn't, we weren't . . . It was only . . .' I couldn't believe this was happening.

'Yeah. Cos I thought you were in love with Elfie Baguley,' said Pinkie. She was chewing on gum, opening and closing her mouth so wide I could see right into her bubble-gum pink mouth as far back as her tonsils.

'And isn't that the immo kid whose dad got a smack in the mouth from Elfie's old man?' said Kirby.

'Don't call her an immo,' I said quietly.

'Guess you're allowed to be mates with immos now your dad turned scab,' Kirby went on. Her hair was scraped back even more tightly than usual so it made the skin around her eyes look all stretched, like she'd had a bad facelift.

'Don't call my dad a scab either,' I said, the words hot in my throat.

Agnes put a hand on my arm but I couldn't look at her.

'Why? What you gonna do, scab-boy?' said Kirby.

They were both staring at me, Pinkie chewing excitedly, Kirby with her hands on her hips, grinning.

I didn't know what to say.

'The immo and the scab, K-I-Double-S-I-N-G!' sing-songed Kirby as she turned to go. 'Can't wait to tell Elfie Baguley about this!'

'And just in case she doesn't believe us –' Pinkie waved a sparkly pink phone in the air – 'we've even got the pix to prove it!'

She giggled and so did Kirby and I felt my stomach sink down to the soles of my shoes.

'See you around, our Jimmy!' called Kirby.

'Yeah, ta-ta, scab-boy!' said Pinkie.

And they both walked off, laughing and me and Agnes just stood there, silently staring after them.

After what felt like ages, Agnes said, 'I'm sorry.'

I didn't know what to say. 'Elfie's gonna be well mad,' I whispered.

'Fireworks,' Agnes whispered.

'What?' I said, turning to look at her. As soon as I caught her eye I found myself thinking of her lips on mine, the way her hair smelt of cherries. I started blushing furiously.

'I'd better go,' she said.

I wanted to say something to make her stay but I had no idea what. So I just said, 'OK.'

'Right,' she said.

And I said, 'I'll see you around.'

And then she went.

Agnes

Kissing Jimmy was nice: damp and soft and sort of sweet. He smelt of chlorine and dandruff shampoo and his lips tasted of Polo Mints. And for a moment, as I kissed him, the sadness went out of his blue eyes and they widened in surprise. It was only afterwards I wondered if he wished it was Elfie he was kissing, not me.

Elfie

My dad looked tired when he got in and the bruising made his face look lopsided. He flopped down on the sofa and flicked on the TV.

'How was it?' I asked.

'No more new scabs today,' he said flatly.

'Oh,' I said. 'That's good.'

He flicked through the TV channels, hardly seeming to look at the images that flashed past.

'Dad?' I said.

'What now, Elfie love.'

'It's just,' I hesitated. 'Jimmy Wigmore . . .'

He looked up. 'That lad and his whole family are off limits now, you know that, right?' His eyes looked fierce, but tired too. 'I mean, I feel sorry for the kid but that's the way it works. I don't want you hanging out with him any more.'

'OK,' I said. 'It's just –'

'You're to have nothing to do with him, you hear?'

He turned and flicked on to the kids' cartoon channel, the one Alfie likes, and sat staring at the pink and blue shapes moving on the screen.

'Dad,' I said, standing in the doorway, half in–half out of the room. 'What about Alfie?'

Just like at the police station, he didn't look up at me. 'Your mam says he's staying with her for the time being,' he said.

'But, Dad . . .'

'She reckons a baby needs its mam.'

'But she can't keep him, can she? I mean, she's not allowed to do that, right?'

He shrugged. 'She is his mam.'

'But she's – you know what she's like, Dad!'

My dad sighed. 'I'm doing my best here, Elfie.'

'Yeah, I know.'

And I hadn't thought it was possible to feel worse than I already did, but the idea of never getting Alfie back made me feel physically sick. I didn't just feel like we were at the bottom of the roller coaster then; I felt like we'd spun off the rails and tumbled out of the carriage. And there was no getting back on again.

Jimmy

Swimming used to be the one time I felt happy. Elfie called the pool my 'happy place' and said I was probably descended from dolphins, but once my dad crossed the line it wasn't so happy any more. He trained me harder and harder each day, and all he did was shout and write down lap times and tell me to do things again and again and again. And even though I was training more, I felt like I was swimming worse than ever.

While I swam I thought of Elfie and Agnes. Agnes and Elfie. Elfie kissing me. Agnes kissing me. In the water it all got muddled up with the stuff at school, the stuff at home, *Pop to the Top*, Elfie's grand media-domination plan. I couldn't seem to empty my brain of thoughts like I used to.

One evening he made me practise sprint finishes for over an hour. When I got out, the lactic acid felt like it was burning my muscles, and I was nearly sick in the shower. I leaned my head against the white tiles, felt the water running over my body and, for the first time, I wondered if I even wanted to do it any more.

I got dressed slowly. The changing room was full of after-work swimmers. My dad reckons one day those are the people who'll say, 'I used to see that kid at the pool, and look where he is now.' But I doubt any of them will even remember me: the scrawny boy with the big feet and chlorine eczema.

When I eventually got out of the changing room, he was waiting for me, sitting on the plastic bench by the vending machine. He got up, put an arm round me and started talking about tomorrow's schedule and tactics for the trials. He seemed pleased with me.

'I've just been told there'll be scouts from a couple of the top independent schools at the national trials,' he said. 'They're looking to offer scholarships to talented youngsters.'

'But I don't want to go to some posh school,' I said. 'I like my school.' I looked down at my feet and thought, *Or I used to – before all this happened.*

'Don't be daft. It'd be an amazing opportunity,' he said.

'But, Dad –'

'I'm glad you're taking the training seriously again,' he said, pulling me closer.

'I want to do well in the trials,' I said. 'For you.'

'Not just for me, son. You need to do this for yourself.'

'Yeah, course I do,' I said. But all I could feel was a strange, tight, sinking feeling in my stomach and a burning in my muscles that didn't give me a buzz like it did most days. It just hurt really, really bad.

Agnes

I didn't like the song Elfie wanted us to sing for the semi-final. It was too fast and upbeat for me. She kept telling me to 'Give it a bit more welly'. I didn't know what she meant so I looked it up. It means *animação:* liveliness, or animation. I liked the word. I imagined painting it on to a pebble, storing it on the pile of words marked 'Elfie' in the back of my head. But I didn't feel lively, animated, full of welly. And it didn't seem like she felt that way either. Ever since Alfie had gone she'd been different. Just as mad as ever, but more brittle too. I tried my hardest to do what she wanted, but she never seemed very impressed.

'You need to chill out a bit and have more fun with it,' she said. It was the night before the semi-final audition – and less than twenty-four hours before the first episode of *Pop to the Top* was due to be aired on TV. It was hard to have fun when we knew our secret was just about to be exposed. Elfie wasn't even supposed to *speak* to Jimmy these days, so we'd had to sneak about more than ever. I'd never lied to my parents about anything before, but it was Elfie's dad we were all mostly worried about. What would he do when he discovered she'd been hanging out with an immo and a scab?

The weather had turned, and that night it was raining so hard we were dancing in puddles and we could hardly hear ourselves over the roar of the downpour. My throat had started to hurt, I had a scratchy little cough that tickled when I sang, and there was a tinny, ringing feeling in my head which wouldn't go away.

Jimmy was late, so Elfie had said we should just get on and rehearse without him. Then, just as we were about to give up, he skidded round the corner and under the bridge. He was so wet, he looked like he'd just got out of the pool and he was panting like he'd run the whole way.

'Where have you been?' Elfie demanded.

'Dad made me do an extra training session,' said Jimmy, glancing at me, colouring, then looking away again. He smelt of chlorine, even though his clothes were soaked with mud and rain. There were bags under his eyes.

'Seriously?' said Elfie, raising her eyebrows. 'The man's gone nuts since he turned scab!'

'He reckons there'll be scouts at the trials, from private schools,' said Jimmy, wiping the raindrops off his nose with his sleeve. The eczema round his eyes looked sore and flaky. 'He thinks I could get a scholarship.'

'What's wrong with our school?' said Elfie.

'Apart from the fact that nobody there is allowed to talk to me, you mean?' said Jimmy. His hair was hanging in long strands over his face, drips of water trickling down his cheeks. 'And the fact I get my head smacked against whiteboards every day and I found slime in my school shoes after P.E.?'

'Yeah, but you can't move to some posh school!' said Elfie. 'I mean, what about your friends?'

'Well, *you're* not supposed to talk to me for a start,' said Jimmy miserably.

'What about Agnes then?'

Jimmy looked at me, went bright red again, and

looked away quickly like I'd given him an electric shock. It was like he hated me suddenly, like he couldn't bear to look at me. I felt my eyes pricking while the buzzing feeling in my head got louder. I blinked hard.

'Oh, for goodness sake! What is it with you two these days?' said Elfie. 'Have you had some kind of bust-up or what?'

'No,' said Jimmy, still not looking at me.

'No,' I said quietly. The pricking in my eyes wouldn't go away.

'I preferred it when you were mooning over each other!' said Elfie.

Jimmy's face flared up like he was on fire and I felt my eyes fill with hot liquid.

'We can't afford conflict within the band,' Elfie went on. 'And there's no need for all this misery and despair either. I mean, things can only get better, right?'

'Except when *Pop to the Top* starts and everyone finds out I'm supposed to be the dad of your love child!' said Jimmy, sliding down the concrete on to the wet ground, facing away from me.

'True.' Elfie shrugged. 'But Plan C should make even that worthwhile. And besides, we don't even know if they'll show our bit. It might *not* be tomorrow.'

'Perhaps they not show it at all?' I said. It was the first sentence I'd uttered since Jimmy arrived. The moths were stirring in my stomach, making me feel sick, and my throat hurt more than ever because Elfie had made me sing the song over and over.

'Duh!' said Elfie. 'We're the best act in the whole flippin' show. Not to mention the fact we've got a smoking hot back story! There's no way they're not going to show us!'

Jimmy suddenly jumped up, sending water droplets flying – like when a dog shakes itself dry. 'No!' he said excitedly. 'They can't!'

'Um – why not?' said Elfie.

'Because they can't show footage of us without parental permission and they know ours was faked!' said Jimmy.

I glanced at Elfie who said nothing. She just tipped her head to one side and smiled.

Jimmy wasn't looking at her. 'And The Legend

said he needed to hear them give permission with his own ears.'

Elfie smiled some more and said, 'Yeah, well, he did.'

Jimmy's face crumpled into a frown. 'What do you mean?'

'It was dead easy, actually,' said Elfie, grinning widely now. 'Way easier than I thought it was gonna be. I just made a couple of phone calls. Putting on the Spanish accent for Agnes's mam was the hardest bit but I reckon I carried it off.'

'She's Portuguese,' he muttered.

'They believe you?' I asked.

Elfie looked at me. 'Yeah. I mean, I had to give 'em a whole long spiel about how angry and disappointed they were with us and that. You know, to make it realistic.'

'And you spoke to The Legend?' said Jimmy, who had slid back down again.

'Nah, he was too busy being legendary, apparently, so I just spoke to that producer girl,' said Elfie. 'It was disappointingly easy – I had way more material planned in case she started asking awkward questions but she just asked me to sign some forms and photocopy some ID to go along with them to prove they weren't faked this time.'

'How did you get ID for Agnes's parents?' asked Jimmy, colouring as he said my name – like even talking about me made him uncomfortable.

'Easy!' Elfie said. 'Her dad left his wallet on the chair when he was at the police station. I nicked his driving licence before I handed it in.'

Jimmy's eyebrows had shot up so high they nearly touched his hair line.

Elfie glanced at me. 'Do you reckon he wants it back? I've got it here somewhere.' She started rummaging around in the pockets of her dad's jacket.

I remembered my dad, the other morning at breakfast, searching in his wallet for his driving licence, saying he must be losing his mind because he always kept it in there. Elfie handed me the card with his photo on. I ran my finger over his face and then tucked it into my pocket without a word. I'd never lied to him before; I knew he was going to hate all this.

'I don't believe you sometimes, Elfie,' Jimmy was saying.

'He had a tenner in there an' all. I could have nicked that, too,' said Elfie, looking very virtuous. 'I figured one good turn deserved another and all that.'

Jimmy was rubbing the chapped skin around his eyes. 'So we *are* going to be on TV then?' he said.

'Yup!' said Elfie with another massive grin.

'And it could be tomorrow's show or any other night this week.'

'Exactly!' said Elfie. 'It's like a ticking time bomb, just waiting to go off! Dead exciting!'

'Yeah,' said Jimmy, dully. 'Exciting.'

The moths shifted again in my belly, fluttering their papery-thin wings nervously. I wished Jimmy would look at me. When he looked at me the moths went away. But he kept on staring at the water and rubbing his eyes.

I coughed again and Elfie looked at me irritably. 'What is it with all the coughing?' she said.

'I have pain in my throat.'

'Sore throat,' Jimmy mumbled. He sort of half

looked at me then. His ears went pink but he didn't look away immediately like he had the other times.

'Yeah, well, you'd better go gargle or suck on some lozenges or whatever,' said Elfie, 'cos we've got to ace it tomorrow at the studio, OK?'

'OK.'

I could feel that Jimmy was still looking at me. I lifted my eyes quickly to meet his. He looked sort of anxious – like he was worried about me. The moths in my stomach stilled their wings for a moment before he looked away again.

'And in the meantime,' Elfie announced, 'I've figured out exactly how to launch Plan C.'

'How?' said Jimmy. He kept flicking little looks in my direction but I didn't lift my eyes to meet his again.

'When I spoke to the producer girlie she said they want to come and film our F and F interviews.'

'F and F?'

'Family and Friends,' said Elfie. 'You know, the bit where they film your mam and your nan and the man from the local sweet shop, saying how proud they are of you and how they always knew you were meant to be a star.'

'And how are they going to do that when none of our families knows we're doing the competition?' said Jimmy.

'Don't you get it? That's what'll make our F and F so tragic and brilliant and launch our campaign of tabloid domination.'

'Right . . .' said Jimmy. 'I still don't really get it.'

'Are you serious? It's front-page stuff,' said Elfie. 'I mean, have you ever seen any Talent TV programme where they turn up to do the F and F and no one's there?'

'Um – no,' Jimmy admitted.

I closed my eyes and imagined the cameraman panning his lens across an empty room. My head buzzed – like the moths had got in there, too.

'Exactly!' Elfie went on. 'And the timing is perfect. They want to do it while me and Agnes are at the semi-finals.'

I opened my eyes. 'What about Jimmy?' I said quietly. 'He no come with us?'

Jimmy went bright red, even his neck flushed.

'That's my whole point,' said Elfie. 'Jimmy'll stay here to meet the F and F crew.'

'What?' Jimmy looked horrified.

'When you break it to them that we're family-and-friendless I guarantee it'll be TV gold.'

'But –' Jimmy started to say.

'Obviously you'll have to bunk off school, but it'll deffo be over before you have to go to training.'

Jimmy gave a groan but he didn't look up. His shoulders sagged and he rubbed his hands over his eyes.

'Don't worry. It won't just be you!' Elfie went on.

'What?' Jimmy looked up quickly, his expression even more pained now.

'I've arranged for a special guest to make an appearance.'

'Who?'

'Can't tell you that!' said Elfie with a grin. 'That would spoil the surprise. All I can say is: expect the unexpected!'

Jimmy looked exhausted, like he was too tired even to ask any more questions, let alone fight Elfie on this.

'Anyway, can't stand round chatting. Don't want me dad getting suspicious,' Elfie said. 'So work on giving that song a bit of welly,' she added. 'We need to show the judges how versatile we are. With your voice and my PR machine we'll be a headline-grabbing act in just a few days time. You just wait and see. Oh, and go suck a throat sweet!'

Rules of Talent TV No. 17:
Show your vulnerability

Elfie

Me and Agnes were sitting on the bus going to the semi-final auditions. The trains were broken or not running or something so we'd had to leg it to the bus station and catch the world's slowest bus into Liverpool, which meant we were going to be late and my hair was totally ruined and Mr Horrocks-Taylor had seen us so now we were gonna get in trouble for bunking school – again. Plus, Agnes said her throat was hurting even more, so the day wasn't exactly going according to plan so far.

Only I figured maybe that wasn't such a bad thing. I'd decided the semis were a good opportunity to show our vulnerable side. After all, the public want to see contestants are human, too; to get a glimpse into their deepest fears and darkest anxieties. And Agnes had been so flipping flawless up till that point, I figured

333

maybe her sore throat was just what we needed: to show that even angels get croaky voices sometimes.

The bus was practically empty apart from a couple of old biddies at the front, but I still insisted Agnes and I sat apart so no one could see we were together. So there was me, right at the back, pressed against one window, and Agnes one seat in front on the other side of the bus, acting like we didn't know each other. Only she'd been looking like she wanted to say summat ever since we left and I figured I couldn't be doing with her coughing and that wide-eyed-and-anxious face any longer.

'Come on,' I said. 'Spit it out. What's up?'

She glanced over at me and opened her mouth to speak, then hesitated. Even without any make-up on, her eyes still looked huge. She had these dark circles under them and her lips were all cracked from where she was always biting them but she was somehow managing to make the sick-chic look work for her.

'What will you do when the judges, they find out?' she said.

'About which bit exactly?'

She coughed a bit and then said, 'That the things you said at the first audition are not true. About Jimmy. And me. And Alfie.'

I stuffed my hand into the pocket of me dad's jacket and fingered Alfie's scrap of blankie. I stroked the silky threadbare seam. I liked the way it felt in my hands. It reminded me of him.

'Not sure yet,' I said. I pulled out one of me dad's tea-bag roll-ups from my coat pocket and stuck it between my lips, cowboy-style. 'I'll think of summat though.'

I pulled a lighter out of the coat pocket and twirled it between my fingers.

'I no understand?' she said. Her voice sounded scratchy, which was good so long as she managed to actually sing a bit. *Nothing like a poorly contestant singing through the pain to wow the judges in the semi-finals*, I thought.

'What don't you get?' I shrugged.

'Jimmy is your friend. Yes?'

'Yeah. So?' I said, flicking the lighter in my hand, sending up a few sparks but never letting it fully catch.

'You make him look . . .' she hesitated, 'bad. On TV.'

I gave her a long look. 'Why do you care about Jimmy Wigmore anyway?'

Agnes looked down at her thin little fingers. 'He is my friend, too.'

I lit up the cigarette and took a quick puff, then shoved it down behind the seat before the bus driver could clock me. 'Yeah, well, me and Jimmy go way back. Our relationship is, like, epic, you know? He knows I'll make it up to him.'

She stretched her sleeves tight over her knuckles.

'We're like blood brothers,' I said. 'Or an old married couple. Nothing – and no one – will ever come between us.'

I gave her a long cool look when I said that and she opened out her fingers, pulling the sleeve even more taut.

'So anyway, I spoke to a man at the *Liverpool Echo* today,' I went on. 'He said if we make it to the finals, he'll deffo do a story on us.' The bus jolted over a speed bump making the old ladies at the front gasp and mutter. 'And from there it's only one step to the tabloids and the big money, and then I figure me and Jimmy are quits for the other stuff.'

Agnes didn't look convinced but she didn't say so.

I took another quick puff of the cigarette. 'Do you want some?' I asked.

Agnes glanced down at the old biddies in front of us and at the cubicle where the driver sat.

'Go on,' I said. 'It won't kill you. It's not even real. Might even sort out your sore throat.'

She loosened her sleeve and reached her hand out across the aisle.

'Oi!' shouted the bus driver. 'I hope you're not smoking back there.'

'No way,' I shouted back, shoving the cigarette in Agnes's direction. 'Don't you know smoking kills?'

Agnes was still looking at me. She has this way of staring sometimes which is kind of freaky and she was holding the cigarette out in front of her like it was some kind of bomb.

'Your dad not be happy that you sing with me, will he?' she asked in a low voice.

'Dunno,' I said. 'Maybe he'll be totally cool about it.'

Agnes looked warily at the cigarette and took one quick puff, pursing her lips and trying not to cough. I laughed as she handed it back.

'Thank you,' she said.

'What for?'

'For getting me to sing,' she said.

'Oh, right. Yeah, well you're OK at it. When you're not chundering and freaking out and stuff.'

'Chundering?' she said, her eyes lighting up at the new word. Jimmy wasn't the only one who'd noticed she had a thing for funny words.

'Vomming,' I explained. 'Throwing up. Being sick.'

'Oh, I see.' She hesitated, coughed again, then smiled a bit. 'Yes. When I not chundering, I like it.'

'Sure.' I shrugged. 'My pleasure then.' And then, because I didn't know what to say after that, I took the tea-bag cigarette and shoved it back in my mouth.

'No smoking on my bus!' the driver yelled.

338

The semi-finals were a bit different to the other rounds. For a start, they were in the TV studio down at the Albert Docks where they used to film all them daytime chat shows. And there was no audience this time, just the judges and a load of TV people.

When we arrived, the skinny producer girl was stressing out cos we were late.

'Bus took forever,' I explained.

'Well at least you're here,' she said, sounding breathless and a bit panicky. 'We're running on a really tight schedule today, so I need you to be ready in five.'

'But we're not even changed!' I squealed. 'Don't we get a chance to do make-up and hair and stuff?'

'So long as you're quick,' she muttered, bundling us into a dressing room. 'Five minutes tops.'

I looked around me. Every square inch of the room was covered in make-up and hair-styling products and there were clothes flung all over the floor and the bed.

'Time to glam up, partner!' I said, turning to Agnes.

I glanced at myself in the mirror and I didn't look anything like I was supposed to. My hair had gone all frizzy on the journey and my make-up had rubbed off. I slapped on some more lipstick but that only made it look worse.

Agnes had insisted on sorting out her own wardrobe this time. She was in skinny jeans and a plain white blouse but she pulled a pair of her mam's heels on and put on a bit of lipgloss and she looked instantly older and beautiful, only in a dead simple way that looked like she'd made no effort at all.

'You look nice,' I said.

'So do you,' she said.

I looked at her then and I sort of wanted to tell her thanks, but I'm no good at that schmaltzy stuff so I just said, 'We've got to ace this, you know that, don't you?'

'Ace?'

'Sing really well. Be the best.'

'I try,' she said.

I paused and then said quickly, 'Like I said, you're actually sort of good.'

Agnes gave me one of her smiles then – like the ones she gives Jimmy, that make her whole face light up. I just scrunched up my nose and looked away so she wouldn't start thinking I'd gone soft. But it felt sort of nice anyway.

Jimmy

I'm not sure how I let her talk me into it. Any divvy could see it wasn't going to work. But then I never was any good at saying no to Elfie Baguley. She kept going on about how this was the only way she was going to get Alfie back, even though I'm not even sure she'd thought the whole thing through herself.

I had to duck out of school at lunchtime and leg it over to Elfie's house, jumping over the back fence so that Mrs Newsround didn't see me. I don't know why I bothered really, cos at half past twelve I opened the door to the presenter and the tattooed cameraman and I could already see Mrs Newsround's curtains twitching across the road, so I knew I was busted. Like Elfie said, 'There's no way she isn't going to clock a film crew turning up in the middle of the estate, right?'

'Can I see your ID?' I said. Cos that's what Elfie said I had to say.

The presenter looked confused, like he wasn't used to being asked for ID. 'What?'

'Elfie said I need to check you're not debt collectors,' I said, blushing deep into the roots of my hair.

'Do we look like debt collectors?' said the presenter, flicking his hair like I've seen him do on TV.

'Um – no.'

I glanced at the cameraman who was carrying a load of equipment. He grinned and said, 'I promise I won't run off with your flat screen, kid.'

'OK,' I said, stepping aside to let them in. Behind them I could see the little ginger kid on his bike, watching. I guess he was bunking off school, too. He was glaring in our direction and it was like when a load of strangers roll up in town in one of them cowboy films my dad likes. I shut the door and pretended I hadn't seen him.

The presenter was glancing anxiously around. 'Um . . . where is everyone?'

I took a deep breath and said, 'Oh, um, it's just me.'

His face fell. It would have been funny if it hadn't been so awful. 'What?'

'I was supposed to have Alfie but '

He was staring at me open-mouthed. 'Didn't the production team explain to you that we need to film interviews with family members?' he said, sounding a lot less smooth than usual. 'And we need a reception party ready to meet Elfie and Agnes when they get back from the audition?'

'Yeah, but like I say, there's only me.'

'Please tell me you're not actually being serious here.'

I glanced at the cameraman who was grinning, his Kylie tattoo pulled taught on his neck.

'Elfie and Agnes they – um – still haven't actually told their families about the competition yet,' I said, repeating what Elfie had told me to say, word for word.

The presenter's face went completely pale.

The cameraman let out a laugh. 'No way!' he said. 'This is class!'

'This is not class, it's a bloody nightmare!' yelled the presenter.

I thought back over the last week – burning newspapers shoved through the letter box, dog mess smeared over our windows, the slow chanting at my dad every morning – and I wondered if the presenter had any idea what a nightmare was really like.

'I was told the permission issue had been cleared up,' said the presenter.

'We sort of faked it,' I said. 'Well, Elfie did.'

The cameraman let out another loud guffaw.

'Faked it!' the presenter yelled, clearly not finding this at all funny.

'She said it was surprisingly easy,' I added, although this probably wasn't very helpful.

'This is a disaster!' yelled the presenter.

'Nah,' said the cameraman, still grinning broadly. 'It's great.'

'And how exactly do you figure that?' the presenter snapped.

'It's a brilliant twist on the F and F section!' he said.

'We get a bit of sad music, play it in the background with a voice-over saying how Elfie and Agnes haven't been able to tell their folks about their dream. How they've had to lie to everyone they care about to make it to the top. That sort of thing. Then I'll take some footage of this kid looking dead small in a massive empty room to show he's all they've got. It could be magic.'

'That's what Elfie reckoned too,' I said.

The presenter sniffed. 'I suppose it has potential.'

'It could be ground-breaking,' said the cameraman. 'Local TV won't have seen nothing like it. I'll probably get a BAFTA!' He grinned again in my direction and Kylie gave another little wiggle on his neck.

'I could ring the studio and see what they think,' the presenter said, tugging his phone out of his pocket.

The cameraman looked at me and winked. 'I should be creative director me!'

'Oh, God! And now we're back to square one with the parental permission issue,' the presenter said with a dramatic sigh.

Only just after he got on the phone to the studio,

the parental permission issue sorted itself out in a way
nobody was expecting . . .

Except maybe Elfie.

Rules of Talent TV No. 18: Stage your own car-crash TV moment

Elfie

There's nothing viewers like more than car-crash TV. I guess it's human nature. We like to see other people messing up spectacularly cos it makes us feel better about ourselves. And because everybody loves an underdog.

The only problem is that car crashes are unpredictable. They can spin out of control. Way out of control.

'Not your best performance, to be honest,' said The Legend, after we'd sung.

'Do you want another turn?' said The Tabloid Princess who was dressed in another outfit that she could have nicked out of me mam's wardrobe.

'Must we?' said The Facelift, whose skin looked

347

even more stretched than usual.

'Give 'em a chance,' said The Tabloid Princess. 'Agnes's voice sounds off. She got a cold or something?'

The cameras weren't rolling at this point. When you watch it on TV it's like it all happens in real time but that's not how it actually is. It all takes flipping hours.

'Have we got time for a second take?' asked The Legend. The producer nodded enthusiastically. She told us earlier that she was a massive 'Juliets' fan and that she'd been so thrilled when our parents agreed to let us take part (I had to do an Agnes and bite my lip to stop myself laughing out loud when she said the last bit!).

The Tabloid Princess grinned and The Facelift gave a long sigh.

'If we must, then,' drawled The Legend. 'From the top, ladies.'

Things weren't exactly going well. Showing a bit of vulnerability is one thing, but we were just being a bit rubbish, to be honest. Agnes's sore throat was playing up and when she started singing her voice came out all weak and scratchy. And it wasn't just that. Without Jimmy and Alfie there, I dunno, it just seemed wrong.

As they sorted out the sound cue, I glanced at Agnes and hissed, 'What's the matter?'

'I don't know, I –'

'We're about to blow it here.'

'I know, but . . . the song. It no feel right. And my throat . . .'

She never got to finish because the producer was whispering something in The Legend's ear.

'Well! Well! Well!' said The Legend, looking slightly less than bored for the first time all morning. 'It seems that there's a bit of a problem with your family and friends!'

'Get the cameras on this,' barked The Legend. Suddenly the lenses were right back on us.

'I've just has a phone call from one of the production team who are filming with your families,' said The Legend, back in his TV voice again. 'Or, rather, NOT filming your families, right?'

I shrugged. I swear I could hear the sound of squealing breaks and burning rubber.

'Yes. Apparently, your little friend Jimmy is the only one who turned up,' said The Legend, narrowing his eyes.

'Surprise, surprise!' said The Facelift, stretching her lips into a smile.

I took a deep breath. 'The thing is –'

'The thing is that you still haven't told them,' The Legend cut in.

'Um, well –'

'And you faked the parental permission – AGAIN!'

The Tabloid Princess gasped and The Facelift gave a little snort of laughter.

I glanced over at the producer who had gone white as a sheet. I felt kind of bad and wondered if she'd get the sack for this.

'Isn't that right?' said The Legend.

I took a deep breath. 'You can edit this, right?' I said, leaning forwards and talking in a false whisper. 'I mean, you can film all I say but you'll only show the bits I want, yeah?'

The Facelift raised a slow eyebrow. 'Are you trying to write the script for us, young lady?'

'No way!' I said, ignoring her and talking straight to The Legend who was still looking unimpressed. 'But I've been thinking about this and I reckon that the whole parental permission stuff doesn't have to be a problem. In fact, it could be an opportunity!'

The Tabloid Princess giggled, a tinkling sound like breaking glass. 'Elfie, you are priceless!' she said.

'Do explain,' said The Legend drily.

'The way I see it, me and Agnes entering the show without our families' permissions, that's TV gold. Because if they don't find out till they see us on TV . . .'

'Which they will tonight!' said The Facelift.

Next to me Agnes inhaled sharply. I hoped she wasn't going to be sick or faint or something. I'd been telling her and Jimmy all week that they probably wouldn't feature us on the very first show, that we probably had a couple of days before our bit went on air.

'Right,' I said, swallowing hard. 'Tonight?'

'Yup. Tonight. So, wouldn't it have been better

351

to give your families a bit of warning?' said The Lingerie Lizard.

'That's one way of looking at it,' I said, trying to give a kooky grin. The Tabloid Princess was the only one who laughed.

I could hear Agnes's shallow breathing next to me and I wondered if perhaps it would cause a good diversion if she threw up on camera.

'Actually, I reckon it's dead class that we're going to be tonight,' I said, sounding much more convincing than I actually felt.

'In what way is that "dead class"?' asked The Facelift sarcastically.

'Cos it'll all kick off big time! I bet it'll make all the front pages round here. And maybe even the tabloids too!'

The Legend paused, narrowed his eyes. 'Are you really telling me that you deliberately postponed telling your family in order to precipitate some kind of crisis and get into the local press.'

'Genius, right!' I said, with my best smile. 'Although I'm aiming for the nationals, me!'

'Oh, God!' said The Legend, raising his eyebrows. 'A child of the reality TV generation telling us how to run the show.'

'Exactly!' I beamed.

'That wasn't meant as a compliment, Elfie,' said The Legend. 'Are you honestly suggesting that we overlook the fact you have lied and faked your way to this point in the competition, and put you forward for the final, just because you've manufactured a bit of drama to make yourselves more interesting?'

'No, I reckon you should put us through because she's got the best voice in the whole competition,' I said, nodding at Agnes, who was breathing really funny next to me.

The Legend stared at me, unsmiling.

'Are you getting this?' The Lingerie Lizard glanced at the cameraman, who nodded.

'But you've gotta admit, it's a top story. Shy girl with the voice of an angel, broken homes, neighbours at war, the whole Romeo and Juliet thing. It's perfect tabloid stuff. Imagine how much the gossip mags will love it.'

'Yes. Thank you, Elfie!' said The Legend. 'You can speak to Spielberg about the rights to the biopic later. Let's concentrate on the present for now.'

'There's just one more thing,' I said.

'What is that exactly?'

I crossed my fingers behind my back and said, 'Just the small fact that this is the only way I'm going to get my baby back.'

Jimmy

'They want to know about the baby,' said the presenter, turning to me, the phone to her ear.

'What about him?' said the cameraman.

'Where is he?'

And I was about to tell her when there was a ring on the doorbell and suddenly I realised who Elfie's mystery guest was. Cos there stood Elfie's mam. With baby Alfie in tow.

Elfie

OK, so I suppose I did know me mam was going to turn up – sort of. I might, for example, have sent her a text on me dad's phone saying he wanted to talk, and it might have suggested that she pop over and pick up Alfie's blanket from our house. Around lunchtime. Right around the time I knew the F and F people were going to be there.

And no, I hadn't warned Jimmy, but that was cos I figured he'd only fret and worry if I told him. And anyway, there was no way of knowing if she'd actually show up, cos when did me mam do anything I wanted her to? I was nearly as shocked as everyone else when The Legend turned round and said she was on the phone.

'Really?' I said. I had a sinking feeling in my tummy, mixed with excitement – this was my car-crash plan after all. 'Where's she calling from?'

'Your house, apparently,' said The Legend. 'She thought Alfie might be missing his "sister"?' He raised an eyebrow. 'Care to explain, Elfie?'

'Here we go!' I muttered. I glanced at the cameras which were still rolling and gave my biggest stage-struck smile. 'It's like I was about to tell you,' I said. 'She's trying to steal my baby!'

Agnes turned to stare at me. The Legend stared at me. The producer stared at me and so did all the members of the camera crew.

'She's gonna claim he's hers and everyone will believe her cos that's what we always told everyone, but it's not true. He's my baby and she's trying to take him away from me, and I won't let her,' I said. I had this tinny taste in my mouth and the sick feeling like I was in a car hurtling out of control but it was too late to stop now. 'Let me talk to her,' I said.

'Be my guest!' The Legend passed me the phone then turned to the cameraman. 'You are getting this, right?'

I took the phone off him and put it to my ear. 'Hi, Mam,' I said, all cool, like I hadn't got a room full of people all listening in.

'Elfie, love!' she gushed. Just hearing her voice

made the sick feeling ten times worse. 'I've missed you so desperately.'

'Is Alfie OK?' I said, trying to make my voice sound as flat and unbothered as possible.

'He's just fine,' she answered, before launching back into her mother-of-the-year act. 'And I've been hearing all about how you're doing on *Pop to the Top*. I'm so proud of you, Elfie. I just knew you'd be a star one day.'

'Probably all those celeb magazines you read while I was in the womb, right?' I said.

'You get your star quality from my side, you know.'

I hate it when she's being like this. When she's pretending to be nice and loving. It's almost easier to deal with her when she's being a cow cos at least I know where I am then. So I made myself think about what her face looked like when she was walking out of that police station with Alfie in her arms, not even bothering to look back. Then I bit my lip. Hard. And said, 'And I'm sure you'll be taking full credit for my success. Right?'

'I can't help it, Elfie. I'm just dead proud. My baby, a star!'

'Just because this is being filmed there's no need to start acting like you're suddenly some perfect mam, you know,' I said.

She paused. Just for a second. 'And you are, I suppose?'

I didn't say anything. I could feel all the judges looking at me. And the technical crew, all staring.

'Cos that's what I'm hearing,' she went on. Her voice sounded metallic and distant on the phone. 'What a great mam you are to Alfie. Do you want to tell me more about that, Elfie?'

I was ready for this. She was playing right into my plan, only for some reason it didn't feel like I thought it would. I felt sick and my heart was thumping. 'I'm more of a mam to him than you are!' I declared loudly.

'Really, Elfie? You sure about that, are you? Strictly – biologically – like?'

I glanced at the judges again. The Legend was watching me, his eyes unblinking. The Facelift was smiling, arms crossed. The Lingerie Lizard was busy texting or tweeting or something and The Tabloid Princess was trying to look sweet and concerned but not quite hiding the curiosity on her face.

'Look, I've told them all about Alfie,' I said. 'They know everything. So you can stop pretending now and give me my baby back.'

Agnes

I listened to everything going on almost as if I was in a dream, or watching it from above. Like I wasn't really there. My throat was sore and scratchy and my head felt like it was filled with cotton wool, my limbs making me feel hot, then cold, then hot again.

'What's going on now, Elfie?' asked The Legend. He sounded completely exasperated.

I glanced at Elfie, wondering what she was going to say next. She had her head tipped to one side and her nose scrunched up. I wondered if sometimes she got tangled up in her own tales, if ever she forgot which strands were truth and which were story.

'Send a camera round to our house tonight and you'll find out everything!' she announced, hands on hips. 'Film the fall-out live. I guarantee it'll be explosive.'

'This is not *American Idol,* Elfie!' said The Facelift acidly.

'No, it could be bigger!' said Elfie. I could almost see the ribbons of lies streaming out of her mouth, twisting themselves round her, trapping her.

'I see!' said The Legend. 'Well, you clearly have a great future in PR or soap operas, young lady, but for now, I need to decide what I'm going to do with you. Do you think you can manage to stop talking for five minutes while I consult with my colleagues?'

'Mmm-mm!' said Elfie, miming zipping her mouth shut.

The Legend looked hard at her for a moment then turned to talk to the other judges. Elfie stopped grinning and looked at me. Without the big smile on her face, you could see she was hot and kind of jittery and a bit all over the place. Her hair was limp and her make-up had already rubbed off, leaving her pale and young looking.

'What happening?' I whispered, my throat catching

painfully as I spoke. 'You are OK?'

'Sure!' she whispered, glancing at The Legend. 'This is all part of the plan. I've got it totally under control, trust me.'

But that wasn't how she looked at all.

'Get me the legal team on the phone,' I heard The Legend say. Elfie tossed her hair and scrunched up her nose and stuffed her hands in her pockets to stop them shaking. Neither of us said anything.

After about five minutes, The Legend turned back to us. 'Well, young lady,' he said, slowly, staring at Elfie like he was trying to make up his mind about something. Then he said, 'I've got to tell you that my fellow judges are unimpressed by your latest little stunt.' Elfie opened her mouth to say something but he put a hand up to stop her. 'And don't try to tell me none of this was a set-up because I don't buy it and neither will they.'

Elfie closed her mouth. My head throbbed some more and my throat felt like it was full of razors.

'The others,' he gestured to the rest of the judging panel. 'Reckon I should send you straight home.' He paused, obviously thinking.

Elfie reached out to squeeze my hand. I turned to her, surprised.

'And you're not exactly my first choice to put through to the finals, to be honest,' he went on. 'There are other acts who've made it this far on talent alone and I don't see why you should do them out of a place just because you've been busy turning everything into a circus. But –' he stopped again.

'But what?' said Elfie impatiently – a little desperately. I squeezed her hand tighter. Her fingers felt hot and clammy.

'I've spoken to legal and they say your mother has signed to say she gave you permission to enter the show,' The Legend said, looking at Elfie.

'Really!' she squeaked then nodded in my direction. 'What about her?'

The Legend narrowed his eyes. 'They tell me there's some loophole about non-UK citizens, which means she never had to get permission anyway.'

Elfie squeaked.

The Legend gave her a look. 'Yes. Well. Some

junior lawyer is going to get strung up by his eyelashes for that one but at least it gets us out of that particular legal conundrum.'

'So?' Elfie looked like she was struggling to stay still and she sounded more nervous than I'd ever heard her sounding before.

'Sooo,' said The Legend, drawing the one syllable out for as long as possible. 'As it stands, there's one more group place in the finals.'

'And?' I could hear Elfie's breath coming quick and shallow. And I realised that I really wanted this to work out. For her. Because she needed this in a way that neither me nor Jimmy did.

'And it could be yours . . .'

'You're putting us through?' she said, her voice cracking on the final word – like she hadn't thought that was what he was going to say.

'Maybe,' he said.

Elfie squeaked again and squeezed my hand so hard I thought she was going to break it.

'But only if . . .'

'Anything,' said Elfie, jumping up and down on

the spot like Alfie does when he's excited. She was still holding my hand really tight. I glanced at her. Her eyes were all twinkly and her freckles seemed almost to have faded into her pale skin. 'We'll do anything. Won't we, Agnes?'

She turned to me, a look of desperation in her eyes. I nodded quickly, thinking that I probably would do anything for Elfie Baguley.

'I'm afraid it's not up to you any more,' said The Legend. 'It's too late to pull the footage that's going out tonight, but legal tell me they won't let you proceed any *further* in the competition until they have personally spoken – face-to-face – with each of your parents and witnessed them putting their signatures to bits of paper.'

'Oh!' Elfie seemed to deflate. 'Even me dad?'

'Yes, even your dad,' said The Legend. 'And hers.'

'But I thought you said . . .'

'Loophole or no loophole, that's what the lawyers are saying they need if you want to proceed. So if . . .' he paused again, '*if* after watching your performance on TV tonight *all* your parents agree, then you are through to the live finals.'

Elfie squealed again. But she looked like she was sort of faking it this time because her eyes were a bit blank and sort of tearful and her fingers were limp in my hand.

'Thank you so much for giving us another chance, Mr Legend, sir!' she said, politely.

The Legend smiled, baring his teeth. 'That's right, Elfie,' he said. 'I'm giving you another chance. So, please, for God's sake don't blow it this time.'

Rules of Talent TV No. 19:
Get your friends and family together
to watch your TV debut

Jimmy

That night, I tried to make training last as long as possible, hoping that if I could string it out enough we'd miss the show altogether. I spent so long in the shower after I'd finished that the manager had to kick me out, because it was time for the pool to close. I glanced at my watch – the programme was due to start in less than half an hour.

Only that wasn't the only thing I was worrying about. I'd been thinking about what Elfie had said about how you've sometimes got to be cruel to be kind, and what she'd said about getting my dad to rejoin the strike. I just knew things would be better if he did. And I knew there was only one way I could get him to do it. Only I wasn't sure he'd ever forgive me for it.

'Much better session today,' said my dad when I finally came out of the changing rooms. He was still grinning. 'If you swim like that next week you'll blow the competition out of the water.'

I tried to focus on what Elfie had said – that grown-ups don't always know what's best for them.

'About that, Dad –' I started.

'We need to keep it up, though,' he said. 'Work hard for the next few days then ease off towards the end of the week to rest your muscles before the trials.'

'But, I –'

'You've nothing to worry about, son. Swim like that and the Team GB selectors would have to be blind not to see your potential.'

I could hear in his voice how much he wanted it. But I could also still hear the chant of 'Scab! Scab!' and see the cut by his left eye where he'd had a broken bottle thrown at him.

'I don't know if I want it enough,' I said slowly.

He hesitated. This wasn't what he was expecting. Behind us, the pool manager locked the door and turned off the light. My dad and I stood in the near dark, in the rain. Opposite each other but avoiding eye contact.

'You're nervous,' he said. 'That's normal. But there's nothing to worry about. You'll ace it.'

'I'm not nervous,' I said.

'What then?' he asked.

Neither of us moved.

Elfie had said I really needed to go for it, or it wouldn't work. 'You've got to stick the knife in,' she'd said. 'No other way, I'm afraid.'

I shifted a little and the security light flicked on.

'You always said I had to really want it,' I said. 'That I had to love what I was doing.'

He cleared his throat, looked down and then up. 'Yeah.'

'Well, I'm not sure I do any more.'

There was another long pause.

When my dad finally spoke, his voice was so quiet it was barely audible. 'You know the sacrifices I've made – that your mam's made – to give you a better future.'

'I know but . . .' I hesitated. 'I'm not sure it's worth it. Not sure I'm worth it. Maybe –' I hesitated again.

'Maybe you should just go back to the picket line.'

The security light timed out and we were in darkness again. My dad stood staring at me for a moment. I could only see the whites of his eyes.

'I'm not listening to this,' he said. 'You're swimming and that's that.' Then he turned and started walking off in the direction of the steps.

'Dad!' I called after him.

But he didn't look back.

When we got back to the house, there was more graffiti over the front walls, and someone had plastered layers of wet toilet roll over the windows. It had dried in sticky clumps, like the papier mache models we used to make in primary school.

'We'll get the hose out later and wash it off,' said my dad.

'But they'll only do it again,' I said. 'Or something worse.'

'They'll get bored of all this eventually.'

I took hold of his arm. 'It's not going to stop, Dad,' I said. 'Not till you go back to the picket line.'

I held his arm firm to stop him walking away.

'It's worth it,' he said.

'No, it's not,' I said. '*I'm* not, Dad.'

'You don't know what you're saying.'

'I'm saying I won't swim until you go back on strike. Not if it means you and mam have to deal with this.'

'We can't keep paying for your training if I'm back on the picket line.' My dad was looking at me. He has to look up because I'm a couple of inches taller than him now, which always feels wrong somehow.

'Then I'll get a paper round or something.'

My dad laughed, only it sounded more like a sob. 'How you gonna manage a paper round if you're training two hours before school?'

'I'll think of something,' I said. I still had hold of his arm.

'It's not your decision to make, son,' he said quietly.

I'm not used to standing up to people, even though everyone's always saying I should: stand up to Elfie, stand up to my dad, stand up to the bullies at school. That's not who I am – not normally.

Only this time it was different. So I took another deep breath and said, 'It is, Dad. I'm not swimming in the trials unless you go back on the picket line. And nothing you can say is going to make me change my mind.'

Elfie

When I got back me dad was in the kitchen, wearing an apron and whistling.

'Hi, Dad,' I said. I could smell furniture polish, mixed with the aroma of beef and onions. 'What're you making?'

'Shepherd's pie,' he said, smiling. 'Your favourite.'

'Oh,' I said. 'Why?'

He'd laid out two trays on the side and even got little pots of trifle for pudding. He looked happier than he had for ages.

'I thought we could have a night in,' he grinned. 'Just the two of us.'

'Oh. Yeah. Right!'

'That *Pop to the Top* thing is on again after the news,' he said.

'Is it?'

'Thought we could watch it together. Just you and me. It's always a good laugh. Seeing the local wannabes parading themselves on TV.'

'Yeah,' I said, weakly. 'That'd be nice.'

'Management at the plant have agreed to talks,' he said, pulling a beer out of the fridge. 'Looks like we might be making some progress.'

'That's great!' I said. I leaned against the kitchen worktop, trying to look totally normal even though that was the last thing I was feeling.

He started dishing the food out on to plates, humming a tune which just so happened to be the song me and Agnes did for our first audition. The one we'd be singing on TV in about – ooh – ten minutes time. I think my English teacher would say that was irony or summat?

'So maybe the strike will end soon?' I said.

'Let's hope so,' he said.

'And then we can ring me mam and tell her we want Alfie back, right?'

He hesitated. 'Maybe,' he said.

I pushed my hand into my pocket and ran my fingers over the silky seam of Alfie's blanket. The food smelled good. And my dad seemed like his old self for the first time in ages. I really, really wished I wasn't about to ruin it all.

We sat down side-by-side on the sofa to eat. Dad flicked on the TV and the opening sequence of *Pop to the Top* appeared on the screen.

'Load of rubbish, this!' he laughed. 'Dunno what the hell possesses anyone to enter!' He put his arm round me, just like he used to when I was little, and squeezed me tight.

'I guess it's like Jimmy with his swimming,' I said quietly. 'They're following a dream, or summat.'

He pulled away a bit and looked at me. 'You've not been seeing that scab kid, have you?'

I shook my head – which didn't feel so much like lying – and crossed my fingers behind my back.

'Good,' he said, landing a kiss on my forehead. 'Oh, here we go!'

He pointed at the TV where the theme tune was playing out while the camera panned across the crowd of contestants who were all waving excitedly. If he'd looked carefully he'd have seen three little figures standing next to a buggy in the top left corner of the picture. One of them looked a lot like me.

As we watched the first few auditions my stomach got tighter and tighter. My dad laughed at Big Hair Lady killing a Marilyn Monroe number, and groaned at the IVF Boys' attempts at break-dancing. I just stared at the screen, my food untouched on the tray in front of me, wondering whether I should leg it while I had the chance. Suddenly this was feeling like my worst plan ever.

'Summat wrong with your food, Elfie love?'

'I'm just not hungry, that's all.'

'You're not sickening for summat, are you?'

'No, I'm fine.' I was trying really, really hard to keep my voice normal.

Then, suddenly, he froze and I knew it had started.

On the TV, the presenter was saying, 'Also hoping to impress the judges today is fourteen-year-old single mam, Elfie Baguley.' Schmaltzy music played and there we were: me, Agnes, Jimmy and Alfie (all looking dead young and kind of cheap in our spangly outfits – not half as glamorous as I imagined) with the presenter (who really does look a lot better on TV) standing beside us. The camera was focusing on me and Alfie and I was saying, 'I was only twelve when I had Alfie but I love him to bits.'

'Dad . . .' I started to say.

The camera panned to Jimmy as the me on screen continued. 'Jimmy's been dead class about it,' I was saying. 'But we're not together. It was just a one-night mistake thing. He might not even be the dad.'

My dad turned to me. 'What have you done, Elfie?'

I wanted to explain that it wasn't as bad as it looked; that I did it for him, and for Alfie. Only I knew there was no point because it was about to get a whole lot worse.

Jimmy

I suppose it was perfectly timed that my dad stepped through the front door the same instant me and The Juliets appeared on the TV. He walked into the hallway and the sitting-room door was open, so he got a direct view of the screen at the very moment our faces flashed up.

My mam was sitting on the sofa. She looked round to greet us. 'Good session?' she said. Behind her, I could see Elfie's smiling face and I heard the presenter saying, 'Also hoping to impress the judges today is fourteen-year-old single mam, Elfie.'

I nearly turned and ran right out of the house.

'Hi, Mam,' I said.

But my dad was already staring at the picture. 'What the –?' he spluttered.

Then my mam caught sight of the expression on his face and she turned to the TV, too. I was still in the hallway, the front door open, rain blowing on to the doormat thinking things couldn't get any worse.

Only just then the TV skipped to footage from the second audition.

'Our families will probably kill us when they find out we're singing together,' Elfie was saying. My heart sank down to my feet. 'A striker, a scab and an immo. This could tear our community apart.'

There was a terrible silence then my dad turned to me. There was disappointment written all over his face and there was nothing I could say.

Elfie

It all kicked off right away, just like I told The Legend it would. Only it didn't happen quite the way I expected it to.

For a start, I couldn't believe they'd shown the bit about the strike. I mean, I'd figured they'd only show stuff from the first audition in the opening show, and we'd have a bit of time before the scab/striker mess hit the fan. Only there I was on screen saying,

'Oh, it's just some stupid scabs-versus-strikers thing – a load of boring politics, basically.' And me dad actually stopped breathing for a second and then he turned to look at me and for the first time in my life I felt almost scared of him. I opened my mouth to say something only the next thing we knew, Jimmy's dad was pounding on our front door, shouting, 'Open up, Baguley, or I'm going to kick this door in.' He sounded like he'd completely lost it, and when me dad flung open the door (seriously, it was like a scene from a dodgy Merseyside soap opera), Jimmy's dad was standing there, wet through, with Jimmy's swim bag in his hand.

His face was blotchy red and white and he stuttered as he said, 'I – I've had enough, Baguley.'

Jimmy was standing behind him, looking like he'd been pickled in chlorine. His face was kind of green and a bit flaky. I've never seen him look quite like that before. 'Dad, don't!' he said.

But his dad ignored him. I don't think I'd ever seen him properly angry and he looked almost crazed with it. 'You can do what you like to me, Baguley, but

I'm not going to let that girl of yours make a laughing stock out of my son.'

Me dad didn't say anything for a moment, then he glanced at me and said quietly, 'I told you I didn't want you hanging out with the scab kid, Elfie.'

'He's my mate, I . . .'

But he wasn't listening. He wasn't even looking at me any more. He was staring straight at Jimmy's dad as he said, 'His father is a scab, Elfie. You know how it works.'

'Don't call my dad a scab,' said Jimmy.

'You don't care who you hurt, do you?' said Jimmy's dad.

Me dad said nothing. He acted like Jimmy's dad wasn't even there – just like the kids do to Agnes at school.

'You're a coward, Baguley,' Jimmy's dad went on, his face scarlet now, like Jimmy's goes when he's embarrassed. 'And a bully, and that daughter of yours is no better than her mother.'

I knew he'd done it then. There was a second when I saw me dad's hands ball into fists and then he lunged at Jimmy's dad. I glanced at Jimmy and he glanced at me and then our two dads started staggering round like a couple of skinny Northern Sumo wrestlers. I probably would have laughed if I hadn't felt so much like flipping crying. Jimmy started trying to drag his dad away and I tried to do the same to mine, only neither of them wanted to be pulled apart.

'Stop it, Dad!' I yelled, grabbing at his arm. He shook me off angrily but I was right back on to him, pulling at him.

'Stop it!' I shouted.

The he swiped out with his arm and I felt myself go flying but it was like everything was suddenly in slow motion. I know he didn't mean to do it, he didn't mean to hurt me. He was just so mad about everything – about the strike and me mam and losing Alfie and the show – and it was like it all just burst out of him and he didn't even notice I was there.

As I lay there on the wet ground I saw half the neighbours had come out on to the street to see what was happening. Mrs Newsround in her dressing gown,

Mrs Winstanley, the biker kids. And they were all staring at me dad and Jimmy's dad trying to beat the stuffing out of each other. And they were gawping at me too as I lay there on the ground with a split lip. Mrs Newsround had her mouth wide open and the ginger biker kid had eyes as big as saucers. But you could tell they were all loving the drama.

Jimmy

My dad was the first to pull away. He staggered backwards. 'You're not worth it,' he spat at Elfie's dad.

Clive Baguley had blood pouring out of his nose and he was panting. Elfie pushed herself to her feet but stayed back. She wasn't badly hurt, but she was staring at her dad like all she wanted was for him to turn round and look at her. Only he didn't.

My dad was breathing really heavily but he didn't look as bad as Elfie's dad. I couldn't quite believe it: my dad landing one on Clive Baguley and coming out looking better.

'Come on, son,' he said, turning to me. 'We're finished here.'

Elfie was still staring at her dad but he still wouldn't look at her.

'We're going to the press, son,' my dad said loudly so that everyone could hear. 'And we're going to set the record straight on a few things.'

Clive Baguley said nothing. He just ran a hand over his bloody nose.

I glanced at Elfie and tried to catch her eye but she didn't seem to notice.

Elfie took a step forwards. 'Dad –'

'Don't talk to me, Elfie,' he said.

'But Dad –'

'You've made a fool of me, Elfie!' he said. 'Just like your mam always does.'

Agnes

When I was little, I couldn't understand how people got to be on TV. I thought they must be in there somehow, actually inside the TV, in some kind of alternate world. And I didn't see how time could be different in the TV set either. How could it be night time there if it was morning when I was watching? How could they be having Christmas when I wasn't?

When I saw me and Elfie and Jimmy and Alfie on TV, I had the same feeling all over again. Like I'd been split in two and half of me was sitting on the sofa, while the other half was trapped behind the screen.

The TV was on mute but I could see Lap-Dancer Girl Band gyrating silently, mouths opening and closing like fishes in a tank.

'You must have realised it would come out eventually,' my dad was saying. He spoke in Portuguese which he'd hardly done at all since we came to England. 'Why didn't you tell us?'

My throat still hurt like mad and my head and limbs were aching. 'Elfie wanted to keep it a secret. Because of the strike, you know.'

My mum put her arm round me and her skin felt incredibly cold against mine. 'I thought you sang beautifully,' she said.

'I still wish you'd told us,' said my dad.

I stared at the screen, which seemed too bright this evening. It hardly felt real. I tried to imagine Jimmy and Elfie watching it. Tried to imagine what was happening to them.

'We got through to the final,' I said. 'Sort of.'

'That's wonderful!' said my mum. 'I'm so proud.'

But I couldn't feel glad. I couldn't stop thinking about Elfie and Jimmy, worrying about them. And I couldn't help wondering if I'd ever get to sing with Elfie again. Because I realised I didn't want it all to end. Not yet.

Grand Final

Rules of Talent TV No. 20:
Never ignore the 'Rules of Talent TV'

Elfie

I lay in bed all night, not sleeping, listening to the sounds of the empty house. I couldn't even remember how it felt to have Alfie's soft body moulded round my own, or to hear the little sucking noises he makes when he sleeps. It was nearly light by the time me dad got back and I had no idea where he'd been. I heard the door slam downstairs and his feet heavy in the sitting room. I thought he might put his head round my door to see if I was asleep. But he didn't.

'Dad?' I called out.

'Go to sleep, Elfie,' was all he said.

I waited a bit before I went downstairs. He was in the sitting room and the TV was on. I heard the sound of the weather forecaster saying, 'Heavy rain right across the north west has led the Met Office to issue a severe weather warning.'

I pushed the door open. Me dad was slumped on the sofa in front of the TV. He still had blood down the front of his T-shirt and he looked like he'd been drinking.

'Areas at risk of flooding include Merseyside, South Cheshire and Lancashire,' said the dark-haired presenter on the TV. The curtains were open and it was still dark outside, but tinges of pink were appearing behind the eight towers.

'Are you OK?' I asked.

He didn't turn round.

'I'm going to ring the competition organisers today and tell them I'm dropping out,' I said.

He didn't say anything.

'Check the Met Office web site for advice if you think your area may be at risk,' said the weatherman.

'That's what you want me to do, right?' I said because his silence was freaking me out more than any amount of shouting would've done. 'Drop out?'

On the sitting room floor, the two trays of food from earlier sat untouched where we'd left them.

It was like I hadn't said anything. Me dad just

kept on staring at the TV. The weather forecaster was signing off in front of a picture of a flooded field, cows stranded in the water.

'I'm going to do a newspaper interview an' all,' I said. 'You know, saying I'm sorry for all the hurt I've caused. I might be able to make a bit of money out of it. Pay off some of our debts.'

He leaned forward and flicked off the TV.

'I'm dead sorry, Dad,' I said.

His eyes were still fixed on the blank screen. 'Elfie, love,' he said quietly. 'I'm not even sure I care any more.'

Agnes

On average, it rains for over 280 days of the year on Merseyside. My dad read that in one of the newspapers he picked up that morning. 'This region is one of the wettest places in the UK!' he laughed. 'Apparently, last year there were never more than two days in a row without rain.'

'That's probably Clive Baguley's fault, too!' said my mum.

My dad laughed again, the serious expression he'd been wearing since last night momentarily washed away. 'He's not going to like all this,' he said, glancing down at all the newspapers spread out over the kitchen table. 'Not one bit.'

I looked at them too. 'Plan C,' I said quietly, only I wasn't so sure if this was really what Elfie'd had in mind.

I looked out the window, wondering what to do. Elfie's Indian summer felt like a distant memory. It was the first week of October and the sky above the eight towers was a dark slate grey; it hadn't stopped raining for days.

I don't mind heavy rain. 'Raining cats and dogs' Jimmy called it; 'pissing it down' was Elfie's phrase. The sort of rain that soaks you in seconds, falling in drops so heavy each one feels like a small water bomb. What I don't like is what Jimmy calls the 'drizzle': the endless grey-sky days when the air is a misty fug of cold moisture. 'It's only spitting,' Elfie says, and that's how it feels, like the sky is spitting on you in dribbles of cold saliva.

That day it was somewhere in between drizzle and cats and dogs but I knew I had to get out of the house. By the time I'd made it to the bridge, my clothes were soaked through and I felt shivery and feverish. I didn't know if the others would even come, but I figured it was the only place to go until the storm blew over.

Jimmy

As I jumped down the embankment I caught sight of her right away, sitting on the pebbly bit underneath the bridge, pouring over a pile of newspapers. I hesitated for a second before saying, 'Hi.'

She looked up. 'Hi,' she said. Her eyes looked extra bright and there were high spots of colour on her cheeks.

I clambered down and sat next to her, just a few inches away. I could see steam rising off her wet clothes. I hadn't spent any time alone with her since the time we'd kissed and I could feel myself starting to go red just thinking about it. She smelt of cough sweets and cherry shampoo.

'Did you see the show then?' I asked, wiping some of the rain out of my hair and glancing down at my sodden trousers.

She nodded. 'You?'

'Yup. My parents are pretty angry.'

'With Elfie?' Her voice still sounded scratchy, though not quite as bad as it had been the day before.

'I think my dad's more mad at me,' I said. I shifted a little to avoid the steady drip of water from one of the steel girders above and ended up brushing against her leg. I could feel my cheeks getting even hotter. 'He says I should have stood up to Elfie. Not let her say all that stuff,' I said.

'Did you speak to Elfie?'

I shook my head. 'Not yet.' I glanced down at the soggy newspapers at her feet. 'What are these?' I asked quickly.

'Stories about us,' she whispered. There was a rasp

in her voice that wasn't usually there. 'My dad picked them up this morning.'

'You're kidding!' I picked up a paper from the top of the pile and saw a picture of Elfie and Agnes on the front page. I read out the headline: 'Pop Go The Strikers – TV talent contest heightens picket-line tensions'.

'Bleedin' hell!' I said. Agnes shrugged and I picked up another one. This one had a picture of me, Alfie and Elfie which looked like it'd been ripped down the middle. The headline read: 'The Scabfather: "My baby's daddy is a scabby," says *Pop to the Top* teen mam'.

'Where have they got all this from?'

Agnes shook her head. 'I don't know.'

'Looks like Elfie's Plan C is working, I suppose.'

Agnes shivered a bit. She was only wearing a thin coat and I noticed she was blue with cold and her hair was still soaking. 'Do you want my jacket?' I said, feeling self-conscious.

'You are sure?' she said.

I nodded, pulling it off. I placed it round her shoulders, doing my best not to touch her or look her in the eye. I could smell the throat sweets on her breath and it made my ears go really hot. I pulled away quickly.

'Hey, losers, what's up?'

I looked up. And there was Elfie.

'Did anyone see you come, d'you reckon?' said Elfie. She was completely wet through. She was wearing some tiny summer dress that I seem to remember her having when she was about nine so it was way too small for her: the waist band was riding high up around her ribs and the hemline barely skirted her knickers. Her legs were splattered with mud and her hair was sticking to her face. She looked like some grubby street kid, but with loads of make-up on.

'I don't think so,' I said. 'Are you OK?'

'Sure,' said Elfie, her fingers skimming over her split lip and the bruising on her cheek which you could still see under all the make-up. She glanced down at the pile of papers and grinned. 'Plan C is going even better than I'd hoped, I see,' she said, changing the subject quickly. 'Have you decided who you're gonna sell your exclusive to?'

'What?'

'Which newspaper are you gonna tell your amazing *Pop to the Top* story to?' she said, flicking casually through the papers like being on the front page was something that happened to her every day. She didn't have her hair in its usual scruffy ponytail: instead it was hanging over her face like she didn't want anyone to see the blue swelling on her cheek.

'None of them,' I said flatly.

'Why not?' she lifted her head and gave me a look like I was being a total mug. 'Haven't you been listening, Jimmy Wigmore? This is the whole point of Plan C! You get a couple of hundred quid for telling some journo what a lying cow I am. What's the problem?' She looked tired and sounded cross and irritable.

I shrugged. I'd thought about this last night and I knew she'd be mad. I knew my dad would be mad too because he was all up for going to the press and setting the record straight, but there was still no way I was going to do it. 'Cos it'll make you look stupid.'

'It'll make me look more stupid if you don't,'

she said, staring at me with an expression I couldn't quite make out, then switching on a too-bright smile. 'Come on, this is the plan! I didn't put myself through all this grief just for you two to throw your chances away.'

'Yeah, but . . .'

'Just because I messed up don't mean you and Agnes should miss out,' she said, scrunching up her nose and shaking her hair. But, although she was trying to act normal, I could tell she wasn't OK. Not really. Her eyes weren't twinkling like they usually do when she's plotting and scheming.

'But you didn't mess up,' I said. 'Your dad –'

'Whatever,' she said quickly, not looking at me. 'Just cos I can't do the competition any more, doesn't mean Agnes has to drop out. Everyone knows she's the one with the real talent anyway. And that was Plan A, right. The original plan – win the competition. She can do that without me.'

'You're dropping out?' said Agnes. Her eyes were wide with shock, and her voice was cracked and husky.

Elfie just shrugged and sniffed loudly.

'Did your dad say you had to?' I asked.

'Not exactly,' she said, peering down at the chipped varnish on her nails.

'What he say?' asked Agnes.

'Nothing much,' said Elfie. 'Actually, nothing at all.' She looked up and I could see myself reflected in her pale eyes. 'But he's not about to sign the permission slip, is he? And I'm not gonna ask him.'

'I don't get it. Isn't he mad?'

She flicked her hair and said, 'He won't be after I quit the band.' She had the same look in her eyes that she gets each time her mam walks out, only more colourless somehow.

'I not want to sing without you,' said Agnes.

'Not that again!' said Elfie. 'Look, this works out for all of us. Jimmy scoops up a nice fee for putting his side of the story straight in the newspapers, and you,' she nodded her head at Agnes, 'go on and win the competition singing solo. Everyone's a winner.'

'What about you?' I asked. It had started raining really heavily and the sky had gone dark. Elfie had her hands up on one of the girders and she looked as if she was hanging there, her figure silhouetted against the sheets of rain behind her.

'I make a packet spilling my guts to a tabloid and apologising for all the hurt I've caused. My dad pays off his debts and forgives me.' She hesitated before adding, 'Hopefully.'

Then she pulled herself up on the girder and swung there for a moment, just like we used to when we were kids, when we had competitions to try and knock each other off – which she nearly always won.

'And what about Alfie?' I asked.

Elfie hung there, silent for a second, and suddenly I remembered the time she fell off and broke her wrist. She was the only kid on the children's ward whose mam didn't sleep over with her. Her dad stayed with her instead because her mam went to see some boy band play in Sheffield and didn't come back for three days.

'Well, I figure if I make us a fat wad of cash, we can bribe me mam to give him back. There's no way her maternal instincts are strong enough to resist that, right?' She was speaking really quickly and I wasn't sure if she was convincing herself but she certainly wasn't convincing me.

'But what if she won't?'

She dropped down on to the concrete and finished like one of those Olympic gymnasts, with her arms in the air. 'Well, Agnes had flipping better win,' she said crossly. 'Cos if everything else is going to go pants, *and* I don't have a Plan D, we might as well make sure one good thing comes of this. If Agnes becomes a star it won't have been a complete waste of time. Right?'

'But this was *your* plan, Elfie,' I said.

She scrunched up her nose then and said quietly, 'Plans change.'

Rules of Talent TV No. 21:
Know when to retire gracefully

Elfie

Me and Jimmy used to hang out on our bikes a lot when we were kids. We'd cycle round and round the close, making ramps off the pavements with old bits of wood and pretending to be stunt riders or policemen chasing baddies or superheroes. We rode the bikes on the marshes too, and the wheels threw up so much white dust we looked like snow men when we got back.

The new little biker gang are nowhere near as crazy and badass as we were. They do a few lame stunts and leave tyre tracks over Mrs Newsround's rhododendrons and that's about it. Kids today aren't what they used to be!

They were hanging round outside our house when I got back. About six of them. One of them had a camera phone and he started clicking when he saw me coming, like he was paparazzi or summat.

'Give us a smile, Elfie,' shouted the fat little ginger kid from number seven.

'Yeah, you're a celebrity now!' said the skinny one with the massive glasses.

I flicked my hair over the left side of my face and posed for a photo. My cheek throbbed painfully but I still gave a massive fake grin and jutted my hips out like all the celebs in me mam's magazines seem to do.

Then I saw Kirby and Pinkie, wearing matching jeggings and knock-off Ugg boots, sitting on Jimmy's front wall. Behind them I could see that someone had stuck a load of pictures of me and him from the newspaper all over the front door of his house.

'Seen you on TV last night, Elfie!' shouted Pinkie with a giant grin.

'Funny, I didn't see you,' I said.

'Is the kid really yours then?' said Kirby.

'What do *you* think?' I said.

'Your mam says you're making it all up,' said Pinkie.

I stopped, put my hands on my hips and narrowed my eyes, like me mam does when she's being hard as nails. 'Is that right?'

'Yeah. Did you see what she was saying about you in the paper?'

Pinkie was holding a copy of the local rag; Agnes's dad hadn't picked that one up so I hadn't seen it. I caught a glimpse of me mam staring into the camera with a wounded expression, wearing a brand-new red dress. My tummy did a sort of hollow flip.

'Yeah. Course I have,' I lied.

'You must be gutted then.'

'Not really,' I shrugged. 'Like I say, don't believe everything you read in the papers.'

Then one of the kids on the bikes – the one who looks like a boy cos her mam shaved all her hair off last month when she got nits – said, 'You were dead class last night, Elfie.'

And another one said, 'Yeah, you and that immo can sing dead well.'

'Ta very much,' I said. I gave Kirby a look and tossed my hair like I get fans coming up to me all the time.

Kirby laughed. 'Bet you wish you had *all* the boys falling over you like that, Elfie Baguley,' she said. 'Specially now fish-boy's gone all native on you.'

I flicked my hair again cos I could feel her staring at my split lip. 'What's that supposed to mean?'

'Check out page seventeen of the *Daily Post* and you'll see,' said Pinkie. She stood up and shoved a newspaper in my direction.

'Whatever,' I said with a shrug.

'Yeah. What do you care, right?' said Kirby. 'He was only your manny, so he can go round snogging who he likes.'

Then she and Pinkie laughed like she'd just made the funniest joke in the world. 'Anyway, gotta go,' she said. 'Happy reading. Oh, and you need to get some better foundation to cover up that shiner your old man gave you.'

They both went off giggling, leaving me with the biker kids who were taking more pictures of me on their camera phones and calling, 'Say cheese, Elfie!'

I put my hands on my hips, pulled a fake grin and posed some more.

I thought Jimmy and me would be best mates forever. Proper BFFs. I figured we'd fall out every now and

then and he'd get mad at me and I'd have to make it up
to him and all that, but basically we'd always be there
for each other, no matter what. I'd also sort of started
to think that me and Agnes were mates, too. Only it
turns out I was wrong about both of them. And it was
all there in black and white on page seventeen.

The weird thing was that I was more upset about
that than I had been about any of the other stuff, even
the thing with me dad. Cos I can cope with me mam
being a flakey cow. I can even cope with me dad being
mad at me. I can cope with all the neighbours staring
at me and the little biker kids going, 'Give us a song,
Elfie,' every time I leave the house. But I can't cope
with losing Jimmy Wigmore. Or maybe even the immo.

And I don't think there's a plan in the world that'd
sort this mess out.

Agnes

'What should we do?' I asked, after Elfie had gone.

'I dunno,' said Jimmy. He was staring in the

direction of Elfie's house with a worried expression on his face.

'Will you sell your story like she said?' I asked.

'No way!' he said, turning to me quickly. 'My dad wants me to. But I told him I won't do it. What about you?' He looked down at me, his eyes blinking as they met mine. 'Will you sing on your own?'

I shook my head.

Jimmy's face creased in concentration. 'We can't just let her drop out.'

'No,' I said.

Jimmy sighed. 'I suppose we've got to find a way to get her dad to sign that permission slip and then we've got to persuade her to sing,' he said. 'Only I've never managed to make Elfie do anything she didn't want to in my whole life. And her dad . . .' He tailed off.

The rain was falling more heavily now; cats and dogs, Elfie would call it.

'We could go round there,' I said. 'To her house.'

Jimmy turned to me. 'You and me?' he said, his face going red. 'Her dad'll kill us.'

'We go when he is not there maybe.'

Jimmy frowned again. 'And what'll we say, anyway?'

I thought of the way Elfie tipped her head on one side when she spun her stories. I inclined my head slightly. 'Maybe we tell her we have new plan,' I said.

'Do we?' he asked. 'Have a plan?'

'No. But we could tell her we do.'

Jimmy gave me a funny look and sort of laughed.

'You say if Elfie no have plan she –' I didn't have the words for what I was trying to say: that if Elfie didn't have a plan she would fall apart, like the moths' wings, papery and broken. Or be caught forever in her own spider's web of tales.

'It's OK. I know what you mean,' he said.

I remembered what Elfie had said about him and her – about them being like siblings, or an old married couple. About knowing each other inside out.

'Everyone reckons she does it for attention and she probably does – a bit,' said Jimmy. 'But that's not the real reason.'

He looked at me then and I nodded.

'OK,' he said with another big sigh. 'So we go and

talk to her, and if her dad kills us, at least we'll have died in a good cause.'

'OK,' I said.

He looked at me and I looked at him and then it suddenly felt really awkward so we both had to look away.

'Let's go then,' said Jimmy.

Jimmy

It felt weird walking along the road with Agnes but there was no need to sneak around any more cos everyone knew about the show anyway. The biker kids all stopped and stared at us as we went past and I heard Mrs Newsround's door swing open. Even though everyone was gawping at us, it was kind of nice not having to act like we didn't know each other, and I almost wanted to reach out and hold Agnes's hand – only I didn't. But as we got close to Elfie's house I still had no idea what we were going to say and I was really, really hoping her dad wouldn't be in.

Elfie came to the door when we knocked, wearing the teddy bear nightshirt and fluffy slippers that she'd had on the day her mam walked out. She'd rubbed all her make-up off and she looked pale and washed out. And really, really mad. She took one look at me and Agnes standing there and said, 'Go away!'

The biker kids had followed us down the road and were hanging around on the pavement just a few metres away and Mrs Winstanley was standing on her doorstep with a duster in her hand. Even Mrs Tyzack was leaning out of her window, smoking a fag and checking us out, so I felt pretty self-conscious but I figured there was no way I could back out now.

'We've come to tell you something,' I said quickly.

'Yeah? Well, if my dad sees you here, he's going to kill you,' said Elfie with a flick of her hair. 'So I'd scram if I were you.'

It was starting to get dark and even though it had stopped raining the sky was full of these big grey clouds with a pinky sheen from the sun setting behind the cooling towers.

'Is he in?' I asked. 'Your dad.'

'No, he went out but he'll be back any minute,' she said.

I breathed a sigh of relief but Elfie was still looking mad as anything and I couldn't work out what had happened to make her like this.

'What's she doing here?' she said, narrowing her eyes and staring at Agnes.

'Everyone knows now, Elfie. There's no point sneaking around any more,' I said, starting to go red.

She squinted harder than ever and said, 'I see.' Then she looked from me to Agnes and back again. 'So, go on, spit it out – whatever it is you've come to say.'

'Oh – um,' I could feel my face burning hotter and hotter. 'Well, we don't think you should drop out,' I said. 'So – um – we've got a new plan.'

Elfie glared. 'I'm supposed to be the man with the plan, Jimmy Wigmore. You know that.'

'I know,' I said, 'but Agnes and me have been talking and we reckon . . .'

'So it's all about you and her now, is it?' she said, shooting evil looks at Agnes. 'I thought we were supposed to be the dream team. You and me, Jimmy Wigmore.'

'Yeah, course, but –' I felt myself blinking madly. 'It's about the three of us, Elfie,' I said. 'We're all mates together, aren't we?'

'So what's all this about then?' She flung the newspaper at me and it hit me in the stomach before falling on to the doorstep. Half the pages came loose and scattered all over the path in front of us.

I glanced down and there was a picture of me and it had been cut round the edges so my ears looked massive and above it the headline said, 'She thinks she's the tart but actually he's two-timing her!'

My stomach sank like a diving bell, down to my stupid flipper feet. I bent down to gather up the bits of scattered paper.

'Well?' demanded Elfie, jabbing at the pages with her fluffy slipper-clad foot.

The grainy photo had obviously been taken on a mobile phone. But you could still clearly see Agnes planting a kiss on my lips. The caption under it read:

'Love rat dad cheating on teen mam with pop partner'.

'It's not what it looks like, Elfie,' I said desperately.

I didn't even dare look at Agnes.

Elfie glared at me. Her eyes looked bluer than usual, and prettier somehow.

'It's not, honest.'

She flicked her head again and wrinkled her freckly nose. The cut on her lip looked red and sore. 'It's not like I care if you want to snog the skinny immo anyway.'

'I – we –' I stammered, but I wasn't even sure what it was I wanted to say.

'You want us to get rid of the scab for you, Elfie?' shouted one of the little biker kids. I turned round to see them all gathered on their bikes, eyes boring into me.

'Nah. S'alright,' she said. 'I can handle these two.' Then she turned to me and said, 'See, I got my own little bouncers now!'

'You can't leave the band, Elfie!' I said hurriedly.

'What?' She peered at me suspiciously.

'It was your plan,' I said hurriedly. 'The Juliets

would never have even happened without you. You should sing in the final.'

Elfie snorted again. 'And that's what you and her –' she spat out the word – 'think, is it?'

'Yes,' I said quietly.

'I always knew you lost half your brains in the swimming pool,' said Elfie. 'And your immo girlfriend can't be all there either if she wants to go round snogging a big-eared chlorine kid like you.'

I couldn't even hear Agnes breathing any more.

'Look, I know you're mad, at me and Agnes, and at your mam and your dad, but –'

'You don't know anything about me, Jimmy Wigmore!' yelled Elfie. She was suddenly more angry than I'd ever seen her before. 'So don't come round here pretending you do.'

'I'm not –'

She cut me off. 'And I don't care about me mam or me dad or about you and her. I don't need any of you.'

She paused for a second, then glanced over at the eight-year-old ginger bouncer who was shifting from one foot to another like he was about to enter a boxing ring. Then she flicked her head again and said, 'I hope you and Agnes will be very happy together. But I'm out!'

She slammed the door in our faces and we were left standing there, with half the street staring at us.

I couldn't move for a minute. I just stared at Elfie's front door and all these pictures of stuff we'd done together flashed through my head. All the crazy plans and all the times we'd been in trouble. And how we said we'd be BFFs forever and ever.

'You heard what the lady said,' yelled the ginger biker kid. 'Get out of here before I have to kick you out!'

I turned to Agnes who looked pale and shaken, and said, 'I'm not sure that went quite according to plan.'

She shook her head and murmured, 'No.'

I glanced round. Mrs Tyzack had gone over to join Kirby's mam and Mrs Newsround and now they were all gossiping loudly and I could hear scraps of what they were saying: 'That scab family!' and 'Crying shame!' and 'Flaunting themselves on TV.' I glanced at Agnes again. She was shivering. Suddenly I just wanted to get her away from there.

'Have you ever been on the Mersey Ferry?' I asked quickly.

Agnes shook her head.

'Do you want to?'

She nodded quickly.

I glanced round at the little knot of people staring at us. 'OK, well – um – let's do that then. If you want?'

She nodded again. She still looked what my mam would call peaky – not quite well – but her eyes were bright and she was smiling.

'OK then. No one should come to Merseyside and not go on the ferry,' I said. 'I reckon it's practically illegal.'

Agnes

Me and Jimmy caught the train into Liverpool. My dad had said it was OK so long as I was back no later than five and I didn't sign up for any more reality TV shows while I was there. Jimmy hadn't told his parents where we were going.

'What about your swimming?' I asked. It was a Saturday so there was no school but I knew he normally did extra training.

He coloured and said, 'I told my dad yesterday I wouldn't swim till he went back to the picket line.'

I stared at him in surprise. 'Really?'

Jimmy nodded, but he didn't look like he wanted to talk about it so I didn't ask him any more.

We got off at Lime Street and walked down the massive stone steps. It had stopped raining for a bit and the sun had come out. My head was starting to clear and my throat didn't hurt so much. Jimmy talked the whole way there about the history of the city, pointing out the two cathedrals, the Albert Docks where ships brought in the coal to be burnt at the power station, the twin Liver-bird statues: one staring out to sea, one keeping an eye on the sprawling city behind. He talked and talked and talked. He talked more in that one morning than I think he had the whole time I'd known him. I think he was talking so much because he was nervous being around me. I didn't say much, just listened.

Then he took me down to the river and we queued up for the ferry. It was quite warm, so we went up on to the open deck and sat down on one of the chairs made out of lifeboats. The sun was glistening off the water. It was hard to believe it was the same river that ran beneath our bridge a few miles inland.

Jimmy and I stood side by side, leaning over the railings. 'That place used to employ sixteen-thousand men,' he said pointing to a vast shipyard that stood rusting further up-river.

'How you know all this?' I asked. My voice still sounded husky, not really like me.

'My dad,' he said. 'He used to talk about all this kind of stuff – before he got obsessed with the swimming.'

'Right,' I said, thinking how my father and Jimmy's father would get on, if they ever had the chance to get to know each other.

'He told me they built hundreds of ships there,' Jimmy went on. 'They were the pride of the seas, once.'

I looked over to the shipyard again. The place looked desolate, empty, the giant rusty cranes disfiguring the skyline.

I leant my body further over the railings so I could feel the metal against my ribs and the wind on my face. 'I been thinking about what you tell me one time,' I said. 'About the things you and Elfie do. When you little.'

He leaned forwards, too. For once we were the same height, our shoulders almost touching.

'Some of it was actually pretty cool,' he said quietly. 'Elfie never does anything unless it's BIG!'

I stared out towards the sea, wondering how far along the coast the Iron Men were, and whether they could see the rusting docks and the dead shipyards. 'Maybe we do something like that.'

'Like what?' said Jimmy.

'Like one of Elfie's crazy plans,' I said. My head felt even clearer out on the water, and my voice sounded more like normal already. 'To persuade her, you know. To rejoin the band.'

'Are you serious?' he said.

I nodded.

The ferry began to turn. Across the water, I could see the city of Liverpool, bathed in sunlight, the two cathedrals shaping the skyline and the buildings climbing up away from the docks.

'Only we'd have to talk to Clive Baguley, too,' said Jimmy. 'Cos I don't reckon Elfie will sing unless he tells her to.'

I nodded. 'And maybe we need to get all the strikers – how you say? – behind us?'

'Only how we gonna do that?'

'I not sure,' I said. 'Something big. So they can not ignore it. We could think of something, you and me?'

I turned to look at him then. I could see myself reflected in his pale anxious eyes. 'Maybe,' he said, uncertainly.

'We can call it Plan D,' I said.

Jimmy grinned. 'You sound like Elfie.'

I laughed. 'We in big trouble then!'

I smiled then, and so did he.

'OK,' said Jimmy. 'So, let's get planning.'

Rules of Talent TV No. 22:
Get the local community behind you

Jimmy

Going down to the picket line was Agnes's idea. I said she was mental when she suggested it, but she pointed out that we'd agreed to do whatever it took, no matter what the risks. We needed to speak to Elfie's dad when Elfie wasn't around and this was the only way to do it. She also reckoned we needed to get all the strikers on side or Clive Baguley would never go for it. 'We need whole community to support us,' she said. And I knew she was probably right – which meant Plan D was almost certainly doomed from the start.

You can see the picket line from my bedroom window: across the marshes, in the shadow of the eight towers, a few dozen men bunched up against the wire fencing, holding banners. You can even hear them chanting when the wind is blowing westwards. But I'd never been down there before; my dad always said I should steer clear in case there was any trouble. And the way I saw it, a scab kid and an immo pitching up and saying they needed a favour was *definitely* going to cause trouble.

The strikers watched us approach in silence. Cos it's so flat round here, they could see us coming from a long way off and it seemed to take ages, walking up that road with them all staring at us. If Elfie had been there she'd have said it was like the big showdown in one of them old cowboy movies. Only it didn't seem half as glamorous as that at the time. It just felt terrifying and like it was probably the most stupid thing I'd ever done.

As we got closer I could see Clive Baguley had stepped to the front of the crowd, his face still swollen from where my dad had punched him. We stopped a few metres off. The wind was blowing, making the wire fencing around the plant rattle and creak.

'What do you want, kid?' shouted one of the men near the back of the crowd.

'That's Brian Wigmore's son,' I heard someone else say.

'And that immo kid. What they doing here?'

'Scabs aren't welcome round here!' shouted a man near the front, just along from Clive Baguley.

'Let the boy speak if he's got summat to say,' said a man just behind him. A face I recognised – Kirby Winstanley's dad. 'What've you got to say, son?'

I opened my mouth only suddenly I thought I was going to be sick, like, properly throw-up-on-my-shoes sick. Because you should have seen the expressions on their faces. Like they wanted to beat us within an inch of our lives and then string us up from the railings. And suddenly I knew how Agnes must feel when she's on stage and everyone's looking at her, waiting for her to sing only nothing is coming out. Because right then I thought I was going to bottle it, I really did.

But then I felt Agnes's fingers weave their way round mine and a pulse of adrenalin went up my arm. I tried to imagine closing my eyes, raising my arms and diving into the blue. 'Don't think about the outcome,' my dad always says. 'Execute the technique and forget about everyone else around you, and you'll come out on top.

And this was for Elfie and Alfie, and Agnes, too, so there was no way I could bail out.

I cleared my throat, took another deep breath and said, 'Mr Baguley, we need some paint.'

A ripple of laughter rose up from the crowd of men. Clive Baguley just stared at me for a second. 'This is a joke, right?'

'No, sir,' I said, my voice catching again. 'We want to borrow some of your red paint.' My voice cracked on the last word and I felt so hot I knew my face must be bright red.

Clive Baguley glanced round at the men standing by him. There was more laugher and shuffling of feet – like they were getting ready to stampede. I imagined being trampled by a load of rioters. I wondered how long it would take to die that way.

'And what will you be needing red paint for, Jimmy?' Clive Baguley said with an expression on his face that reminded me of Elfie's when she'd chucked the newspaper at me.

I could feel myself getting hotter and hotter. 'The thing is we think Elfie should sing in the finals,'

I said. 'With Agnes,' I added quickly.

'You having a laugh, son?' shouted a short bald man, who was standing near the railings.

Elfie's dad's expression didn't change. 'Your old man send you down here, did he?'

There was an angry muttering around him at the mention of my dad and I heard scraps of words: 'Dirty scab!', 'Traitor' – that sort of thing.

Agnes curled her fingers tighter into my own until I could hardly feel where mine started and hers began. I looked down at our hands, hanging in the air between us.

'No,' I said. 'He told me I couldn't have anything to do with Elfie.'

Agnes was staring hard at Clive Baguley, her dark eyes bright. I wondered what she really thought about all this, whether she wished she were back on the beach at home. She still looked pale and ill and suddenly I really wished I hadn't let her come. I should have come on my own.

Clive Baguley sniffed loudly. A few of the men around him were still muttering stuff about my dad.

'At least me and your old man agree on something then!' he said at last.

'But I told him I wasn't just going to just drop her, not for you or for him,' I said, trying to sound a lot braver than I felt.

Clive Baguley raised an eyebrow. 'Fighting talk, eh, son! Looking for a punch-up, like your dad?'

'No, sir.'

'What you come here for then?' yelled a man on his right.

Clive Baguley continued to stare hard at me.

I still had the sick feeling in my stomach as I glanced around the sea of faces, and then back at Agnes. I knew I didn't want to let her down. Or Elfie.

'You've all seen me and Elfie and Agnes on the TV,' I said.

'Yeah, and in the papers and all!' shouted a voice from over by the gates. I didn't look to see where it was coming from. And I didn't look at Clive Baguley because I knew if I did, I'd lose my nerve.

'So – um –' I stammered, suddenly not sure what I was actually going to say even though me and Agnes had talked about it all the way here. 'Well, um – if there's one thing Elfie's taught me, it's the power of TV,' I said.

'I heard she taught you a few other things, an' all, son,' said another voice.

A light ripple of laughter from the crowd. The wind whipped up quickly and sent a shudder down the railings.

Agnes's hand suddenly felt cold and small in my giant sweaty palm. 'So the thing is – um – I reckon Elfie Baguley's – um – done you all a favour,' I went on. I could hear my own heart beat, amplified loud in my ears like it is underwater, the wind swirling it about my head.

'How do you reckon that then?' said Elfie's dad.

'She made the whole strike look stupid!' yelled a man who lives down our street – one of the ones who'd been screaming 'Scab!' at my dad every opportunity he got.

'But she got the strike on the front page of the nationals,' I said. 'And on the news, an' all.'

'So what?' shouted another voice.

'So maybe that will help with the negotiations,' I said. 'Maybe management can find jobs for the immos and for some local men, too.' I said hopefully. I could feel impatience growing all around me and I knew I didn't have long before they all started shouting me down. I kept trying to imagine like I was swimming, just one stroke after another. 'And anyway, I think we should all set aside our differences and show that we can come together as a community. You know, to support two local kids, help them follow their dreams.'

'Why?' said a massive man standing in front of Clive Baguley.

Everyone waited for me to reply. The air around me seemed quieter suddenly.

'Cos Elfie's had a hard time,' I said, feeling myself getting hotter and hotter. 'With her mam and Alfie. And –' I hesitated and looked at Clive Baguley – 'and worrying about money, and her dad and . . .'

A shadow crossed over Elfie's dad's face. I stared at the purple bruising round his jaw where my dad had punched him. I was still sort of surprised that my dad could do so much damage.

'She was worried about you,' I said, talking directly to him now. The wind had picked up and I had to shout to make myself heard. 'She entered the competition to try and make things right,' I went on, knowing it was too late to stop now. 'She thought if she won then you wouldn't have to fret about money any more. You could say she was doing her bit for the strike effort,' I added.

'Is that so?' said Clive Baguley.

My hands felt numb – I could hardly even feel Agnes's fingers. 'Yeah. She did it for you,' I said. I was speaking way too fast and my voice was coming out a bit squeaky but I knew I had to say what I'd come to say quickly before I lost my nerve, or they went for us, or both. 'And Alfie. She knew you'd be mad but she figured you'd realise she was only trying to help in the end. Only now she's saying she won't sing because she thinks you don't want her to. And it seems to me,' I glanced up at the eight towers – the cause of all this bother – and tried to pretend there weren't forty angry strikers all staring at me as I looked Clive Baguley straight in the eye, 'it's time somebody looked out for Elfie a bit. And so that's what I'm doing. And Agnes, too.'

Elfie's dad glanced at Agnes for the first time. She went pink and her fingers started to slip out of mine so I gripped them tight. Above us a couple of seagulls wheeled and screamed, their voices angry, barking.

The strikers were still now, staring at us. Clive Baguley didn't say anything for a very long moment. I braced myself for getting punched in the face. But when he finally spoke all he said was, 'My Elfie know you're here?'

'No,' I said.

'Reckon she'll be mad when she finds out, do you?'

'Yup,' I said. Then I added quietly, 'You know Elfie.'

Another burst of laughter erupted from the crowd, louder this time. I heard a voice say, 'Like father, like daughter, eh, Clive!'

Elfie's dad gave another grim smile but kept staring at me. 'But you came anyway?'

'Yes, sir,' I said.

He let out a short quick laugh. 'Well, you've got more guts than I put you down for, that's for sure.'

A voice from the back of the crowd called out, 'Watch out, Clive, or he might plant one on you, like his old man!'

More noisy laughter. I tried to keep my head up and maintain eye contact but I could feel myself blinking furiously.

Clive Baguley narrowed his eyes at me as another gust of wind rattled through the railings. 'I always figured my Elfie had you under the thumb,' he said. 'But maybe I was wrong.'

He glanced at the other men around him and I wondered what I'd do if they just went for us. 'What makes you think I've got red paint, anyway?' he said.

I felt a pulse of adrenaline in my stomach, the feeling I get when I can see the finish line but my muscles are screaming and I don't know if I can even make it. 'You painted "Scab" on our house,' I said. 'I figured you must have some left over.'

He eyeballed me for a long moment and I tried really, really hard not to look away. This was it: he was either going to kill me or – or . . . or I didn't know what exactly.

He let out a long low sigh, glanced back at the eight towers then turned to look at me. 'Maybe the kid's got a point,' he said slowly.

'What about, exactly?' shouted a bald man to his left. The seagulls screeched overhead.

'About what we're supposed to be doing this for anyway – to give our kids a better future,' Clive Baguley said.

'Yeah. It's not the kids' fight, is it?' said Mr Winstanley.

'That's not what you was saying earlier,' said the short bald man.

'Well I'm the first to admit I'm wrong then,' said Clive Baguley.

The crowd were muttering again but lower than before – less hostile.

'Can't exactly do any harm supporting a couple of kids in a singing show, can it?' I heard Mr Winstanley say.

'Not unless Clive starts singing himself,' said a red-faced man in the front row. 'Voice like a flippin' foghorn, he's got!'

There was laughter then, lots of it. Clive Baguley turned round to me and Agnes and he still didn't look exactly happy but his expression had softened. 'OK, so what exactly have you got in mind for this paint, huh?'

Agnes held on to my hand the whole time I was explaining about our plan: Plan D. I couldn't quite believe we might be about to pull it off. After I'd explained and Clive Baguley had agreed to help us my whole body felt drained, like I'd done a mega session in the pool.

Then one of the strikers yelled, 'Give us a song then.'

Everyone was looking at me and Agnes again. Blood shot up into my cheeks and I felt her fingers tighten around mine. 'Um – I can't sing,' I muttered.

'Not you! The immo kid!' said the red-faced man on the front row with a lopsided grin.

Agnes's fingers seemed to go cold suddenly. She looked up at me. 'I can't,' she said. 'Not without Elfie.'

'Come on!' shouted another voice.

'We might even vote for you then!' shouted the bald man who'd been so angry earlier.

'Sing us that one you did on the telly,' said Mr Winstanley. 'The one you did with his Elfie.'

Agnes looked up, met Clive Baguley's eye.

He nodded. 'It were nice that were,' he said.

For a moment I wasn't sure if she was going to faint in my arms or be sick on my shoes.

Then she said the last thing I expected. She looked at me and said, 'OK.'

So she sang 'You'll never walk alone' – not the song Elfie and her did on the first audition show but the one they'd been practising recently. It was a pretty inspired choice, given the circumstances. I don't think even Elfie could have scripted it better.

She sang quietly at first, her eyes closed, every single one of the men hushed and still watching her. Then gradually her voice began to rise, clear and pure, carrying over the sound of the wind and the seagulls, soaring up towards the sky where the white smoke belched endlessly in the blue.

All the strikers cheered after she finished and

some of them called for an encore. Even Clive Baguley was clapping.

I couldn't quite believe it – and I had no idea exactly how we'd managed it but it seemed like Elfie's dad and the strikers were now behind The Juliets all the way.

Now all we had to do was get Elfie back on side.

Agnes

Jimmy said it was just like the stuff him and Elfie had done when they were kids. The only difference was that this time we really, really needed it to work.

We used all of Jimmy's swimming towels (Jimmy said his dad was mad enough at him already so it could hardly get any worse) and some of Elfie's mam's favourite pink satin sheets. And we used most of the can of red paint, too.

It took hours and we got red paint all over ourselves – in our hair and splattered across our clothes. When we'd finished we both stood back, tired and grubby, and looked at what we'd done.

'Do you reckon it'll work?' Jimmy said.

'I don't know,' I replied.

'Me neither,' said Jimmy.

And we really didn't. The thing with Elfie Baguley is, you just never know what to expect.

Rules of Talent TV No. 23:
Never give up on your dreams

Elfie

Last night I had this dream about when me and
Jimmy were kids. Only I dreamt Agnes was with us,
too, and Alfie – all four of us playing on the marshes.
It was one of them dreams that was so nice that when
I woke up and remembered they were all gone, I felt
worse than ever.

Then me dad pushed open the door. He was
holding a cup of tea and a slice of toast. 'Breakfast in
bed?' he said.

I couldn't work out if he was still mad at me or
what, so I sat up quickly and took the mug off him.
'Thanks,' I said. I took a sip and watched him, trying
to work out from his face what was going on but he
wasn't giving much away.

He sat down on the end of the bed. 'This the little

man's?' he asked, picking up Alfie's bit of blankie from beside me.

I nodded. 'It doesn't smell of him now though,' I said.

'Not as good as the real thing, eh?'

I shook my head. My stomach was tight and I could feel the bruising on my face where he had caught me with his fist.

He was still looking down and fingering the scrap of blanket. 'I'm sorry,' he said. 'You know, about me and your mam – the way things are . . .'

'It's not your fault, Dad, she –'

He looked up. 'Yes it is. Mine as much as your mam's. What is it they say? It takes two to tango.'

I stared down at my cup of tea and said nothing. I could feel my dad looking at me. My face hurt all over and my stomach ached the way it had after Alfie had gone away. He reached out his hand and touched my left cheek where the bruising was. I looked up at him.

'And I'm sorry about this, an' all,' he said.

I could feel the tears coming then and I didn't want them to so I blinked hard – only that made me think of Jimmy and his blinking and I felt even worse.

'I was mad as hell about everything but I never should have –' He broke off. 'I never should have blamed you.'

'But I let you down.'

'You were only trying to help,' he said. 'Only I was too stupid to see that. I'm sorry, love.'

I was holding on so tight to my cup of tea that my hand was shaking.

My dad lowered his hand and lifted up the scrap of blankie. 'I've asked your mam if I can take him along to the finals,' he said. 'So he can watch his big sister sing.'

My heart leaped and I nearly spilled my cup of tea all over the place. Only then I remembered.

'I told you. I'm not going, Dad.'

'Sure you are,' he said quietly. 'I hear it's being shown on live TV across the north west – maybe even the whole country. Least that's what the papers are saying. You can't go missing that. '

I looked down again, stared into the brown liquid. 'But the strike –'

'You reckon a couple of kids singing on TV can destroy my legendary strike force?' me dad said. I looked up and he was smiling. 'I'm sorry, kid. You were good but not that good!'

'But –'

'But nothing.' He took the cup of tea out of my hand and put it down on the table next to me. 'Listen, I've been so caught up in my own stuff I haven't been a great father lately.'

'You've had a lot on,' I said, the tears caught up in my throat making me talk funny.

'So have you from what I hear,' he said. He ran his hand over my hair like he used to when I was little.

I shrugged and sniffed back a load of tears that were getting clogged up in my nose. 'I guess.'

'But us Baguleys, we're tough, right?' he said. 'Can't knock us down easily.'

I nodded, my eyes forcing their way up to meet his. He was smiling.

'Exactly,' he said. 'And now you got to show the world we can sing an' all.'

The tears started to come properly then and I

couldn't stop them, and I didn't even know why I was crying because for a moment it was like everything was all right again. Me dad wasn't mad at me and I was gonna sing in the final and maybe Alfie would come along and watch and I'd get to hold him afterwards.

Only then I remembered about the picture in the newspaper, Jimmy and Agnes hooking up behind my back. My heart sank.

'I can't,' I said. 'Jimmy and Agnes . . .'

He grinned. 'Who do you think made me see sense?' he said.

I looked up and I reckon I must have had one of them comedy surprised expressions on my face cos my dad laughed.

'You spoke to Jimmy and Agnes?' I said.

'More like they spoke to me,' he said. 'Or your friend Jimmy did. I couldn't get a word in edgeways.'

'Jimmy Wigmore?' I said, trying to imagine Jimmy out-talking anyone, let alone me dad. 'What did he say?'

'Never mind that,' he said. 'Just go and look out your window.' His eyes were twinkling, like I'd not seen them do for ages.

'What're you going on about, Dad?' I said.

'Just for once, Elfie Baguley, will you stop asking questions and do as your old man tells you!' he said with a grin. 'Go on. Go and take a look.'

Jimmy

Elfie always says you've got to go for big gestures. No use doing things by halves, she reckons, not if you want to get noticed. Me, I'm usually more of a head-down kind of person. But I reckon Elfie's right: sometimes you've got to make a splash – stand up and be counted. The bigger the better.

Elfie

The letters were painted six-feet high on me mam's silk bed sheets and a load of swimming towels which'd been hung from the fences around the plant where the strikers usually stood. The blood-red words were so big you could read them from a mile off: 'Please Sing Elfie!'

And I'm not sure what I was expecting, but it wasn't that. Not in a million years. For a start, I never thought Jimmy had it in him to carry off a grand plan without me around – and how did they get the strikers to agree to it anyway? And how'd he get me mam's best sheets? And wasn't that the paint Jimmy's house got covered with?

'Took a lot of guts to do what they did,' me dad was saying. I was just staring at the letters, wondering what Jimmy's dad was going to say when he found out what Jimmy had done to all his swimming towels.

'Reckon you got a couple of pretty good mates there,' said me dad.

My tummy did a little leap. 'I suppose I've got to sing now,' I said.

'Yup,' he said, with a grin. 'I think you do.'

Jimmy

My dad went nuts about the towels. And he was even more mad when he heard about me and Agnes going down to the picket line to confront the strikers. 'You could have caused a riot!' he said. 'Anything could have happened to you.'

I stared down at my hands which were covered in red paint (Elfie had called me and Agnes 'the red-hand gang' and said there was no way she was hugging either of us till we had a shower).

'And I've been thinking about what you said the other day, an' all.'

I looked up.

'There's no way I'm going back to the picket line,' he said. 'D' you hear me?'

I thought about the way the men on the line had stared at us, thought of my dad facing that every day. I nodded.

'If you want to stop swimming that's your decision son. Just like whether I decide to strike is mine.' He looked me right in the eye when he said that. 'I won't go telling you what to do with your life; and you can do the same for me,' he said. 'Are we agreed?'

I nodded.

I thought of Elfie again and how she'd said that it was her decision to rejoin The Juliets and it had nothing to do with me and Agnes's 'silly plan'. She said she'd already decided to be the bigger person and forgive us for betraying her trust even before she saw a load of flipping towels hanging over the railings.

'So you don't mind if I give up the swimming?' I asked.

'I never said that, son. I just said it was your decision.'

'Right,' I said.

'I appreciate what you're trying to do for me,' he said quietly. 'And for your mam. But we're grown-ups. We can take the heat. And we want you to have this chance – if it's what you want, that is.'

'Thanks, Dad,' I said. I was so tired after staying up nearly all night doing Plan D that I wasn't even sure what I wanted any more.

'No need to decide straight away,' said my dad, looking right at me, his pale grey eyes just like mine only with more lines around them. 'A couple of days off training won't do you any harm. And if you tell me you really don't want to swim I promise to try and respect that. Although I'm not promising to find it easy!' He grinned then.

And so did I.

Rules of Talent TV No. 24: Put your heart and soul into the Grand Final!

Elfie

So, obviously the grand final is what it's all about when it comes to TV talent shows, right? And we had less than a week to practise. Jimmy and Agnes's big banner stunt might have been all very cool (not that I told them that: I couldn't have them thinking they'd saved the day now, could I?), only all their secret snogging meant we'd lost valuable rehearsal time. Jimmy reckoned it was easier training with his dad the lunatic swimming coach than it was with me these days.

The rest of the audition footage was being shown on TV every night that week after the news, and it felt like *Pop to the Top* was the only thing anyone ever talked about at school. People even started asking Agnes about it – like, actually talking to her in lessons and stuff. It was weird. And they'd laid off her and

Jimmy, too – which just goes to show the power of celebrity.

Tickets for the final at the Empire Theatre had totally sold out. There'd been loads of media hype about it and not just on Merseyside either. It was like the presenter bloke on *North West Tonight* said: me and Agnes's story had captured the nation's hearts (which was a bit of a cliché but I wasn't complaining). We were on the six o'clock news and the front of the tabloids and everything, and the strike even got a mention in Prime Minister's Question Time (me dad was well chuffed about that). Me, I was more excited about having our photo on the front of me mam's fave gossip mag. Oh, and the fact that cos of all the hoo-ha they were gonna show the final live on national TV – right across the nation!

It was basically just like I always planned!

The day of the final was totally mental. Proper Talent-TV whirlwind, roller coaster stuff. We got to rehearse on the massive stage with the lights and the TV cameras and all the sound effects and smoke machines and everything. Then there were all these hair and make-up people to transform us into dazzling pop icons (well, that was how Agnes looked – I just ended up looking like a young version of me mam, worse luck!). Back stage, all the contestants were running round shrieking and hugging each other and going on about how their lives were about to change forever, and the producer girl was panicking about lighting cues, and the presenter guy was going round with the tattooed cameraman filming backstage interview thingies while we got ready. Oh, and we also had to sort out the whole parental permission thing – boring – but apart from that it was all totally showbiz and brilliant.

And the whole time I was trying to work out what our chances were. Cos when it comes to live finals, anything can happen – the Rules of Talent TV go out of the window. But I did have one last plan up my sleeve (Plan E it was called, although I hadn't mentioned it to Jimmy and Agnes because it was topper than top secret).

Then finally it was show time and I figured we must be in with a shot when we stepped out on to the stage and the audience went totally mental. There were spotlights on us so we couldn't see much but the cheering was really loud and when I squinted out into the distance I could just make out loads of banners saying stuff like 'We love The Juliets' and 'Go Elfie!' and 'Agnes rocks'. And I don't know what was weirder – that all those people were there for us, or the fact that me dad was in the crowd, sitting next to Agnes's mam and dad and they were all wearing T-shirts saying 'Agnes and Elfie: Strikers' Choice' on them. I mean, who'd have bet on that happening two weeks ago, right?

The crowd just kept cheering and we hadn't even done anything. I couldn't stop meself from grinning, while Agnes – looking pale as a ghost in a white sheath dress (I knew she should have let me slap some of me mam's fake tan on her) – was doing some deep-sea diver breathing technique that Jimmy taught her. Finally, after what felt like about ten minutes, the clapping died down and the spotlight focused on the judges.

'You certainly know how to create a scene, I'll give you that!' said The Facelift. She didn't look like she hated us quite as much as usual. And a few whoops and cheers and a cry of 'Go Elfie!' came up from the audience.

'Welcome back, ladies,' said The Legend who was wearing a white tuxedo and a silver bow tie for the occasion. 'I wasn't sure if we were going to get to see you tonight.'

The audience laughed.

'Now, before you sing again, can I ask you the question we all want to know the answer to?' He paused. 'Why all the lies, Elfie?'

The crowd fell silent.

'Because with a voice like Agnes's, you don't need a wacky back story,' The Legend went on. 'Or a big soap-opera drama.'

I shrugged. 'Me mam once told me that lies are usually so much more interesting than the truth,' I said. And it occurred to me then that me mam wasn't exactly the best person in the world to take advice from.

'Didn't you tell *The Liverpool Echo* you'd like to sell your mam on eBay, only nobody'd buy her?' said The

Lingerie Lizard who was glowing luminous orange under the lights.

The audience laughed and there were a few whoops from the back row.

'It's just . . . once you've started spinning a story, it gets kind of hard to stop,' I said.

'That's about the most truthful thing you've said since the process started,' said The Facelift.

More laughter from the crowd.

The Legend waited for it to stop before he said, 'So, given everything that's happened, can you give me one good reason why you think you deserve to win this competition?'

I'd rehearsed this bit. I grinned. 'Because we've united a divided community,' I said brightly. 'And brought harmony and happiness where before there was hatred.' I paused. 'And because Agnes here is a proper little star – and I make great TV!'

I heard another laugh from the crowd, plus a few cheers, and another cry of 'Go, Elfie!' in a voice which sounded a lot like my dad.

'I suppose I can't argue with that!' said The Legend.

The Facelift looked as if she might like to, but she just pursed her lips and said nothing.

'So, now you've got the whole nation on tenterhooks, what are you going to sing for us?' said The Legend.

I glanced at Agnes. In the pale-blue lighting she looked like an ultra violet ghost and she was shivering a bit, but she was staring straight into the crowd with a really determined expression on her face, like she was looking for someone. It didn't take a genius to work out who.

'I thought maybe "You'll Never Walk Alone",' I said.

Big cheer from the audience!

'Well, you know what they say,' I said. 'When in Liverpool, and all that!'

The Legend raised an eyebrow for the camera. 'OK, let's hear it,' he said. And then all the lights dimmed.

The audience went mad for our performance. And no wonder cos it was totally brilliant – Agnes was dazzling and I was pretty flipping hot too if you must know. And the cheering went on and on for so long afterwards, even Agnes couldn't help smiling.

I reckon they should just have announced that we'd won it there and then; but instead we had to endure the whole long drum roll, voting-off-half-the-acts, eeking-out-the-suspense-as-long-as-possible process. Just the usual Grand Final clichés!

So before the half-time break they ditched Lap-Dancer Girl Band, Big Hair Lady and Handsome Student. The lap dancers all cried so much their faces looked like pandas, Big Hair Lady got gobby and shouted that it was a stitch-up and Handsome Student went round backstage saying he wasn't that bothered anyway cos he was already through to bootcamp on *Britain's Got Talent*. Then he started snogging one of the lap dancers and that seemed to cheer her up too.

So then there were only three acts left and we all had to sing again before they announced the overall winner. The IVF Boys had already sung, Girl-Who-Used-To-Be-A-Guy was on stage doing some kind of Spice Girls tribute medley and we were up next.

Standing next to me in the wings, waiting to go on, Agnes looked completely amazing in the white dress her mam lent her. Apparently she used to be a bit of a clubber in the eighties. 'So, you and Jimmy,' I said, looking down at the sparkly platform shoes Mrs Tyzack had lent me to go with Mrs Newsround's neon-pink playsuit (you would not believe what the women on our estate keep in the back of their wardrobes!).

'We just friends,' she said quickly.

I shrugged. 'Whatever. Doesn't bother me either way. Personally I think you make a good couple.'

I looked sidelong at her and I could see she was blushing slightly.

I stared straight ahead at Girl-Who-Used-To-Be-A-Guy who was doing some kind of samba wiggle to 'Spice Up Your Life'. 'So long as you know that Jimmy Wigmore is like family to me,' I said, in my best Merseyside Mafia voice. 'I love him like a brother. So if you hurt him, I won't just cut off your pinkie finger; I'll kill you. Got it?'

'Yes,' she said. I glanced at her quickly. She'd gone bright red but she was sort of smiling.

And that really should have been the end of everything. Me and Agnes would have made our peace and we'd all have had a big reunion then gone on to win the final. That's how I'd have written the script, if it was a soap opera.

Only in Talent TV – and in soap operas, I guess – there's always one more twist in the tale. Just when the contestants think it's all over, the organisers spring some last minute surprise on them. Or the press leak a story about the favourite being the love child of one of the judges, or the phone vote turns out to be rigged. There's always something to keep the public hooked right till the final seconds. And this was no exception.

Cos that was when me mam pitched up.

Agnes

I had never met Elfie's mother but even if I hadn't seen her in the papers, I'd still have known who she was right away. She looked just like Elfie, only without the freckles and with different eyes. Elfie has her dad's eyes; her mum's are flatter, more cat-like, with none of Elfie's sparkle to them. Janice Baguley was holding Alfie whose face lit up as soon as he saw Elfie. He stretched out his arms and fought to get free from Elfie's mam and cried out, 'Effie!'

Elfie froze. She looked like one of the Iron Men on the beach – stuck in the sand, unable to escape the tide.

On stage, Girl-Who-Used-To-Be-A-Guy was singing 'Mama' by the Spice Girls in a weird twisty voice that veered between tenor and soprano.

'Elfie, you were brilliant!' her mum was saying, moving towards us in what seemed like slow motion. She'd dyed her hair platinum blonde and she was wearing a green sequinned dress that made her look like a mermaid. Alfie was still struggling to get free from her arms, stretching out his fat little hands towards Elfie.

'I'm kinda in the middle of summat here, Mam,' said Elfie, staring at Alfie with bright, teary eyes.

'I know, Elfie love, but I need to tell you I've made a terrible mistake,' her mam said in a loud whisper. 'I want you and your dad to take me back. I want us to be a family again.'

Elfie was white as a sheet. She didn't scrunch up her nose or shake her hair or put her hands on her hips. She just stood totally still and reached out her hand to touch Alfie's little chubby one.

'Effie!' he said again. And a single black mascara tear trickled slowly out of her eye and made its way down her glittery face.

Elfie

I hate it when me mam walks out but I hate it even more when she comes back. Even when I was little and I missed her like crazy and all I wanted was for her to pitch up on the doorstep and beg me dad to give her one more chance – even then, I always hated it when she actually did come back. Cos I knew it'd only start all over again. So I'd start crying and she'd end up having a go at me because I wasn't glad to see her.

Only that wasn't why I cried this time. It was because of Alfie. The way his little eyes shone when he saw me, the way his tiny fingers grasped mine and the way he clung on to my neck so tight it almost frightened me. I buried my face into his cheeks and breathed in his little baby smell and realised he was shivering in my arms.

Everyone was staring at us. The IVF Boys and Big Hair Lady and Handsome Student (who'd stopped snogging the lap dancer and come up for air briefly) and all the other finalists, plus the tech crew and the producer with her clipboard. None of them were watching the stage any more; instead they were checking out the drama unfolding backstage.

Me mam was waving a newspaper around. 'This is my way of saying sorry,' she said, forgetting to whisper again.

I stared at the newspaper. On the front was a picture of me mam with her new platinum hair, under a headline saying: 'Take me back, Elfie!'

I looked at it for a long moment, as Alfie started to lick my nose with his warm little tongue.

'So, Elfie love, what do you say?' me mam purred, glancing round at the contestants and crew, clearly enjoying the audience. 'Can you forgive me?'

Just then a voice from behind her said, 'Are you for real?'

Girl-Who-Used-To-Be-A-Guy was belting out the high note of 'Mama' on stage but no one backstage was taking any notice. Everyone swung round to see me dad appear from the direction of the dressing rooms. He'd shaved properly for the first time in weeks and even though he was wearing the daft T-shirt with a picture of me and Agnes on it, he still looked good. Just like he did in the photos of him and me mam when they were young.

I didn't even stop to think what on earth he was doing backstage because I'd never been so glad to see him in my life. I had no idea how me mam had made it past security either. It all just seemed part of the soap opera that my life was turning out to be.

'I just want another chance, Clive,' said me mam, taking a step towards him. 'Let me come back and show you I've changed.'

Me dad glanced at the little audience which had collected around us in the wings. Girl-Who-Used-To-

Be-A-Guy was launching into her final chorus so, by my reckoning, we had about sixty seconds before we were due back on stage. 'Haven't you messed these kids around enough already, Janice?' he said.

'I was only a kid meself when I become a mam,' she said, too loud again.

'That's our fault, not theirs,' me dad replied quietly.

'You know what I'm like,' me mam said, taking another step towards him. 'I'm not good at all the mumsy stuff. I'm a free spirit. But it doesn't mean I don't love you all.' She reached out and put a hand on his lapel and smoothed it down, then glanced up into his eyes.

'I know,' me dad sighed. 'I'm just not sure that's enough any more.'

'Come on, Clive,' me mam said, moving closer still, so that they were nearly touching. 'You know it'll never be over between you and me, don't you?'

The moment before he answered seemed to last forever.

'Actually, I'm not sure that I do any more.'

Me mam's face fell. 'You what?'

I couldn't quite believe what I was hearing. I took a deep breath as Alfie started nibbling on my left ear.

On the stage, Girl-Who-Used-To-Be-A-Guy was warbling out the final note of her ballad.

'You heard what I said. It's over, Janice. I'm done.'

'But . . .'

Girl-Who-Used-To-Be-A-Guy was still holding on to that final note for all she was worth.

'I'm not letting you hurt the kids any more. We're divorcing you. And fighting for full custody of Alfie.' Me dad turned to me and said, 'In't that right, Elfie?'

I nodded as the music on stage came crashing to an end and the audience erupted into applause – which seemed completely appropriate.

Me dad put an arm round me as Alfie stirred contentedly in my arms. And I could smell his warm baby smell mingled with me dad's aftershave. And in the auditorium the applause went on and on and on.

Jimmy

I stood on the edge of the pool and glanced along at the other contestants. In my head I ran through all my dad had taught me – about starts and turns and breath control and sprint finishes. I remembered what he'd said about not focusing on the outcome: just concentrating on perfecting the technique then everything else would fall into place.

I had to miss Elfie and Agnes's Grand Final. My dad might have got his head round the idea of me hanging out with Elfie Baguley (it probably helped that all the stuff got cleaned off our house and the abuse sort of stopped – on Clive Baguley's orders), but after I'd said I wanted to swim again, there was no way he was going to let me miss Nationals, not for anything on this earth – and certainly not so I could go and watch the *Pop to the Top* final.

So, while Elfie and Agnes went off to Liverpool, me and my dad were on a train to Wolverhampton. I had my kit bag in one hand, energy drink in the other, and my dad was so nervous he looked like he was going to be sick. He didn't say much. But when the guard announced that we were approaching Wolverhampton station, he turned and looked me straight in the eye. 'You know your mam and me are dead proud of you, son,' he said.

'Oh – um – yeah,' I said awkwardly, reaching for my kit bag.

'I know I always go on at you about the swimming – sometimes too much,' he went on. 'But it doesn't matter to me how you do today. I'm proud of you, whatever happens.'

'Really?' I said. The woman sitting opposite us was listening and so was the old man across the aisle. I could feel my ears burning.

'You and that crazy girlfriend of yours –'

'She's not my girlfriend, Dad!' I said quickly.

'OK, you and Elfie – and the other lass, Agnes –' he pronounced it 'Agg-ness'. 'You made a load of grown men see sense and I'm proud of you.'

'Thanks, Dad,' I said. And then, as the train pulled into the station, I said, 'And I'm sorry – you know – about saying I wouldn't swim.'

'I was pushing you too hard,' he said.

'No,' I said, 'you weren't. I mean, you were pushing me but I'm glad you did. And I want to do this. For me.'

He just nodded.

That's what I was thinking of when I was waiting for the race to start: about how I'd missed the water. Then the starter horn blew and the flag came down and suddenly I remembered the look on Elfie's face when she'd told us she was rejoining the band, and Agnes laughing with red paint all over her hair. The smell of cherries and cough sweets and the taste of tea-bag cigarettes. Then I launched myself into the water.

Agnes

Elfie said the way to keep the public on your side is to keep them guessing right till the end. 'The more twists and turns in your story the better,' she said. But I don't know if she planned what happened or whether she took herself by surprise, too. She said it was Plan E, but I'm not so sure.

Elfie still had mascara streaks down her face and her hair was all messed up from where Alfie had tangled his fingers in it. But the audience went mad again when our names were announced, and when the cheering died down Elfie stepped forward and grabbed the microphone from the presenter before he had time to speak.

'I just want to say something,' she said.

The microphone made a weird tinny whistle.

'What now?' said The Legend.

I glanced at Elfie, alarmed. There were butterflies in my stomach that night – not moths. Butterflies with multi-coloured wings that caught in the flickering stage lights.

'It's pretty obvious to everyone here who the real talent in this double act is, right?' said Elfie. She nodded her head significantly in my direction and I felt my breath catch in my chest.

'Plus, we all know the judges think Agnes would stand a better chance if she sang solo.'

'Elfie!' I said, my voice barely a whisper.

Elfie ignored me and went on. 'Only you probably know about the stuff her and Jimmy did to get me to rejoin the band, which was actually –' she paused and scrunched up her nose like she really didn't want to have to say the next bit – 'well it was probably the nicest thing anyone's ever done for me,' she said hurriedly.

The audience laughed and Elfie scrunched up her nose some more and didn't look at me.

'Yeah, well, it might have been dead class, but it was also well daft!' she said. 'I mean, it's not like I even want to be a singer – I was only in it for the prize money and the headlines.'

The audience laughed even louder and I could see The Legend leaning back on his seat and watching with a bemused smile on his face. The producer was clutching his earpiece and looking worried.

'But Agnes . . . ' for once she actually pronounced my name properly and she turned to look at me as she said it. The butterflies paused momentarily in their dance. 'Well, Agnes is a proper star and she deserves to win this. And that,' she paused. 'That is the only reason I agreed to come here tonight.'

The audience had gone silent. The presenter was hovering uncertainly to Elfie's left, his hand up to his earpiece, clearly wondering what he was supposed to be doing.

'What's going on, Elfie?' I whispered. The disco ball hanging above us was making little light spots dance and leap across the stage, and over me and Elfie like butterflies fluttering all about us.

She turned to look at me. 'We both know you'd never have come on your own,' she said. 'So I figured somebody needed to give you a little push. Cos that's what mates do for each other, right?'

She kept looking right at me, her green eyes ringed with smudged mascara and twinkly purple eyeshadow. I looked right back at her and said nothing.

'Elfie!' said The Legend. 'What exactly are you saying?'

'I'm saying,' said Elfie, turning back to the audience and speaking in a strangely grown-up voice. The butterflies in my stomach were completely still and I felt as if my heart had stopped beating too. 'That it's time for me to step aside and let you all listen to Agnes's amazing voice. Solo.'

'Elfie, no!' I breathed, the words barely audible. The butterfly lights' coloured wings fluttered above me but the wings in my stomach were still.

'So, just to be clear,' said The Legend. 'You are saying you quit?'

'Again?' said The Facelift, raising an eyebrow.

'Yes,' said Elfie. 'I'm saying I quit.' Then before I could say anything, she turned to me and whispered, 'You'll thank me for this one day. Knock 'em dead, kid.'

Stage fright, Jimmy called it. But it's more than just fright, or fear. Fear is an emotion but what I feel when I'm standing on stage and everyone is waiting for me to sing is more than that, more than just something in my head and my heart. It's physical; it takes over my whole body. It's like being paralysed – a numbness that travels through every bit of me, clamps my mouth shut, tightens like an iron fist around my stomach and pounds so hard in my brain I see light spots dancing before my eyes, and feel papery wings clogging my throat.

But not that day. When Elfie stepped off the stage I panicked for a moment, but then I watched the coloured lights dance over the stage and I thought of rain under the bridge, Alfie eating cheesy Wotsits, and the way Jimmy smelled of chlorine when I kissed him. I thought of the Iron Men on the beach, the taste of tannin cigarettes, Alfie clinging to his sister in the wings.

Then I opened my mouth and I started to sing.

Jimmy

I turned up just in time. I missed Elfie's big speech (which meant I had to watch it on YouTube about a million times the next day and tell her how awesome she was) but I did get to see Agnes's final performance.

When me and my dad slipped in the back of the theatre, she was standing in the middle of an empty stage, a giant disco ball suspended above sending hundreds of coloured lights dancing over her. She was wearing a white dress that had belonged to her mam and her hair was down over her shoulders. She looked like an angel and when she started to sing she shone like a star. Nobody moved, everyone in the audience seemed to hold their breath. And I felt like I do when I'm underwater – suspended, for a few moments, caught up in the current of something timeless, ageless, utterly beautiful.

I don't think she'd ever sung as well as she did that night. Elfie said it was her inspirational speech and act of extreme selflessness which elevated Agnes's singing on to a whole new plane. And she might have been right, I suppose – although there is *definitely* no way I'm ever gonna tell her so.

Rules of Talent TV No. 25: Always look like you don't think you're going to win, even if you reckon you're a dead cert

Elfie

Jimmy Wigmore reckons I've got a tale-telling face. He reckons he can always tell if I'm making stuff up by some expression I make, or something I do with my head or whatever. Before the final, he said I needed to work on my results face, cos apparently I never looked worried enough when I was waiting to hear if we were through, and I never seemed surprised enough when I found out we were. He thought it'd make the public think I was smug or arrogant. And he might have had a point, only it wasn't exactly helpful. Cos the more you think about what your face is doing when you've got a load of TV cameras pointed at you and about 2,000 people in the audience watching, the harder it is to make it do what you want.

They hauled me on stage for the big results announcement, even though I kept saying that Agnes was a solo artist now. It wasn't until we were standing up there on stage, with the presenter guy saying, 'And the winner of *Pop to the Top* is . . .' that it kind of dawned on me what a dumb plan this had all been anyway. I mean, what were the chances of us actually scooping the big prize money? About a million to one, probably.

I could see Agnes's mum and dad in the crowd. And in the wings I could see me dad with Alfie in his arms (me mam had stormed off earlier – I figured we'd see her face in the papers again the next day, but she was gone for now and that was all that mattered). They had the theme tune to *Star Wars* playing and flashing lights were moving between me and Agnes, the IVF Boys and Girl-Who-Used-To-Be-A-Guy.

'And the winner of *Pop to the Top*, recipient of a cheque for £25,000 and a recording contract with Legend Studios is . . .' The presenter paused. There was a drum roll in the background.

The presenter stood mute, waiting for the signal

in his ear to deliver the final verdict.

'How much longer do you think they can string it out!' I whispered.

Agnes giggled.

That was when I spotted Jimmy and his dad; they must have slipped in at the back. I half expected him to still have wet hair, and his trunks and goggles still on, but of course he didn't. He was in his usual scruffy T-shirt and jeans but I noticed he was wearing a medal and a big grin on his face. He had his dad with him, too, and he was beaming from ear to ear.

'I suppose we're friends now, or whatever,' I whispered to Agnes.

'I suppose so,' she said.

'I might even talk to you when we go back to school after half-term if you're lucky.'

'That would be good,' she said.

'And the winner is . . .'

Jimmy

It all started on the day Elfie's mam left (for the fourteenth time – or was it fifteenth?). And it all came to an end the day she tried to come back. Elfie's plans have always been about her walkabout mam, one way or another.

The TV people threw this after-show celebration thing. Elfie reckoned it wasn't really much of a party. She said drinks and nibbles down at the daytime TV studios on the Albert Docks wasn't her idea of getting the party started. But there was sparkling wine in plastic cups and Elfie even managed to nick a glass for us to share, mixed in with our orange juice so no one would notice.

Then the three of us ducked out of the party and went to sit down on the docks, staring out at the lights over the River Mersey, Agnes on one side, me on the other, Elfie in the middle.

'So how did your dad even know what your mam was up to?' I asked.

'My little bouncer tipped him off,' Elfie said.

'Said he'd seen her going round by the stage door.'

'Which kid?'

'The ginger one. He reckons he's my personal bodyguard or summat.'

'Bet he wants to be your boyfriend an' all,' I said, grinning. Cos the funny thing about standing up to my dad and Elfie's dad was that I didn't feel like it was so hard to stand up to Elfie any more either. I mean, I figured I'd probably still do whatever she asked ninety-nine per cent of the time, but when it came to the things that really mattered, I didn't feel like a total pushover.

'Yeeuk! He's about eight years old!' said Elfie, scrunching up her nose so that all her freckles ran into each other. Her feet were dangling down towards the dark water below and I reckoned that any minute one of her platform sandals was going to go flying off into the black depths – and if it did she'd probably send me in after it. And I'd probably go, too. I might not be a pushover any more, but you've got to choose your battles, right?

'I hear you did good in your swim thing, Jimmy

Wigmore,' Elfie said.

'Yeah. I sort of won,' I said. I glanced at Agnes who was sitting on the other side of Elfie. She looked luminous under the lights. She caught my eye and smiled.

'Will you get your funding now?' Agnes said quietly.

She hadn't spoken much since the show finished and I could feel myself colouring, just hearing her voice.

'Yeah, and you'll get in that Olympic target squad thingie, right?' Elfie cut in.

'Um – yeah – at least my dad reckons so.' I glanced back into the brightly lit room behind us where my dad was standing next to my mam, looking awkward in a shirt and tie, talking to The Legend. He had my medal in his pocket now and I could see his hand resting on it the whole time.

'Not going off to some poncey school, I hope?' said Elfie.

'Nah,' I said. 'I told my dad I want to stay where I am.'

475

'Good call,' said Elfie. 'We'd probably sort of miss you if you weren't around.'

I figured this was the closest I was going to get to Elfie saying we were mates again, so I just grinned down into the dark water below and said nothing.

'And if he does try to drag you off to Malory Towers or Hogwarts or wherever, we'll come up with a plan to save you, won't we, Agnes?' Elfie went on, flicking her hair and checking out her reflection in the Mersey.

I looked at Agnes, who didn't catch my eye but just muttered, 'Um – yes.'

I sighed. 'No more plans, Elfie, please!'

'Only kidding, Jimmy Wigmore,' Elfie grinned. 'I've had enough of plans, me. I'm going into PR. Hey! You should sign me. I could get you loads of exposure. Interviews for a few teen mags, half-naked photos in *Heat* – that sort of thing.'

'No, thanks. I've been in the papers enough to last me a lifetime,' I said.

'You're a wimp, Jimmy Wigmore,' said Elfie, taking another slug of her stolen wine and orange juice and then passing it to me. 'No such thing as too much publicity, I say. You wait till you see the interview I'm doing in the *Sun*.'

I groaned and looked across at Agnes again. She was smiling a faraway smile now, like she was thinking of her home in Portugal, bathed in sunshine. 'What have you said this time, Elfie?'

Elfie swivelled her eyes towards me. 'Nothing you need to worry about,' she said. 'Only that me dad's on the lookout for a new girlfriend.' She kicked her legs and grinned. 'And that I wish you two love birds would get on with it and snog each other again cos this whole 'will-they-won't-they?' thing is just getting boring now!'

The final rule of Talent TV:
Second place is the new first!

Elfie

In the end, it turned out better than I could have planned. The Juliets didn't actually win *Pop to the Top*; we were pipped to the top spot by Girl-Who-Used-To-Be-A-Guy, only everyone reckoned it was a stitch up by the TV company. The *Liverpool Echo* said they fiddled it cos they didn't think it looked good if we won after all the lies and stuff, which of course they totally denied. So what can you do? Anyway, I reckon if we'd come first it would've have been a bit too cheesy, so I figure it's better this way. You know what they say: first the worst, second the best. And second is the new first when it comes to Talent TV, if you ask me – and if anyone would know, it's me!

The press obviously thought so too, cos they were queuing up to interview me and Agnes afterwards. Agnes was suddenly the most bankable act in the whole show. And nobody cared that Alfie wasn't mine and that I'd made half the other stuff up, too. The 'community united by teen stars' story sold so many papers that nobody gave a monkeys about a few white lies along the way – which just goes to prove my point that a great story will get you a long way in life.

And we might not have won the twenty-five grand – which was the only downside to coming second – but I did make a bit of cash from all the interviews which I put in a special bank account for Alfie, for when he's older. *And* we got to do a recording of 'You'll Never Walk Alone' (B-side: 'Ferry Cross The Mersey') as a charity record in aid of the Strikers' Relief Fund. Now there's talk of Agnes getting a record deal with The Legend. She says she's not sure she wants one, though. Seriously, we might be mates these days, but I'll never get that girl.

But the best bit was when me dad served divorce papers on me mam and filed for sole custody of me and Alfie at the same time. Happy ever afters don't usually involve divorce and custody battles but, if you ask me, more of them should.

The strike is still dragging on, so no happy endings on that front just yet. But some other good stuff came out of my grand plans. Me dad joined an online dating site and got loads and loads of hits (he lets me vet which ones he's allowed to go on dates with), Jimmy and Agnes are sort of boyfriend and girlfriend these days – they didn't get much choice really once I'd decided they should be, and I suppose the three of us are mates now, an' all.

What else can I say about the whole *Pop to the Top* experience? Why not roll out a few more clichés for old times' sake. It's been an emotional roller coaster . . . an incredible journey . . . I've learned so much about myself . . . I gave a hundred and ten per cent . . . I put my heart and soul into it . . . and I'd like to thank everyone who's supported me along the way!

And if there's one thing this whole experience has taught me, it's this: you should never ignore the Rules of Talent TV!

Acknowledgements

While the events of this novel were initially inspired by the 2009 Lindsey Oil Refinery strikes and the subsequent wildcat industrial action that affected the energy industry across the United Kingdom that year, the characters and events of the novel are entirely fictional. I have also simplified the detail of those disputes in my narrative. Nonetheless, my thanks go to the authors of the various accounts of the strikes I read, and my apologies for not doing justice to all the issues they raised.

Thanks also to all the striking teachers I know. I wrote this before the 2011 strikes started but you imbued it with your spirit in the editing process and it comes to you with love and solidarity from the Bruton strike crèche!

Huge thanks also to my big sister and my little-big bro, and to Jackie and Ian Johnson for the endless summers of frog hospitals, secret fires, woodlouse racing, granny exorcisms and the War against One.

Special thanks to Clare for fish-finger ear-piercing and many other secret adventures (that Mum still knows nothing of!), and to Tim for never letting me forget I'm a Northerner!

Big thanks to the Roller-Rink Gang (R.I.P.!), especially Claires Hendry and Baguley; to Dave Baguley and Gramp (because lovely characters need lovely people to borrow names from!); to my ever-wonderful mum for Anthony Gormley, Crosby Beach and the Fiddler's Ferry research. To Leila Rodriguez for helping me with the Portuguese; to the teachers at Bradford pool for swimming input; to Will Galinsky for *A Taste of Honey*; and Elizabeth Gaskell (via Richard Armitage – swoon!) who gave me the germ of the idea in the first place. Also to the girl who inspired Elfie, who I hope made her peace with her mum in the end.

Oh, and massive thanks to many years' worth of Talent TV contestants – I have loved you all! It's been fabulous to be able to claim that my X-Factor/BGT addiction is actually 'research'. How will I justify it from now on?

As always a huge thank you to all my pupils, especially this time to my lovely Year 10s (2011–12) who helped me find Agnes and Jimmy – and to 7J and 7L who always make me giggle!

I am so grateful as always to everyone at Rupert Crew and Egmont, especially Tom Hartley, Vicki Berwick and Doreen Montgomery.

Biggest thanks go to Caroline Montgomery and Ali Dougal who make me a far better writer than I could ever be without them (although please remind me never to do a three-part narrative again!). And to my lovely family, especially Jonny, Joe-Joe and Elsie Maudie, who bring all the love and the laughter to my writing – and to my life!

ALSO BY CATHERINE BRUTON

EVERYBODY'S TALKING ABOUT IT. DON'T MISS OUT.

'Witty, wise and compelling.' *The Sunday Times*

'Deserves high praise.' *Evening Standard*

'An important book: brave, honest and funny.' *Bookbag*

EGMONT PRESS: ETHICAL PUBLISHING

Egmont Press is about turning writers into successful authors and children into passionate readers – producing books that enrich and entertain. As a responsible children's publisher, we go even further, considering the world in which our consumers are growing up.

Safety First
Naturally, all of our books meet legal safety requirements. But we go further than this; every book with play value is tested to the highest standards – if it fails, it's back to the drawing-board.

Made Fairly
We are working to ensure that the workers involved in our supply chain – the people that make our books – are treated with fairness and respect.

Responsible Forestry
We are committed to ensuring all our papers come from environmentally and socially responsible forest sources.

For more information, please visit our website at www.egmont.co.uk/ethical

MIX
Paper
FSC FSC® C018306

Egmont is passionate about helping to preserve the world's remaining ancient forests. We only use paper from legal and sustainable forest sources, so we know where every single tree comes from that goes into every paper that makes up every book.

This book is made from paper certified by the Forestry Stewardship Council (FSC®), an organisation dedicated to promoting responsible management of forest resources. For more information on the FSC, please visit **www.fsc.org**. To learn more about Egmont's sustainable paper policy, please visit **www.egmont.co.uk/ethical**.